AS JENNY KNELT TO UNLOCK THE TRUNK, SHE COULD FEEL THE EVIL OF THE MASTER.

It was like a bone-chilling ache. The stench of something rotten pervaded the air.

This place has been defiled, she thought.

"So much evil," Willow whispered.

"Of the bad," Xander added softy. "I can feel it now, too."

Jenny opened the trunk. With sickening dread, she peered in. The arms were folded in on themselves. The hands were positioned palms up. Finger bones had separated and were nestled on either side of the skull like huge, macabre earrings.

Then the Master's left hand shot straight up and wrapped itself around her throat.

Buffy the Vampire Slayer™

Available from ARCHWAY Paperbacks and POCKET PULSE

Buffy the Vampire Slayer adult books

Available from POCKET BOOKS

BUFFY THE VAMPIRE SLAYER™

HOW I SURVIVED
MY SUMMER VACATION

Vol. 1

A collection of original short stories based on the hit TV series
created by Joss Whedon

POCKET
PULSE

POCKET PULSE
New York   London   Toronto   Sydney   Singapore

Historian's Note:
These stories take place between
the first and second seasons.

An *Original* Publication of POCKET BOOKS

 POCKET PULSE, published by
Pocket Books, a division of Simon & Schuster Inc.
1230 Avenue of the Americas, New York, NY 10020

™ and © 2000 by Twentieth Century Fox Film
Corporation. All rights reserved.

ISBN: 0-7434-0040-2

First Pocket Pulse printing August 2000

10 9 8 7 6 5 4 3 2 1

POCKET PULSE and colophon are registered trademarks of
Simon & Schuster Inc.

Printed in the U.S.A.

CONTENTS

DUST

MICHELLE WEST

It was a modern picture: Girl in a water-stained dress surrounded by friends in a loose, roving pack. Cars held at bay by the presence of people spilling into the streets on their way to and from the dance that marked some unfathomable human ritual. And in the folds of wind, dispersing as the night waned, the dust that had been a small army of vampires.

Then again, in war, the losers rarely had a choice of how they left the battlefield.

The girl paused for just a moment—not enough to break stride. She glanced at a small boy walking with his father, out far past his bedtime. Glanced, and passed, although on closer inspection, the tall man beside the boy wouldn't have passed for *anyone's* father on a day that wasn't Halloween. He wore dark robes that seemed to reach for dust-heavy wind, as if to grasp the dead and contain them.

Still, it was a tense moment; although the man

didn't worry at all, the boy held his breath, figuratively speaking, until the girl's attention was caught by the words of the oldest friend present. By about two hundred years. She shook her head slightly and picked up her step to catch up with the friends that had moved on while she hesitated, father and son—such as they were—forgotten.

"I told you, Anointed One," the older man said quietly. "Unless she knows what she is looking for—*exactly* what she's looking for—the spell I've cast prevents our detection."

"She looked this way, anyway."

The robed man frowned. "And did not see."

"I don't understand," the boy said at last, staring at her back, at the way the folds of fabric skirted the surface of concrete and asphalt. "The prophecy . . . she beat it."

"There is no way to defeat prophecy; it is a simple statement of fact."

The boy raised a brow. "You haven't tried reading it lately."

"I'm not a reader, I'm a writer." The man looked at the boy for a moment. "You have great power, Anointed One, but perhaps *your* reading skills were not as well honed as they might have been." He raised his head; the night had diminished the passing figures until only a white dress could be clearly seen in the distance. "The prophecy was correct. The Slayer *did* die."

"I know dead when I see it. That's not it."

"Ah, I forget. You cannot see." He lowered his head for a moment, lifting his hands and spreading them slowly, as if his palms were touching a glass wall. Then he blew into the air, and his breath came out in fine mist, as if it were suddenly very, very cold. That mist touched the flat air beneath his palms, and frost, swirling and glowing, thinned out between the man, the boy, and the Slayer.

She was glowing.

At her back, like some bizarre shadow, some outcropping of malignant light trailed after her, arms moving slightly out of sync with hers, long, angular fingers reached for her hair . . . or perhaps the back of her neck.

"What does it mean?"

"Anointed One, she walked the edge between life and death. She crossed it. Something pulled her back, but . . . there is a vacuum that surrounds her. Any normal mortal would not have had the strength to return to the living. See?"

The Slayer turned again, and for a moment, her face was as clear as . . . glass. The light that had followed her pawed at her face; she frowned. The creature that had once been Angelus spoke to her and she lifted a hand, looking through the invisible attacker; the light retreated.

"She struggles with death. There is a possibility that she will still lose."

"And if she loses?"

"Death will take her back. But she is not aware of the struggle."

"*Make* her aware of it."

"It can be done."

"Good."

"But I require the blood of one who had physical contact with her on the night of her death."

"Any of them," the small vampire said, pointing.

"I'm not a fool. Take one of them, and we will all meet the Master's fate."

Collin frowned for a moment, and then offered his companion the sunny expression of a boy eight or nine years old. He held out his hand to his companion in silence.

Just as he had when he led Buffy to the Master.

"How many deaths have you seen, Anointed One?"

The small vampire shrugged. "Not enough."

But the demon mage was no longer listening. He worked for a moment, trading silence for the cadence of stilted chant, trading chant for the motion of hand over the stone surface of a small altar. Then he paused and gestured to Collin. He had tried to choose a working area that would be convenient, but in the end, Collin—as if he were a mortal child—was forced to pull a chair over to the altar's side so he could better see what was happening.

"Watch carefully. Timing is everything."

The stone bubbled where the mage passed hands over it, becoming molten, and then becoming a still, slick liquid with an unusual sheen. A very familiar face came into focus as they watched.

She really was a very pretty girl.

The young woman who Rupert Giles had, by dint of birth and twist of fortune, been given to train, stood in the middle of his flat, lost in thought. It seldom happened. Although she stood in the light cast by long windows, her face was shadowed, her chin lowered.

"Buffy, have you been listening to a word I've said?"

"Yes?" She looked up from the flat, old book in her hands with a guilty start. Giles walked across the room and very carefully closed the book. It was one of several that he had been forced to relocate to his personal quarters while the school library underwent extensive renovations.

"That would be the right answer, if it happened to contain any truth. If you're worried about the Hellmouth, it's closed. The vampires were only drawn to the school because of the Master and the Hellmouth. There has been no sign whatsoever of vampire activity since that night. I must again point out that you were quite thorough.

"You needn't worry about your absence."

"I am *not* worried. What makes you think I'm worried?"

"For a start, that's probably the third book I've seen you open all school year."

"So?"

"It's in Latin."

"Latin?"

"And it's upside down."

"Oh."

"Buffy, I realize that it's been a . . . difficult year. The worst of it is over. The Hellmouth has been closed, thanks to your efforts here. You deserve . . . well, you deserve a vacation, inasmuch as traveling to a city that defined the words 'road rage' *can* be a vacation."

"Now. Watch." The man's hands moved over the altar.

She took a piece of paper out of her pocket. "This is my father's phone number. If anything goes wrong—"

"What could possibly go wrong?" He held the folded piece of paper out to her.

She looked at it pointedly. "You want a list? I could spend my entire vacation making one, and I got a C in English this term for 'poor use of imagination.' "

"Uh, yes, well. Maybe I will keep this. As a precaution."

"Good. I have to get going. Dad's going to pick me up at home. It'll be our first summer together. I mean, since their divorce." Her smile stretched, thinned and disappeared. "You know, there's a whole lot of silence going on here. Help me out a bit, Giles."

"Uh, yes, well. I'm certain that you'll have a wonderful summer doing whatever it is young girls do."

"I bet you got a lot of A's for effort when you were my age. If you were ever my age. Don't get killed while I'm gone." She held out her hand.

After a slight hesitation, he took it. "Buffy—"

Giles.

He lay on the ground, right fist still clenched, left leg clearly broken; the front of his jacket shredded, dull tweed brightened by blood that had not yet dried and stiffened. There was so much of it.

But worse: his glasses were cracked, and beneath the fine vein of forked lines she could see his eyes, devoid of disapproval, surprise, or the subtleties of very British anger. His left hand lay in shadow; it seemed that he had been reaching for something.

"Giles!"

"Buffy?"
"Giles?"
"Buffy! Are you all right?"
"I . . . I'm fine."

He frowned, his brows bunching slightly as he raised them. "Is something wrong with your hand?"

She was cradling it as if it were burned. "No. I . . . I have to go now."

The lights were off; the hum of neon was absent; the sound of hungry young musicians wouldn't be heard for hours yet. But the Bronze had a life of its own, even outside of normal hours.

A slim girl with long, pale hair stood in its shadows.

Angel recognized her at once. He knew a lot about living in shadows, and he didn't miss much that happened in them. "Buffy?"

She looked up at the sound of his voice. "Angel."

"I got here as soon as I could."

"Well . . . I'm glad the place was open. I think the management is doing the once-a-decade post-dance fumigation." She looked down again. "I wasn't sure you could make it. It's . . . it's morning." She walked over to the bar, turned her back toward it, rested her shoulder blades against its edge. Neither the Slayer nor the vampire spoke, and the silence was almost as pointed as any of Buffy's other weapons.

"Why did you—"

"I'm leaving—"

They stopped; the words echoed and stilled. "I can see we're going for awkward here." She put her hand into her pocket; Angel could hear the crinkle of paper before she pulled her hand out. Empty.

"Leaving for—"

"I wanted to say—"

They stopped again. "We should have taken a number at the door," Buffy said at last. "You want to go first, or should I?"

9

He didn't answer.

She looked away. "I'm leaving Sunnydale for the summer. I wanted to . . . to say good-bye."

"Why?"

"Why what?"

"Why are you leaving?"

"You might have noticed that I live with my mother. My father's in L.A. They worked this thing out between them like civilized adults—civilized adults who couldn't stand to live under the same roof. Mom puts up with the weirdness of my life for the school year, Dad gets it when other parents are supposed to be relaxing. It keeps me in the family. Sort of like built-in summer camp.

"And that was probably more than you wanted to know."

"Buffy—"

"So now tell me more than I want to know. Tell me anything at all about you. Tell me that you used to have pimples and a terrible complexion before you . . ."

"Died?"

Silence.

"Why did you pick here?" they said, in perfect unison.

Angel answered after another awkward pause. "Because this was the place," he said softly.

"The place?"

"The place I killed Darla." He took a step toward her, and then another; she took a step away from the bar, and then stood her ground, her gaze caught by his, in the shadows. "For you."

"For me . . ."

"Was that more than you wanted to know?"

"I . . . don't know." She reached out, slowly, to touch the side of his face—

—and then she was standing in a smelly, dank street as Angel, arm around his friend's shoulder, walked right past her. The strong stench of alcohol was almost welcome, the rest of the street smelled so bad. She turned to follow Angel, and then stopped as she saw someone in the distance beyond him.

Someone in a dress straight out of a museum, with its fitted bodice and a skirt that could only be rounded in that unnatural feminine circle with multiple hoops. The stranger stood, with perfect poise and complete confidence, in an alley that was only barely lit by torches from a nearby tavern. Buffy knew her.

Darla.

At her back, Buffy could hear the rickety sounds of wheels over cobbled stone; she turned; saw shadows and mist.

It was cold. Buffy was cold.

"Angel?"

Something was wrong with him. He was speaking, but she couldn't quite make out what he said because his voice sounded so wrong. And his clothes . . .

It took a moment before she realized what it was. A Slayer knows a vampire in the same way she knows how to breathe; instinctively. And this Angel *wasn't* a vampire.

But the woman in the alley was. He walked toward her, leaving behind first his friend and then everything he'd thought he'd known.

Darla was elegant; one of the most beautiful women that Buffy had ever seen. He was mesmerized—and why wouldn't he be? She opened her mouth to warn him, but her throat was dry; no sound came out.

Angel . . .

He closed his eyes as Darla smiled.

He died.

And then he was on his way to being undead, his lips against the curve of her flawless skin, his head cradled in the infinitely strong and unnaturally gentle hands of his sire.

Buffy had never seen a vampire in the making before. It was worse than accidentally stumbling into a bedroom in active use.

She cried out, pulled back, broke free—

And stood in the Bronze, clutching her hand, eyes wide. Certain of one thing: He had *wanted* Darla.

"Buffy?"

"I'll—I have to go. My father's going to be at my house any minute."

He reached out; she stiffened; he let his hand fall. They walked into separate shadows.

"Buffy, where have you been? Your father's going to be here any minute—" Joyce Summers came out of the kitchen, wiping her hands on her apron as if the word *frazzled* had been coined only for her personal use.

"Mom, I know when Dad's coming. I packed last night, remember? Eight o'clock? You were standing over my shoulder handing me underwear and socks?"

"I just—I want you to be on time. I want things to get off to a perfect start for you."

"You worry about you, okay? I can take care of myself."

"I know, dear," her mother said, with a soft smile. "Did you bring the suitcase down?"

"Mom—"

"I'm sorry. I know. It's just . . ." She smiled in that brightly forced way that wasn't all that cheerful. "I think we've made a really good start this year. I know it was hard, leaving all your friends behind, going to a new school, dealing with things. I think you've done well. I think we've both done well. And I'm going to miss you. There." She lifted a hand as her daughter started to speak. "I know I promised I wouldn't say it, but it's true. I've never spent eight weeks without you before."

She opened her arms and swept her daughter into a hug—

And her daughter stiffened and paled, overwhelmed by the sudden smell of antiseptic cleaners that couldn't quite mask the scent of less pleasant things. She stood at the foot of a hospital bed that had been decorated superficially—different sheets, a nonstandard bedspread—to look as if it were anything else. In that bed, head in the center of a pillow, was a withered old woman. It took a second.

Mom . . .

Her mother. Her lips were sunken over a jawline that clearly had no teeth; her eyes were closed. She was struggling for breath; failing to catch it.

Not a pretty sight, is it? But that's mortality's ugly little secret. You might be lucky enough to be spared, Slayer. I believe it's unusual for someone in your vocation to survive their first quarter century.

I know I've done my best to give you a death you deserve. And isn't any death better than this one?

She turned slowly, her eyes wide in that unblinking stare that was halfway between disbelief and fear.

In the light through the door, a shadow lay, long and thin against the ground. The familiar voice accompanied a familiar shadow. But nothing seemed to cast it, and when she turned back to the bed, she was alone with her mother's death.

And the fear of the Master.

Rigor mortis would have left Buffy more flexible than the shock of her mother's death. She had never thought of her mother as particularly young. But she couldn't see how the woman in front of her could somehow disintegrate into whatever it was that had been left in that bed.

"Buffy?"

She had never really thought about her mother's death before. Her mother was the single constant in a life that suddenly didn't seem all that long. She wanted to shout, or to cry, or to fight *something*, but there was nothing at all she could do: age was age. It wasn't a vampire, a demon, or a man-eating insect. It was a . . . fate.

God, she hated that word.

"Buffy, are you all right?"

No.

"I'm . . . I'm fine. I just remembered that I . . . I forgot to . . . to pack something I need. Dad'll be here any minute." She didn't push her mother away because she'd been taught, over and over again, that Slayer strength against normal person could lead to permanent injury, but the desire to *shove* and escape was visceral. Desperate.

She escaped, fleeing up the familiar stairs, ducking

into the familiar room, and closing the door behind her. Then she stopped. Leaned into it, palms against the pale surface of painted wood. Wondered if she had been—no, would be—one of those daughters who said, "I can't visit my mom in the nursing home because I want to remember her as she was," thereby forgetting everything that she ultimately had shared with her mother: company, time, even arguments.

The doorbell rang.

"Buffy!" Her mother's voice, muffled by the door, was clear and strong. "Your father's here!"

She came down the stairs quietly, a jacket that she hadn't packed—and probably wouldn't wear—slung over folded arms.

"Buffy!" Hank Summers opened his arms in that prelude to bearhug that was so familiar.

She stopped at the foot of the stairs. The distance between the last step and her father was about fifteen feet, and she made no move to lessen it. "Hi, Dad."

She knew what was coming, and she did not want to see it. She wanted to see her dad like this, like a whole person, like someone young and vital and *aware* of her.

His smile went from open and natural to frozen and stiff in the amount of time it would have taken her to walk that stretch of space. He lowered his arms. Empty arms.

"Buffy." Her mother's voice dropped slightly at the end of the first syllable. "Is something wrong?"

"No. No, nothing's wrong."

The man and the woman whose only common bond now was the young woman at the foot of the stairs watched her a little too carefully. The man looked away.

"Dad . . . I'm fine, it's just . . . I—"

He bent down and picked up her suitcases. "I'll see you in the car."

The car was about as comfortable as a car could be when occupied by two people and a large, awkward silence. After the first three attempts to point out interesting trees, a billboard, and the weather, father and daughter settled into an unspoken agreement: Buffy's half of the car was the passenger side; her father's was the driver's. The parking break in the center was the great divide.

It was a two hour drive that might as well have lasted two weeks. And in between one of them, Hank Summers said to his daughter, his brows drawn in, his teeth slightly clenched, "Did Joyce—did your mother tell you anything recently?"

"How to pack enough underwear for a decade of clean living?"

He chuckled in a way that made his smile seem natural. "Did she tell you anything about me?"

"That she wanted us to get off on the right foot, which I guess we haven't." She closed her eyes, then opened them, and caught her father's eyes in the mirror as if that were the only safe way to look at them. Which, given that he was driving, was probably true. "Look, Dad—I'm sorry I was so distant. I haven't—"

"Because I told her about Wendy in strict confidence, and I asked her to let me break it to you in my own way. I guess she didn't think my own way would be gentle enough."

"—been myself lately. I really had to . . . Wendy?"

"Wendy."

"We don't even have Dave Thomas commercials in

Sunnydale. Are you telling me something in your life besides a fast-food franchise is using that name?"

He was silent for a long time, driving quickly absorbing his attention the way paper towels in cheesy commercials absorb spills. "It looks like I owe your mother an apology."

"And me an explanation?"

"And you an explanation. I've—" He chuckled again. Buffy had heard fingernails and blackboards that sounded more pleasant. "I've recently started seeing someone."

"Seeing someone."

"A woman I met at the office. A client of a friend."

"A client. Of a friend."

"Buffy—"

"When exactly is recently?"

"In the last couple of weeks. She's a great person, Buffy. I think you'll both get along really well."

"Are we going to be seeing a lot of each other?"

The smile cracked. "We haven't finalized any plans yet," he said quietly, "but if things work out in the next month or two, Wendy and I will probably be moving in together."

"Oh." Buffy leaned forward and hit the automatic button on the armrest that dragged the window from the top of the frame to the bottom. The air that rushed past her face was smoggy and full of car exhaust—but it was loud. Familiar.

When L.A. had proved a little too hot for comfort—the distinct aftermath of burning down a school—the Summers' marriage began the process of being consigned to paper, along with the house that Buffy had called home in the simple years before some lunatic with a death wish had found her on the steps of her old high school.

She wasn't particularly fond of guilt, and she didn't indulge in it often, but she wondered from time to time if her parents could have fixed what was wrong with their marriage if they hadn't had to deal with what was wrong with their daughter's life.

How much of her parents' marital problems had been Slayer problems? How often had they argued about the hours she kept when she'd had a later-than-midnight rendezvous she couldn't avoid making if she didn't want the city to wind up as a mobile blood bank for vampires?

And when *exactly* had her father been planning on telling her about the new girlfriend?

"Buffy?" Hank Summers, bent by the weight of a summer's worth of his daughter's clothing, stopped at the foot of his property line. "Do you like it?"

"Wow, Dad. I knew you never liked yard work, but this is a big change." There it was again, that "change" word.

No house greeted her; the grounds that stretched out from one end of the block to the other fronted a stretch of apartments. One of which was her father's.

"I know it's not . . . not home."

She nodded. It wasn't home. She hadn't thought it would bother her. And it hadn't—until she looked at this building, at this building that she might be happy to live in one day, on her own, and realized that she *could not* go home. Not to the home she had had before she had been discovered as the Slayer. Not to the time when her biggest tragedy was who the best friend of the day was.

"I kept your room. I mean, I have a room here that's just for you."

She smiled, and if the smile was a bit stiff, it was genuine. She didn't even ask him who decorated it. But as she walked toward the building's entrance, other thoughts intruded. The girl on vacation with her father moved over and the Slayer stepped in. She knew just how far she could jump, how thick a window she could expect to break with her fist, foot or elbow, and how much of a midair recovery she could make if she didn't have a chance to slow her momentum when she was going *out* the window. These were the things she looked for in a place these days. She followed her father, absently, looking at glass, at light—at how *much* light—streaming through the uncurtained windows.

"These are yours," he said quietly.

"Hmmm? Oh. Keys." She took them carefully, trying not to touch him. Trying not to show how hard she was trying.

"I thought I'd let you try them out."

"Here?"

"Here. This is home in L.A. from now on."

"Dad?"

He stopped.

"I can carry one of those." Buffy held out a slender hand.

"I'm fine." Which was true, if one counted struggling with suitcases that weighed maybe a little too much to be fine.

"But I—"

"You haven't changed much, have you?"

She froze.

"You haven't wanted my help since you turned thirteen."

"Thirteen?"

"Give or take a few months. You got so independent so quickly. It seems like I took a business trip one month and came back to a whole new girl."

"I think I was older than thirteen." She let him carry the suitcase. She even made it down the hall to the door he seemed to be aiming at before she finally turned to see him struggling slightly. "When were you planning on telling me about Wendy?" She put her hand on the door; it was solid; thick. The knob was standard brass.

On the other hand, maybe it was cheap aluminium with a brass enamel. *Real* brass doorknobs didn't usually bend when someone gripped them a little too hard.

"Does it matter? I didn't mean to hide it. I'm not ashamed of Wendy. I just thought you'd rather hear about it in person than over a phone line."

"But you could tell Mom."

"Buffy—"

"You couldn't live with her, but you could tell her."

There wasn't much he could say.

The room was large.

The window was half the size of the west wall with curtains that matched the bed. The bed itself . . . was a canopy bed. She had loved canopy beds as a child, and although it had been years since anyone had called her a child, some echo of excitement remained.

"I know I should have let you choose your own things," her father said, watching her expression. "I'm sorry. But I—"

"No, Dad, it's perfect. It's like my old room. I

mean, my *old* room. It's . . . it looks like it's even the same bed."

"It is the same bed."

"But you said—"

"I said I was going to get rid of it because you said you never wanted to see it again. But I remembered going to buy it for you. I remembered how happy you were when it arrived. I wanted to hold on to that. And I just . . . I put it into storage."

"You kept it?"

"I kept it." He exhaled, a big man who seemed inches shorter than the last time she'd *really* looked at him. "Buffy . . . I don't know what we did wrong as parents. You should have been that happy for all of your life. That's all we wanted for you. But—God, you're so much better with words than I am."

He'd put the suitcases down.

And she wasn't thinking clearly.

When he opened his arms, she walked right into them. It was like coming home.

If home was a morgue.

The carpet was bright. Her father had been lying against it, thrashing, ten years older than he was at this moment, but heavier. No obvious signs of violence, there. Heart attack, maybe. And against the body in motion, a shadow in stillness.

You haven't really escaped me, you know. You were meant to die, and you can't cheat death without consequences.

"I didn't cheat death. *I* have friends."

True. And look at how they end up. In fact, you will look at how they end their pathetic lives for the rest of your life.

"You're dead."

I am. But that didn't stop you, and you're just a little girl with delusions of grandeur.

"Well, at least *I'm* not ugly."

True. But you will be. Just think about your mother. Or your father, for that matter. There's only one way to stay young and beautiful forever.

She would have told him to go to hell, but it occurred to her that she'd already sent him there once.

She had watched her father die in silence because she hadn't been about to share her pain in front of witnesses. Especially this one.

"Buffy?"

"I'm . . . I'm fine."

"Buffy, if you're angry at me, could you just come out and say it?"

"If I was angry at you, I'd tell you. I just . . . have car sickness. I'm still car sick."

"Car sick?" He hadn't mustered much in the way of belief.

"It's a new thing. I get car sick a lot. Put me in a car for longer than five minutes, and—you don't want to hear the messy details. I just need a half an hour to lie down."

"Fine." He walked toward the door.

"Dad?"

Stopped.

"I . . . I'm really glad that you kept the bed."

"Buffy, the Master *is* dead."

Her hands were shaking. The bed was shaking. "Giles—every time I touch somebody, I see them die." She gripped the phone a little harder.

"You died yourself, Buffy. It's just possible that you may have ... issues ... that need to be dealt with."

"It's not a matter of issues—"

"You've come face to face with mortality in a way that very few people your age ever have to. It's not pleasant. It's not gradual. You haven't had a chance to grow 'into' it the way the rest of us have. But there's nothing about the deaths that you've witnessed that suggest absolute truth."

"Angel's death."

The voice on the other end of the phone was quiet for a while. "Are you so certain? You know that Darla sired him. You know that she was in love with him, that at some time he must have returned that love, in a demonic fashion. You know how old Angel is ... you could easily have filled in those details."

"With my grades in history this year?"

"Good point. But still ... Buffy, I don't mean to trivialize your experiences, and I am worried, but not about the supernatural in this case."

"And the Master?"

"If you hadn't seen or heard the Master, I'd consider this more threatening. I will do research—I *am* doing it—but the Master is *dead*, Buffy. Put your mind at rest. He's gone."

"Buffy," Her father's voice came out of the wall—or rather, the intercom speaker imbedded in it. Buffy jumped and walked over to the wall to look at the buttons. The panel was flat and devoid of any useful instructions, like "press here to answer."

"There's a message on the answering machine for you."

She pressed a button. "And the answering machine is where?" He didn't answer. She pressed the next button. Then the next. That one worked.

"It's an answering service. The code is beside the phone. You have your own voicemail box, if you want to use it."

"Thanks, Dad. I didn't expect to get much in the way of calls here."

"It's one of your old high school friends," he said, sounding slightly surprised that she still had any. Which was a lot less surprised than Buffy was.

"It's been *months*," Amber Theirsen said. "I mean, *months and months*. You wouldn't believe what's happened since you've been gone. Well, I mean, after the renovations to the school. Anyway, what was I saying? Oh, right. Claudia? She's going out with Jeff Thompson now. He dumped Laurie and she's on the warpath. She's done this thing with her hair that has to be seen to be believed. You're gonna be with your dad for the summer, right? I stay with my dad for the summer, but at least both my parents still live in L.A. I mean, isn't Sunnydale a one-street town?"

"Two. Well, one and a half."

"So it'll be a relief to be back where things are happening, right? I thought we could get together and maybe go shopping or something. My dad's—I don't mind staying here, but it's *so* boring. You can come out, right?"

"I'd really like that. It's been way too long."

"Well, great! Because it has been *so* dead here, you know what I mean?"

"I think I have a pretty good idea of what dead means."

"So come and save me from boredom. When did you want to do the see-me-in-person thing?"

"Well, I have—"

"Tonight is good."

"I'm not sure tonight is great for me but—"

"Good. Got a pencil? I don't think you've been to my dad's place before. Let me give you the address."

"You're going out tonight?" On the off chance that Buffy had forgotten how much like an accusation a question could be, her father chose to remind her.

She stood beneath the arch that marked the midpoint between the living room and the hall that bisected the apartment while her father slowly rose from a couch that still smelled of new leather.

"Why? Were you planning on inviting Wendy to dinner?"

There was a long, awkward pause.

"You *were* planning on inviting Wendy to dinner."

"I thought you'd want to meet her."

"Maybe you could let me do my own thinking."

"Buffy—"

She looked across the room at a conveniently placed section of wall. "I know. I haven't changed at all."

"That's not what I was going to say."

"Good. Because if I heard much more of it, I'd start to think there was something wrong with the 'old' me." She lifted a hand before he could say another word. "You've just started a thing with someone new. Why don't you spend a quiet, private evening with her, while I catch up on old friends?"

"Well—"

"I've pretty much got to leave now if I'm going to make it there on time."

"Do you need any money?"

"Mom gave me an allowance for the summer, but thanks." She slung her bag over her shoulder, turned on well-heeled shoes, and walked out of the living room.

Hank Summers watched her go. He heard the front door open. It was a lot louder when it closed. He sat in the quiet, empty apartment for a while, and then he reached over the armrest and picked up the phone.

Hard to believe she had ever felt at home in this city. She had gotten used to Sunnydale, where a walk in the darkness wasn't an invitation for anything but a handful of vampires and a quick workout. That was the good thing about vampires: It wasn't illegal to kill them. Technically they were already dead, and legally they didn't exist. But legally, neither did she.

Oh, Buffy Summers did, but The Slayer—the role that defined her life in every conceivable way—was material for long psychiatric sessions if she started talking about it seriously. It had been hard not to talk about it.

Of course, it had been hard not to talk, period, when she had lived in L.A. When she had had normal friends, and a normal life, and her own phone. When she had had crushes on people with heartbeats.

And maybe she'd have a little bit of that back tonight.

Amber's father lived in a neighborhood that wasn't the best and the brightest L.A. had to offer. Too close to the highway, for one. Not enough lawn, buildings too tall and a little too close together, for two. But this was the right address, if she'd been paying attention. She slid her hand into her bag as she walked up the street to number 67–01. Left it there when she knocked on the door. It swung open.

"Amber?"

"Buffy! Eeeuw. You have last year's hair." She wrinkled her nose. A nose that was a third the size of her previous one. "But you've got this year's shoes, at least. C'mon in."

"This is where your father lives?"

"Yeah. Dirty little Theirsen secret: Mommy makes all the money. Daddy still wears pants, though." She ran her hands through this year's hair, which was short, straight, and a shade of red that you'd only find in an expensive boutique. Only on the East Coast was black or pink an acceptable substitute for things that looked natural. "I'll tell you," she added, as she stepped out of the way, "that my father's ego was pretty fragile about the whole losing-the-job thing, and when they divorced, things got *ug*ly." She shrugged. "It was a long time ago."

"A long time?"

"Sure. They've been divorced for years. When it mattered—during the school year—I lived with my mother. When it didn't matter, I lived with my dad. This place," she added, swinging her arm in a wide arc, "was a big step down, though." She laughed, the sound pretty forced. "But it was worse when he started desperation dating."

"Desperation dating?"

"Yeah, he'd bring home any old woman who showed the slightest interest in him. It was pathetic."

"I . . . I'm sorry. I had no idea."

27

"No, well. You probably will. Or is your dad a hermit?"

"He's . . . he's just started dating."

"Good date? Bad date?"

"I don't know. I haven't met her yet."

"Well, she *must* be new, then. I mean, my dad was pretty careful the first couple of times, too. Like, when he cared what I thought. This way. My room—such as it is—is upstairs. *I* have a car, but I have a few things to get ready before we leave."

Buffy followed her friend up the stairs. She had been afraid they would have to do the kiss-the-cheeks thing, and that would have been awkward. She did *not* want to spend an evening watching someone else's death with the Master as Greek chorus. "Amber?"

In the narrow hall, the girl turned. "What?"

"How did you deal with the whole father thing?"

"Well, at the beginning, I tried the good-girl approach. I tried to be friendly with all of his girl-friends."

"Why?"

"Dunno. He had a really ugly depressive streak."

"My dad's always been Mr. Cheerful or Mr. Angry. Not much depression in between."

"Well then, he might not be annoying enough."

"Enough?"

"For you to do what I eventually did."

"Oh?"

"Yeah. I killed him."

Buffy froze in mid-step. "You what?"

"Well, technically," Amber said, her voice changing slightly as she looked over her shoulder, "I *ate* him."

Buffy was already on the move when the vampire's

game face took over what had been a very pretty human one.

Amber . . .

The hall was really narrow. The walls were really thin. She discovered the truth of both things the hard way. Luckily, being put through wallboard wasn't a whole lot worse than being put through a window; it just left very little maneuvering room. But it was enough. New vamp. Tougher Slayer. She leapt out of the way and rolled down the stairs, landing on her feet. No contest.

"What is it with you, anyway?" Amber snarled down the stairs, tensing to follow Buffy's leap. "You always thought you were something special, but you're just another nothing. You know what? You're going to get *old*. You're going to get *ugly*. And you're going to die."

"*I'm* going to get ugly? Have you looked in a mirror lately? Oh wait," she added, ducking the fist that put a hole in the small partition between living room—such as it was—and dining room. "You can't actually see what you look like anymore. No reflections in the mirror. You must be in hell."

She rolled with the punch that followed. Threw her bag across the floor, but not before she'd grabbed the stake that was her best defense. *How long? How long have you been like this?*

"What's the matter, Buffy?" Amber put the game face away.

She really did have this years' hair, so it wasn't likely she'd been a vamp for long. *Just long enough,* Buffy thought bitterly. What was the point of burning down an entire gymnasium and losing all your friends as a result if in the end you didn't *win?*

Amber sensed the momentary hesitation, but then

again, she'd always been a predator. She leapt. Grabbed Buffy's face in her hands.

Buffy brought her knee up and then doubled over.

The girl was weeping. Her features were blurred by fear and blood; a slender incision across her forehead was new and wet. Buffy recognized her. Amber. She froze. She did not recognize the back of the creature that held Amber, but she pretty much knew the end of the story.

Do you want to live, little girl?

Yes, yes, please—I don't know what you want. But I'll do anything—I'll give you anything I have. Please—don't hurt me. Don't hurt me.

Well, the creature said, *that's not really an option.* He pulled her head back by her hair—yes, this year's hair, forever this year's hair, now—and sank teeth into her pale neck, and she cried piteously while she had any strength at all. Which thankfully wasn't long.

"But it was, Slayer," a very familiar voice said. She looked up. Standing in the shadows, long fingers like branches or bone stripped of flesh tapping out an impatient staccato against black leather, was her death.

The Master.

"It was the whole of her life. Or don't you remember how long dying can be?"

She cried out at a sudden inexplicable pain.

"You were right, Master," she heard a young voice say. "This was pathetically easy."

Buffy looked up to see what was no longer—would never be—Amber, leaning over her, her teeth a stretch of white in a wide, wide mouth. And she gave Amber the next best thing to life: real death.

* * *

"You're home early."

Buffy slid around the open door and shut it. Her father stood beneath the cut shadows and light of an expensive chandelier, hands in his pocket. He hadn't changed. He really hadn't changed.

"Did you have dinner? If you didn't—"

"I ate. Thanks, Dad. No date?"

"No date."

"Sorry."

He started to cross the distance between them, and she backed into the door. "Buffy, I think we should talk."

"I'd love to talk. Tomorrow. The day after. Whenever. But tonight I . . . I just don't have anything left to say."

"How was your friend?"

"Not what I expected."

"I'm sorry to hear that. But at your age, people change."

Or they stop changing, forever.

She opened her eyes to the Master. He was standing just out of the sunlight, in the shadows cast by the mixture of sun and a bank of trees. There was sidewalk beneath her feet, and grass between them, but the silence spoke indirectly of isolation; they were alone. She rolled to her feet.

"Oh, don't run," he said quietly.

"I wasn't going to run, exactly." She snapped her wrist and a stake fell into the palm of her hand.

He rolled his eyes. "Why do you even bother? We both know this isn't real. It's what you call dreaming. But I have some control of it."

"Then you should really do something about your fashion consultant."

"I could," he said, looking down the length of what

31

passed for his nose, "but fashions are like their creators: mortal. I endure. Do you have any idea how many Slayers there have been since I first woke to the night sky and the power of eternity?"

"Enough."

"Many."

"I mean, enough as in enough to kill you."

"You think I'm dead? Do you honestly think *I'm* dead? You died, Slayer, and yet you walk—and you weren't even the strongest little girl I've faced. If you can escape death so easily, when you march toward it day by day, how hard do you think it could be for me?" He walked out of the shadows, and darkness clung to him as if it had a will and a life of its own. "This isn't real, not yet. But it doesn't mean we can't have any fun. . . . Oh, and don't look around for help. There isn't any. It's just you and me—as it always is, in the end. You never meet your death with company."

"I'm not dead."

"Not yet. But you will be, again. And again. Until your death bores me, which, it may surprise you to know, might take a while."

"Buffy?"

She looked up from whatever it was she'd been trying to feed herself. The sun through the windows was hazy, the sky the pale gray that comes with heat inversion in the summer in L.A. "What?"

"I thought we could go shopping today."

She looked back down at the bowl. Bran flakes had been drowned in skim milk. "You hate shopping, Dad."

"I used to hate it when I had to do it all the time.

But it's been a long time since I've gone shopping. I almost miss it."

A smile worked its way over stiff lips. "Sure. But I have one thing I want to do first."

"I have the day off. We can do whatever you want."

"It's not a 'we' thing."

"Oh." Then, "What is it?"

"I want to get rid of last year's hair."

Buffy's grip on her crossbow was so tight it wasn't clear that she and the weapon were separate entities. She had spent a week trying to vary her sleeping hours to see if she could avoid these nighttime encounters, but without success.

She had also spent a week and a half trying to avoid touching any other human being. The death of the hairdresser had been brutal, long, and entirely human. The deaths of the women who had fitted her in the shoe store—all three of them—had been pathetic and whimpering.

The hardest random encounter was with a thief, a small, emaciated child with sun-dark skin and flat, black hair. His death brought her closer to murderous rage than she'd ever been, although he'd been trying to cut open the bottom of her purse with a small knife and she'd caught his wrist in a Slayer grip without thinking. She dropped it as if it burned and he got away with a pocketknife that wouldn't stop a few months of abuse and a brutal death.

No more, no more, no more.

She spent a lot of time in the dark, with the door that had seemed solid her only protection against the death of everyone around her. Her bed had a permanent dimple in the middle that matched her back. Her father had moved the television into her room without saying a word. She had been more grateful than she could say, so she hadn't said much.

Unfortunately, she wasn't watching television at the moment. She was dreaming.

"Why do you do it, I wonder?" the Master said quietly. He rarely raised his voice.

"I wonder the same thing," she said, holding her weapon, watching him. "Maybe it's because you're big, ugly and evil, not necessarily in that order. You kill things—which isn't a problem—and people, which is. I kill you."

"And why is it *your* duty, little Slayer? Why is it your burden? The world sacrifices Slayers, you know. Isn't it tiring to carry the world on your pretty little shoulders day after day?" He smiled, showing fangs. "Why don't you shrug?"

She shrugged. But the movement was stiff and hesitant. "There. Didn't seem to change much."

"You have no vision," he replied. "But you also have no lifespan, so vision would be wasted on you. Do you know what your life expectancy is? Do you know what the average life expectancy of a Slayer is?"

Buffy shrugged, deflecting the words.

"Oh well. Shall we start?"

"Why not? I'm not sure what's worse—dying, or listening to you talk."

He laughed. "Yes you are. But I like your bravado. Your ignorance is less appealing." He gestured, earth beneath his feet split; she could see flames lap at grass as if they were waves, scorching it as they passed. "They'll tell you that I left a skeleton because I was ancient. They lie. I left a skeleton because our lives are tied. Neither of us met the fate we deserved."

"No, Dad. I don't want to go to the beach."

"Young lady, you've been sitting in this house for two weeks in front of that stupid box."

Familiar terrain. A mixed blessing.

"You don't understand. I really really don't want to go the beach today."

"You don't understand. You are getting out of the house one way or the other. You can come to the beach, or you can spend the day on the front steps until *I* get back from the beach to let you in. Understood?"

"Are we doing this for you or for me?"

"Does it matter?"

"Dad—"

"Tell me *why,* Buffy. Tell me why. Talk to me."

"I just get caustrophobic—"

"Is that like claustrophobic?"

"—whatever. I get claustrophobic with all those people around me. And I—"

"You're the stand-in-large-crowds and move-around-to-deafening-music girl. You've never been claustrophobic in your life. Try again."

Because I don't want to see another large body of water again for the rest of my life. I don't even want to sit in a bath; I'll take a shower, thank you. Because I don't want to go into the water. I don't want to think about—She swallowed. Looked at her father as if seeing him for the first time—as if not liking what she saw.

She couldn't explain why she didn't want to go into the water, of course. She couldn't tell him any more than she could tell her mother. But once, *just once,* it would be nice if he could just trust that she had a *reason* for behaving the way she did.

"Dad—"

"Buffy, just once—just this once—I'd like it if you could trust that I have a reason for what I'm asking."

She stopped in mid-motion—and there hadn't been a whole lot of motion to begin with—and stared across the table at the man she had seen die the single time she'd lowered her guard and actually hugged him since she'd arrived.

"Could you—could you tell me why?"

He looked at her and frowned. "Because I'm worried about you. About this sitting around in your room as if your room is the entire world."

Buffy stood up. "Dad—"

"Look, I'm not good with words, Buffy, but I try." The implication of course being that she didn't. And he was right. She didn't. For just a minute she could actually understand how he felt, and she held on to that as if—as if it were a lifeboat and she were on the verge of going under. *Water metaphors. Great.*

"Yeah, okay, it's a great day to go to the beach."

That turned out to be a popular sentiment; the Summers showed up at the beach along with the other half of L.A.

Her father had brought the usual beach things with him, and she absently picked up the cooler and the beach umbrella and strode lightly across the sand while he struggled with the hamper and the camera bag. She didn't have to worry about keeping a hand free for a weapon because it was broad daylight, and although she was always the Slayer, the slayees were notably absent.

A year ago, and she would have been quite happy here. But the intricate dance required to avoid coming into contact with strangers was not the only complication the beach brought with it. She stared at the tufts of foam on a relatively quiet ocean and realized that she had not gone swimming once since the night she faced the Master and prevented the Hellmouth from swallowing the town whole.

Not since the night I—she could think the word now, but only barely, and only when she was so tired she couldn't force herself to think of something else—*drowned.*

"Do you remember how much you hated water when you were small?" her father asked. Somehow he'd managed to catch up with her. She handed him the cooler and the umbrella, and left him to struggle with them both at a safe, discrete distance.

"No. No, I don't remember."

"You did hate it. You particularly hated to be submerged. Even in the bathtub, if your face got wet, you'd whimper or cry. You honestly don't remember?"

"Why would I have to when I have you to do it for me?" She stopped herself from speaking with effort, forcing the words to flow into less familiar channels. "I'm sorry, Dad. I'm just not up to this today."

But if he'd taken offense at her words, he didn't show it. He was caught, she realized, by the need to offer her the explanation she had asked for. "You weren't up to it then. Friends of ours said it was best just to throw you in the water and let you figure it out for yourself—and you were so headstrong, Buffy, it almost seemed like the right thing to do."

"And you did?"

"No. No, I went in the water with you. I got thrown out of more toddler wading pools than I care to remember." He smiled. "But it worked."

And in spite of herself, she smiled back.

"Whenever things were tough, we'd go swimming. I think . . . I think the water is the only place in the world that you were willing to trust me."

She couldn't think of anything to say. It was painful to look at him, because even though he was no longer looking directly at her—even though he had busied himself with the umbrella and the beach blankets—she could see the expression on his face.

"It's not you," she said abruptly. "I mean, it's not specifically you. There are just things that I can't talk about with anyone."

"I had those," he said quietly. "I don't remember when they happened, and I don't remember when they went away. Maybe never."

She almost hugged him. But she didn't, because seeing a loved one die as a reward for a sign of affection was a poor incentive. There was only one other thing she could offer. "I think I will take that swim now." He nodded without looking up.

The water was salty. That was good, because it was different. It hit her skin like a shock or a slap, but that was also good; bracing. It cleared the mind.

She didn't actually want to dive in or submerge her face, but it was all she could offer her father. She would have bet money he was watching it all. She teetered for a moment in cold water—the girl who killed monsters afraid of a few feet of crowded surf. And then, holding her breath, she started to run, to build up momentum for a knife-clean dive into the ocean.

She stayed under just long enough to make her point; the water against her skin was uncomfortable.

She could still feel it. Paralyzed, she had held her breath until she could not hold her breath, and then, with the world getting darker and darker, she felt the sharp sting of water in her nose and her throat as her body defied what little control she had over it in a desperate search for air.

She forced herself out of the water.

And found herself crouched before a black pool in a familiar grotto. The bathing suit was gone; the white dress of both dream and nightmare flowed over her knees, its sheen unmarred by water. The crossbow that she had carried from the library to this small wedge between worlds was pointed toward wet stone.

She blinked. Reached up with one shaking hand to touch last year's hair. Last year's face. Heard words so familiar she would never forget them.

"You're not going to kill me with that thing."

"Don't be too sure." She struggled to reload the crossbow—and then stopped. Held the bolt in her hand instead. She continued through steps memory had carved and enlarged, searching in shadows too deep too penetrate. Hearing his voice come from all directions, as if he were moving at incredible speed.

It hasn't happened. It hasn't happened yet. She swallowed. She had seen so many deaths—so many disturbing, horrible deaths. And it almost shamed her to say that the one that still terrified her the most . . . was her own. Maybe that would change. God, she hoped that would change. But—she *hadn't* died. She was here. He was here. And she didn't want to die, ever. Now that she knew how it had happened, she had a chance to prevent it.

"You still don't understand your part in all this, do you? You are not the hunter. You're the lamb." The words came from everywhere, the sentence fragmented syllable by syllable with echoes and varying distances. As if he were circling her from above, waiting for the right moment to start his dive, like a bird of prey.

"You know, for someone who's all powerful, you sure do like to hide." She clutched the bolt, waiting. Waiting now. Knowing the moment—the only moment—when he would be vulnerable.

"I'm waiting for you. I want this moment to last."

"Well, I don't."

"I understand."

And he was there, behind her, beside her, moving so damned *fast;* she gave up the crossbow almost instantly; gave up the fight as she had done that night. *There's no disgrace in flight, Buffy. Retreat, and you can fight again. Fail to retreat when it's necessary . . .*

Who had said that? Did it matter?

She felt the pull of something old, strong, something that had roots on the wrong side of the demon/human divide. The scent of death and decay was stronger than it had ever been as she froze at his command. He sauntered elegantly behind her; he removed the jacket that Angel had given her, the talisman of protection and connection, exposing her throat over the thin white straps of the dress she had wanted so badly.

God, her heartbeat was so *loud* in this place, in this packed terrible space, at this moment. She heard his voice beside her ear. She struggled for air, for breath, for calm. Dropped her arm, then stiffened the hand that held the bolt that she hadn't put into the crossbow.

When he bent, she struck. She heard a soft grunt, and she could move, could turn to witness the slight widening of the eyes that passed for surprise in a dead person. She wanted to say something clever. But nothing clever came to mind as the Master disintegrated, leaving only dust and night in his wake.

The Hellmouth hadn't opened.

And Buffy Summers, the Slayer, hadn't died. She waited for the sound of footsteps. She knew that Angel and Xander would be rounding the bend in the sewer tunnels at any moment. She wanted to see them.

She wanted to see her friends. To see friends who hadn't failed her; friends who hadn't expected her to come here like the sacrificial lamb the Master had spoken of. But it was silent in the grotto; silent as the dead. She picked up her crossbow carefully, and turned toward the stairs enclosed by tunnels. Toward freedom. And then she noticed that the lights were dimming and flickering.

It made sense. Not that the lights in this ruined space had ever been spectacular; they set the mood and tone for the encounter; hundreds of candles burning slowly into oblivion. The Master's magic was no longer present to maintain them. But . . . something was wrong. She listened for a sound . . . any sound. But not even the rats were in an obliging mood. The candles were wrong. The space was wrong.

"Hello?"

She walked toward the stairs. Stopped. Turned to look at the pool in the grotto's heart. And she heard voices. Voices that she liked, even, but raised in a way that made them unpleasant.

But this is the Codex. There is nothing in that that does not come to pass.

Then you're reading it wrong.

I wish to God I were. But it's very plain. Tomorrow night, Buffy will face the Master and she will die.

Giles. Angel. Giles.

Like the tolling of a bell.

She turned away from the stairs and began to walk toward the pool. Knowing that this was a dream. And that it wasn't.

"I did die," she said softly.

"You did," the dust said. It began to rise and whirl, coalescing into a horror that was so thoroughly familiar it should have lost its edge. It hadn't.

"I did die. But so did you." She swallowed. Her throat was thick and swollen, and her heartbeat had become such a constant white noise she could almost pretend it wasn't racing wildly out of control. Could almost pretend he couldn't hear it, that he didn't know just how frightened she was. She was still sixteen years old and she didn't want to die.

I've got a way around it. I quit.

It's not that simple. Angel's voice. Angel's concern. But it wasn't important. She raced over it, pain speaking, fear taking her words and forcing them out.

I'm making it that simple. I quit. I resign. I'm fired. You can find someone else to stop the Master from taking over!

I'm not sure that anyone else can. The signs indicate...

She hadn't let him finish. But she understood now. She could never have beaten the Master had she not died. She didn't know why, and she *hated* it, but it felt true. She *had* died. And she had come back, and in between those two—dying and coming back—she had found the strength to beat the Master and send him to Hell.

"You're the avenue for my return," he said softly. "And the roadblock. You would have made an amusing consort."

She ignored him, sweating now. There was no air. No air.

"You're too late, little Slayer. You're already dead." The Master stepped between Buffy and the water. His voice was a moving whisper again. "Or have you forgotten? I've *seen* your nightmares. I know what frightens you. You're trapped here, with me, while the lights go out because there's only one other way back."

"If I were already dead, you wouldn't be trying so hard. And you shouldn't. It doesn't suit you."

He snarled; she ran. Past him. Through him. She felt a terrible chill, and then a familiar horror, a physical terror, as she hit the water and passed beneath its surface, cheek striking the debris that littered the rock inches below. She did not know if this was real. Didn't know if she was in the past, and the drowning had yet to take place, or in the present, in Hell. But she had *done* this once. She had come through it. And she had had to do it; she could see that now. Yes, her death had served his purpose—the humiliation of that left a scar of its own—but it had served hers as well.

How hard could it be to face it again?

Easy question; she had the answer. Harder than anything she had ever done.

His fingers were on her shoulders, as if he could somehow force her from the water; she could feel them as if they were the brush of moths' wings. And then she could feel nothing but the burning sensation of water down her throat, water in her lungs, the terrible darkness that comes without something so simple people never think about the action at all. *Breathing.*

But there was some small solace, some small gift: she could hear the cry of rage and frustration somewhere in the halls of the dead, in the beyond that the living couldn't see or touch. But the tenor of the screaming changed; rage and frustration gave way to terror and pain.

She didn't like it.

"Buffy!"

She didn't like it at all. It wasn't his voice anymore. It was the voice of someone she cared about. Someone—

Who had always been there, in the water, near the surface; someone who had taught her that the water was nothing to fear. She felt his hands on her shoulders, and then she felt nothing at all.

She woke in a bed, in a sterile room. Or rather, in a room that smelled enough like antiseptics that it should be sterile. That's how it worked in television. Her throat felt raw, her eyes ached, her mouth tasted not like the salt water she'd swallowed by the gallon—which would have been bad enough—but like anything living in that water had given up on life, died, and decomposed there.

Her father sat beside her bed, head bowed, forehead caught in his hands.

"Don't tell me. I'm wearing one of those really awful hospital gowns and you've suddenly developed enough fashion sense that you don't want to see it, right?"

The head snapped up fast enough she was surprised he didn't get whiplash.

He hugged her.

She stiffened, waiting for his death. But if it was coming, it stayed where it belonged: in the future.

"I'm sorry. I'm sorry, Buffy. I should have listened. I should have listened. It was easier when you were two. I could be right there, all the time."

"Dad?"

He didn't say another word.

And she didn't say another word. But she let him hold her, and for a minute memory opened its vast curtains and she could clearly remember being pulled from the water, in tears, by a huge bear of a man with a voice deep enough that it almost always sounded slightly scary.

You can trust me, Buffy. I'll never let the water hurt you.

She wasn't that girl. Could never be that girl again.

"Dad, I was wrong. I *do* remember," she told him softly.

The good thing about the human world, the demon mage reflected, as he sat back into the wide curve of a first-class plane seat, *was the ease with which one could disappear into it.* Failure in Hell had its consequences, but failure here was . . . different. For one, the people who one failed had to have the resources and the abilities to hunt you down. Two, the old vampires were exceedingly rare, and the young ones were bound by darkness, their movements curtailed by the poverty of their limited imagination and their pathetic power.

Had it not been for the possibility of the Master's revivification, he wouldn't have felt a pressing need to be half a globe away from Sunnydale. But he was curious. The Slayer was formidable almost by accident—and accidents of a certain type rarely happened without cause or purpose. He picked up a dark, wide bowl and stared into it for a long time.

"Did you want a refill, sir?"

"You noticed."

ABSALOM RISING

NANCY HOLDER

It was a warm summer night. Rupert Giles stood in the courtyard of his condo complex and waited for the others to arrive. His hands in his pockets, he listened to the gentle bubbling of the tiled fountain beside him. Birds of paradise rustled in the breeze. The scent of night-blooming jasmine wafted around him like the signature perfume of an affectionate ghost.

Despite the tranquillity, Giles was not tranquil. The scent of death hung in the air as well. Evil crept along the concrete on clawed talons, ready to slash, eager to kill. A sense of dread pushed against Giles's spine until he was afraid it would crack. Each day, each night, the things in his apartment drove him out here, to the courtyard. It was as far away from them as he could get, and still stand guard over them. It was getting worse. He could no longer rest. He had been this way ever since Buffy had killed the Master.

Ever since his apartment had become a reliquary for the Master's bones.

It was late June. The other faculty members at Sunnydale High School, blissfully unaware of the rampant evils in their midst, had spoken of nothing but their upcoming holidays for weeks. The students had practically gone mad with the waiting. Giles was new to the academic world. *If working as the school librarian at Sunnydale High counted as academic in any sense of the word.* Having a job that came with three months' vacation was a novelty.

Novel as well was the departure of the Slayer, who had left Sunnydale to spend the summer in Los Angeles with her father. No Watcher had ever had a Slayer who went on holiday before. The Watchers Council were extremely put off by it. *No surprise there.*

There was quite a lot about Buffy that put them off—her lack of discipline, her unorthodox approach to training, and, of course, her insistence upon having a social life. Giles had been unprepared for her as well. He had known since age ten that one day he would become a Watcher, and once having accepted his fate—not an easy task—he had done all he could to ensure he would be the best.

At present, Buffy Summers did not share the same . . . enthusiasm . . . toward her destiny. One girl in all her generation was chosen to be the Slayer. It was she who must battle the forces of darkness—the demons, the vampires, the monsters. Buffy was that Chosen One. But as she had pointed out more than once, choice had nothing to do with it.

"Which sucks," as she'd so eloquently put it.

When one is only sixteen, it does suck. There had to be a few compromises to keep her going, help her survive. So Giles had surreptitiously smoothed the way for her summer visit with her father. He'd pointed out to the Council that Buffy had become the Slayer while living in Los Angeles. Before her expulsion from Hemery High School (for burning down the gymnasium, according to the official record), she had killed any number of vampires in that balmy metropolis. One could expect her to have as productive a summer there as here in Sunnydale.

"And I shall remain in town, and keep vigilant," Giles had promised the Council. He had not mentioned the presence of the Master's bones in his home. He didn't want Quentin Travers—who was turning out to be no friend to Buffy in the Council—to use it as a reason to forbid her trip. She desperately needed a break from Sunnydale.

Sunnydale. What an ironic name for this dark place.

The Spanish who had first settled it had called it by a more suitable name: *Boca del Infierno.* Quite literally, "the mouth of hell." The small, seemingly dull little town was situated on a Hellmouth—a portal through which evil sought to enter this dimension. It was a constant fight to keep it closed; even so, its energy attracted monsters, demons, and vampires from all over this dimension. Sunnydale was a magnet for death and destruction. No wonder it was home base for the Chosen One.

The last time the Hellmouth had opened, Buffy had died.

Mere weeks ago, Giles thought. *I wonder what kind of toll that's taken on her.* At first she'd called him plagued by visions of death, which he assured her was normal given her recent brush with it. All the while he was researching like mad to find a correlation. Then she called to briefly say it—whatever it was—had passed and she was fine. Since then he'd heard nothing from her and was content to let her keep her distance from all things Sunnydale.

And memories of the Master.

In life, the Master had been Joseph Heinrich Nest. He'd been a monster, a brutal, sadistic man whose joy in life consisted in seeing just how far he could push other brutal, sadistic men—and women. His tests of loyalty required his followers to commit atrocities unparalleled in the annals of human history. It had often been said of him that he was born without a soul.

As a vampire the Master tried to open the Hellmouth and failed, trapping himself deep below the earth. He couldn't leave, but his followers could.

It's true we killed the Master, but what about his followers?

The soft breeze whipped to an unexpectedly sharp wind. Giles told himself that that was the cause of his sudden chill.

"So, Will," Xander said to his best friend, as they caught up with each other at the corner near her house. "Smile on the face, spring in the step. I'm seeing computer camp."

She smiled at him. "Two more days till. What are you taking in summer school?"

He gave her a very broad pout. "What makes you think I'm going?"

"You always go to summer school."

"Ah." He held up a finger. "Correction, my dear

Watson. I always *enroll*. I rarely go." He sighed and rolled his shoulders. "Slayer's out of town, which I'm guessing means no big bad, and I'm thinking beach, sand, babes, and a third-degree sunburn. The simple life of the marginally unemployed."

"With cherry Icees," Willow said dreamily. "But not near the keyboard."

"My keyboard shall remain Icee-free," he assured her, moving his brows up and down. "So, do you think Slayers lay out and tan? 'Cause, hey, Will, no freckling indoors where *you* surf."

Willow sighed. *Xander never gives up,* she thought. *He'll always have a crush on Buffy. And when he looks at me, all he'll see is his best friend who is not Buffy, and never will be.*

"It's too bad Buffy doesn't have a computer at her dad's," Willow said. "We could exchange e-mails."

"Oh, she'll call. She'll write," Xander said breezily. "She'll miss us and she'll come back early because Los Angeles is deadly dull, and we will rejoice by watching the primer dry on my Uncle Rory's car."

Willow shrugged. "I'm actually looking forward to a little boredom," she confessed. "I've had enough vampires and hellmouthy things to last me all summer and the fall semester, too."

"Yeah." Xander looked at her sheepishly. "I'm glad Buffy's having a real vacation. I guess we need one, too. It'll be good to have a nice, normal, endlessly endless summer of endlessness."

"Endlessness," Willow murmured. "Yes. I wonder what Giles wants, anyway?"

"Probably to say cheery-bye. I'll bet he's hitting the road for England."

"I'll miss him," Willow said.

Xander smiled shyly. "Me, too, gotta admit."

"Fi, fi, fo, fo, fum. Look out, baby, cuz here I come!"

Giles smiled faintly at the exuberant falsetto of Xander Harris as it carried from the sidewalk. Buffy was also unusual for a Slayer in that she had friends who knew her secret. At first Giles had worried—it just wasn't *done*—but time and again Buffy's best friends, Xander Harris and Willow Rosenberg, had proven to be of invaluable help to the Slayer.

"Hey." Willow appeared first, gently pushing aside the overhanging fronds of an elephant-ear plant. Dressed in a long-sleeved T-shirt and overalls, she was smiling her sweet, shy smile. Her long red hair would have gotten her burned at the stake a couple of centuries ago. Being a redhead was supposedly a clear sign that one was a witch. Thank God *that* didn't prove to be the case.

In an oversized plaid shirt and baggy pants, his dark hair curling at his neck, Xander trailed in her wake.

"Hey, G-man," Xander said merrily.

"I do believe I've asked you not to call me that."

"And I will go through the entire summer G-man-free," Xander shot back. He frowned slightly. "Not meaning that literally. Or I am, if you're planning to blow this pop stand, the way Buffy did."

"Alas, no, I'm not. That is, I've no plans at present," Giles said. He took off his glasses and wiped them. He felt a headache coming on.

Willow made a face. "Giles, what is that?" she asked, wrapping her arms around herself. "Oooh, creepy. Not good."

"You can feel that?"

"Yes."

Giles cocked his head at her, a bit surprised that the miasma had penetrated her consciousness. *Perhaps there is a bit of the witch in her, after all,* he thought.

"They're his bones. The Master's," Giles explained. "In my house."

"For . . . sentimental reasons?" Xander asked. "And, hello? Not feeling them," he added.

"You're lucky. It's icky." Willow shuddered. "And these are just his bones. Think what it was like to be near him. Then he puts his mouth on your throat . . ."

"And his *fangs* in your neck," Xander finished. The Master had, indeed, bitten Buffy. That had alarmed Giles more than the fact that she had temporarily died, but he had kept his own counsel. He was researching that event as well, and thus far, had no evidence that Buffy would suffer any dire effects for it.

"Why are we here?" Willow queried in a small, anxious voice as she settled on a low wall bordering the patio.

"We're going to conduct a ritual cleansing of the bones," Giles said. "I believe the Master's essence is clinging to them. We must perform a ritual over them that will dissipate the miasma."

"Just us three?" Willow looked anxious.

"Miss Calendar's at the magic shop," Giles answered. "I was fresh out of mugwort, and this cleansing will take quite a bit of it."

"Mugwort. I like the name. Sounds like some kind of really classy root beer." Xander struck a pose. "Fill your mug with a mug of Mugwort!"

"How can you joke?" Willow asked, hugging herself tighter. "This is scary stuff, Xander."

Xander's smile faded. "That's *why* I joke, Will." His voice was gentle, and Giles was proud of him. Xander Harris might act like a mindless American teenager most of the time, but there were times Giles was certain there was far more to the boy than met the eye.

"Right," Giles said. "Now, I've done a bit of research on the situation. As you both know, when a vampire is staked, it disintegrates immediately."

"Kind of explodes," Willow added, nodding.

"But the Master did not dust," Xander put in.

"No, he did not."

There was a silence.

"Because . . . ?" Xander prodded.

"I don't know." Giles hated those three words more than any others in the English language. *Except, perhaps, for G-man.* "It's often been speculated that Nest was born without a soul. Nest the man, I mean. In which case, when he was transformed into a vampire, there was no means through which a demon could inhabit his body."

"Then how did he become a vampire?" Willow asked. " 'Cause, you know, vampire, dead body inhabited by a demon. All the books we've read gives that as the only definition."

"Yes." Giles pushed up his glasses. "He was an extraordinary sorcerer in his day. He clearly possessed powers other vampires don't. Take the Harvest, for example. From miles away, he was able to absorb the energy of his chosen Vessel as the Vessel fed upon the humans in the Bronze. Yet the Master was still imprisoned inside the church."

"Not normal vamp stuff, huh," Willow mused.

"And he looked like a rat," Xander added, dropping into a lawn chair. "He looked a lot whiter and grosser than your average vamp. Angel even looked pretty good next to him."

"Thanks," said a voice behind Giles.

Giles turned quickly. He hadn't heard so much as a footfall, but there stood Angel, the vampire who did have a soul. Tall and pale, with dark hair and eyes, he must have been a strapping young man in life. The long black coat he wore reminded Giles of bats' wings. He was another anomaly: a vampire who worked for the side of good. He repeatedly risked his existence to help humans. And he was quite smitten with the Slayer.

Rather poetic, that's what Giles himself had said of their budding love. But it was also very tragic. *What could ever come of it?*

"Angel. Thank you for coming," Giles said.

"Dead Boy got an invite?" Xander asked, perturbed. Xander wasn't fond at all of the object of Buffy's affections. He clearly saw Angel as an unwelcome rival. And, quite sensibly, Xander didn't trust Angel. Giles still wasn't certain that he did, either.

"Yes," Giles replied. "As he's the one who helped me with the prophecy about the Master in the first place."

"Hi, Angel," Willow said softly.

Angel gravely nodded in her direction.

"Any luck?" Giles asked.

Angel shrugged. "I can't improve on your plan. Sanctify the bones and destroy them."

Giles nodded. "Right. Then that's what we'll do. Miss Calendar went to the magic shop for supplies."

"Hocus-pocus root beer," Xander offered, waving his hands.

"She should get here soon." Angel looked concerned. "It's a full moon."

"Excuse me, but I don't think the Master's bones are a werewolf?" Xander zinged.

Willow looked thoughtful. "I wonder if there are werewolves. We've never seen a werewolf—"

"There are werewolves. And like werewolves, magickal forces are often stronger with the full moon," Giles said, looking to Angel.

Angel shifted. "The Master loved the full moon. He could feel it even under the ground."

Xander nodded, glaring at Angel. "Oh, that's *right*. You spent a little *time* with him. A few decades or so, maiming and killing little kids and kittens and puppies."

"Xander," Willow admonished. "Be polite."

"Well, he did, and, okay, I'm saying it because no one else is." He pointed at Angel. "He was not going to go save Buffy. He was too afraid of the Master. Or so he *said*. I'm the one who talked him into going. How do we know he's not going to try to revive the Master? Fool us into saying our spell backward or something?"

"Xander," Willow said again, a bit painfully. She glanced at Angel with embarrassment. "Angel helped you save Buffy. And he tried to help her kill the Master."

"Yeah, well." Xander crossed his arms. "All that proves is that he knows how to be a survivor. Seeing as he's been doing it for over two hundred and forty years."

"I can leave," Angel said bluntly.

"No, ah, Angel." Giles raised his hand. "If something goes awry, we could use a good strong—"

"—vampire—" Xander cut in.

"—*fighter* in our midst."

"Who's a vampire," Xander insisted. "Who used to hang out with the other dead guys we are not currently loving."

Angel gave Xander a look. "Don't worry, Xander. If anything happens, I won't save you."

"He's just kidding." Willow knit her brows. "Right, Angel?"

Angel looked up at the sky. "She'd better hurry."

The neon sign in the window read DRAGON'S COVE. It was the best magick shop in town.

Jenny Calendar had the mugwort on the counter and a gentle smile on her face. The boy who was chattering nervously beside her was Jay Nichols, the most socially awkward of the many socially awkward boys in her computer classes at Sunnydale High. In the dim store light, he looked pale and wan. He would probably look the same at summer's end. Boys like Jay didn't get out much. They stayed on their computers night and day, jacked in and loving it.

"Wow, I can't believe you're in here," Jay babbled. "I mean, it's so weird to see your teacher, you know, at the grocery store, much less a place like this."

"I buy herbs for tea here," she ventured.

The beaded curtains that led to the back room parted and the proprietor appeared. The back of his head was reflected in the mirror facing the register.

"May I help you?" the proprietor asked, looking from one to the other. He was a nice middle-aged man.

Jenny gestured to the small paper bag beside the cash register. "Just this mugwort, please."

"Oh. Doing a ritual cleansing?" The man picked up the paper bag of mugwort, hefting it. "You must have at least a pound of it here. You sure you need this much?"

Jay watched with excitement. "Maybe I should buy some, too."

"Why? You got evil spirits?" the proprietor asked, then guffawed. "Kids," he said to Jenny. "They usually come in here for black lights and incense burners. It's like the sixties never died." He looked at Jay. "What do you need, kid?"

Jay ignored him. He looked at Jenny. "Evil spirits?"

But Jenny was looking in the mirror. Her blood ran cold at what she saw there. Or didn't see.

"Indigestion," Jenny said blithely. She smiled pleasantly at him. "Have a nice summer."

He looked crestfallen. "I graduated, remember?"

"Oh, of course." She didn't.

Jay Nichols watched Miss Calendar leave the magic shop with her mugwort. *She's a hottie. My heart would be pounding,* he thought, *if it still had a beat.*

The proprietor of Dragon's Cove said to him, "Is there anything I can help you find? I've got some really nice psychedelic posters."

Jay shook his head without turning to look at the man. He went outside. Turning right, he began walking down the street, in the same direction as Jenny Calendar.

A flash of white caught his attention. Hidden in the privet hedge, a vampire stood menacingly, staring at him.

Jay let his face transform.

"Dude," the other vampire said. His name was Corvelle "the Corvette" DuMont, and as a human being, he could fix any kind of car that had ever been built. Jay figured he still could. "Something big's going down."

"No kidding." Jay grimaced. "Kevin was right. They've got the bones."

Corvelle's vampiric features angled more sharply as he frowned. "So it's true. The Master didn't dust out."

"I guess."

Corvelle still chewed tobacco; he spit some brown juice out one side of his mouth. Jay was grossed out, but he didn't say a word. Along with his knowledge of mechanics, Corvelle's wicked temper was also still intact.

"Some new guy's in town." Corvelle's voice fell to a whisper. "His name's Absalom. Mean. Powerful. Very old. The Anointed One summoned him. He used to be part of the Master's inner circle."

Jay's eyes widened. "Does he know? What if Kevin gave us up?"

Corvelle looked wigged. "I'm thinking, maybe we shouldn't go back. If the Anointed One finds out we're disloyal—"

"Ssh," Jay said anxiously. "If any of *them* hear you, we're dead meat."

"We're already dead meat, you moron." Corvelle spit juice. "We'd better go back. I was sent to find you. Everyone's supposed to greet Absalom when he shows tonight."

Jay sighed. "You learn something new every day."

Corvelle lifted a brow. "What?" he asked finally.

"Being undead's worse than being in high school."

"Tell me about it," the other vampire said glumly.

The two kept to the shadows as they crept back to the lair. The large cavern was lit with candles, casting flickering shadows on the rock walls. The water in the stagnant pool gave up a stench; the Anointed One had thrown a couple of second-string varsity football players in there after feeding on them.

Jay stumbled; a rock dislodged from the path to strike a piece of wood from the ruined church. The ribs of the building reminded Jay of stakes. He didn't like so many broken pieces of wood sticking up.

Everybody looked at him and Corvelle, who was chewing his tobacco plug for all he was worth.

"Where have you been?" the Anointed One demanded.

"Hunting." Jay kept the tremor out of his voice. They were allowed to hunt.

Their imperious leader narrowed his eyes. He looked as he always did, just a little human boy with dark hair. Jay had to remind himself to be afraid of him. It was easy to forget that he was really powerful. The Master's secret weapon.

Yeah, and? The Master's dead, he thought. *Some secret weapon.*

But the boy was; that was the kicker. You turned your head, you could fill an ashtray.

Jay felt eyes on him and looked up. Kevin met Jay's gaze with a calm, steady expression. Kevin used to be a sophomore at U.C. Sunnydale. He'd planned to major in political science before he'd been changed.

Kevin was a genius, and he was a really great vampire. He kept his posse well-fed. He was incredibly strong.

And he was extremely ambitious. He'd been talking about breaking away from the Master's group even before the Master had died.

"He doesn't feed us, and he doesn't watch our backs. All the Anointed One does is order us around, and kill us if we screw up," Kevin had said to Jay and Corvelle. "What's the benefit to us? We're only following him because we're afraid of him. But there's safety in numbers, my friends. You join us, we'll be two stronger than we were. And someday, we'll take over this lair."

"What about the Anointed One?" Jay had asked, in a terrified whisper.

Kevin shrugged. "We kill him. Just part B of the word problem."

Only now, it was not the same equation. Even though there were about a dozen vampires who had joined Kevin's side, and the Master was dead, the field had just tilted again.

In the center of the cavern, a tall, dark vampire stood alone. Jay could just feel the bad karma surrounding him. He was scary.

It had to be Absalom.

The dude was dressed in a sort of old-fashioned outfit, like a preacher from the olden days, or something. Jay wasn't too big on history. Absalom's face was tricked out, and he looked hungry. Everyone was taking a step or two away from him.

The Anointed One scooted his evil little backside off the Master's throne and walked to the newcomer. The vampire bent down on one knee and gave him a hug. The Anointed One hugged him back, the way a little kid might hug a favorite uncle.

Shivers ran up and down Jay's back.

"Absalom has come at our request," the Anointed One announced like a freakin' king. *Which he is,* Jay reminded himself. *Don't forget that. Don't ever forget that. Dude can gouge your eyes out and behead you, if he wants to. If he tells these guys to tear you to pieces, they will.*

Jay said weakly, "Cool." Heads swiveled in his direction, including Kevin's. Jay clamped his mouth shut and cleared his throat.

"I greet you, my brothers and sisters," Absalom said in a booming voice. "This has been a tragic time of loss and grief. But no more. I'm here to bring our people back to a time of plenty. A new harvest." He smiled at the Anointed One. "I am here to fulfill the mission laid before me, and I will not fail our leader, or you, my brethren."

Absalom raised his arms toward the ceiling of the cave.

"Praise be, I am here to resurrect the Master."

There was a collective gasp. Then silence. Then cheers.

One of the other vampires, a sweet little redhead dressed in purple, raised her hand. "How?"

"Do not question my acolyte," the Anointed One growled. His voice thundered like a hellish chorus, echoing and reverberating off the walls of the cavern.

"No, my lord. Let us rejoice that your flock is careful and cautious. The Master left you goodly sheep." Absalom bowed to the young leader, but didn't lower his gaze. "We have need of vampires who can think."

"So many can't," the Anointed One said, sighing heavily.

Jay thought about that. He didn't know why some came back with all their faculties—like him and Corvelle, and Kevin, too—and some were simple, ravening beasts. He didn't know if it was luck of the draw or some weakness in life or the strength of your demon, or what.

"Now, to answer your question." Absalom smiled at the redhead. "I have wonderful news." He spread his arms wide. "A miracle has occurred. When the Slayer struck down our Master—"

Boos rose up and drowned him out.

The Anointed One stomped his foot and shouted, "Silence!"

The boos died down. Absalom's smile grew. "I am truly touched by your loyalty. It speaks of your great love for the Master. Now, when she pushed him through that skylight, and he fell, it is true that he turned to dust."

Kevin looked directly at Jay, as if willing him to keep quiet. *No problem,* Jay thought, trying hard to swallow. Talk about dust. It was in his throat.

"But . . ." Absalom held up a finger. "Unholiest of miracles, his bones remained intact."

There was dead silence.

"But his enemies, the ones who smote our great leader down, they gathered them up. They have them now."

"How . . . how do you know all this?" the redhead stammered. *Go, chick,* Jay thought. Of course, that was the question on everybody's mind. His, especially.

"I know all, see all," Absalom said, grinning. He

winked at her. "The power of the Master is alive in me, as I live in him."

She frowned. "But nobody here knows that stuff. And you're from out of town."

Jay stared straight ahead. He was dizzy with fear. Kevin had assured him that no one else but he, Kevin, had seen the Slayer's friends take the Master's bones out of the Sunnydale High School library. *Just how reliable is that guy?* he worried.

Absalom looked casually at the Anointed One. The child nodded gravely.

Absalom walked calmly toward the redhead, pulled a stake from his vest, and smoothly, quickly stabbed her in the heart. The beginning of her scream signaled the end of her life.

"The time has come to trust in me," Absalom said. His eyes were golden, his fangs long and glistening-sharp. And he was smiling. "For he—or she—who is not with me, is against me. We will find those bones. And as I stand here tonight, witnessing to his might and his glory, we will have our Master back."

No one cheered louder than Kevin.

Unless it was Corvelle and Jay.

Yeah, I'm cheering like my life depends on it, Jay thought, totally freaking out. *'Cause it does.*

Jay slid his glance toward Corvelle, who was chewing his tobacco for all he was worth. He flashed Jay a secret signal, thumb out to the side, like they were hitching.

It meant, *We need to get the hell out of here.*

Slowly, Jake started sidling toward the tunnel exit to the lair.

Then he looked up, and saw Kevin staring at him.

Kevin made the same signal as Corvelle. Jay's eyes bulged. Kevin shouldn't know that signal, but he did.

This sucks, he thought.

Giles's heart skipped a beat when Jenny glided into the courtyard, a paper bag cradled in her arm. Her dark hair was clipped atop her head, with tendrils curling beneath her chin. She had on a beaded gray, clinging blouse and a long black skirt.

Here's the affectionate ghost, he thought as she beamed at him. A score of poems about beautiful phantoms by Englishmen long dead sprang to mind. *She walks in beauty, like the night.*

"Giles." She was breathless. She greeted the others with a nod. "There was a vampire in the magic shop. He was a student of mine." She patted her chest to catch her breath. "I think he started to follow me."

"A vampire?" Willow echoed. "How did you know?"

"No reflection in the mirror," Jenny answered.

Giles was alarmed. "Do you suppose they know?"

"That we have the Master's bones?" she said in a quiet voice. "We were so careful. I did that protection spell before we gathered them."

"I placed wards," Giles murmured.

"You two have been busy. Alone," Xander said, wagging a finger. "Funny cars, I can let that go. But this is sounding pretty much like something two young people in love should be refraining from."

"Xander," Willow muttered, "please. They're *teachers.*"

"Teachers in lust, I think. And, oh, Angel, you wouldn't have, by any chance, mentioned this bone-collecting to any vamp buddies of yours? Engaged in a little pillow talk with some toothy hottie, perhaps?"

Angel simply stared at Xander. Giles stepped forward. "Now is not the time to point fingers at each other," he said. "It doesn't matter at the moment how they found out. It only matters if they do indeed know we have the bones."

"We've got to cleanse them asap," Xander said. "I say, bring on the mugwort!"

"I had a thought," Jenny said hesitantly. "We don't know why the bones haven't disintegrated, and we can feel the Master's demonic presence."

"*Some* of us can," Xander cut in.

Jenny looked confused, then continued on. "But what if cleansing the bones is the wrong thing to do? What if it actually frees the Master, like—" She gestured with her hand as she searched for the right words. "—like letting the *jinn* out of the bottle?"

"Gin?" Xander echoed.

"A genie," Giles said slowly. "That's a possibility."

"We might be doing the exact wrong thing," Jenny continued, "if we cleanse these bones."

Giles thought for a moment. Then he said, "So we bury them. In consecrated ground. We place wards all around them so the vampires can't even hope to touch them."

"Excuse me? Shovels?" Xander offered.

"Lots of consecrated ground," Willow said anxiously. "Lots of it. Hectares of it."

"And I would expect you, Will, to know precisely what a hectare is," Xander said fondly.

"We've got to move them now, then," Angel spoke up. "If that vampire in the shop suspected anything, they'll be all over this place."

"If," Jenny replied, looking at Giles.

"We can't take that chance." Giles headed for his front door.

Xander followed after him. "But I thought we'd decided cleansing the bones was the action item on our agenda du jour."

"We're changing the menu," Giles informed him.

"You teachers. You're just so chummy," Xander grumped.

"Xander," Willow said.

Giles felt his face flush. Truth be told, he was rather liking how chummy Miss Calendar had become. And he was delighted she hadn't yet left Sunnydale. She'd made mention of some rather dreadful New Age be-in or whatever they were called these days—convocation?—and he'd somehow assumed she'd planned to leave the second school was out. But here they were, saving the world yet again—hopefully—and, as usual, her nearness was intoxicating and distracting.

Giles led the way to his weapons trunk. His various cudgels and battleaxes were strewn about. Knives, maces, and swords lay across the divan. The Master's bones were locked inside the trunk, with chains and padlocks securely bound around the outside.

"Wow, it's Houdini," Xander said.

"Angel, please come in," Giles said, when he counted heads and found Willow, Xander, and Jenny in his living room, but not the vampire.

"Angel?"

"Silence is not golden," Xander breathed.

Giles looked at the faces of the two young people.
I shouldn't have let Buffy go, he thought.

* * *

Jay and Corvelle emerged from the manhole and stood across from Sunnydale High School in a state of shock.

"Damn. We made it," Corvelle said. He looked at Jay. "Nobody stopped us. Nobody so much as blinked."

Jay nodded. "Always said I'd leave Sunnydale one day. I guess it's time."

He broke into a run. Corvelle shouted, "Hey! Wait up!" and joined him.

They were only a few yards down the road when something moved into their path. It was tall, and solid.

And it was not a some*thing*. It was a some*one*.

It was Absalom. He had his hands behind his back.

Jay and Corvelle screeched to a halt.

"Dear brothers, where could you be going on such a fine night?" the vampire asked pleasantly.

"Um," Jay answered. "Just, uh . . ." He looked at Corvelle.

Absalom rocked on his heels. "I believe the correct answer is, 'Brother Absalom, we're going to fetch the Master's bones and bring them home.' "

Jay croaked, "Huh?"

Absalom just smiled. He took a step forward.

Corvelle said quicky, "We're going to fetch the Master's bones."

"And bring them home," Jay added.

"For his works are mighty," Absalom said. "Brothers, we'll come with you."

From the bushes on either side of the road, vampires emerged. One, two . . . a dozen.

But no sign of Kevin.

Absalom's eyes glowed in the black night. "Onward, brothers. For the weak who falter are as dust."

He brought his fists from around his back and lifted them to eye level. With a cheery smile, he opened them. Dust sprinkled onto the blacktop.

"Ashes to ashes, brothers. And the weak are as dust to—"

Jay swallowed hard. *Kevin?*

"Miss Calendar was flirting a lot with Mr. Giles," he ventured.

"The Slayer's Watcher. Praise be." Absalom looked pleased. "The moon is full, and she shines down upon this revelation. Oh, how she smiles."

"Angel?" Rupert said again.

Willow and Xander looked at each other in silence.

They're just children, Jenny thought. *Buffy is, too. So young to be mixed up in things like this.*

Willow slid her glance toward her, almost as if she could read her mind. Rupert moved slowly toward the open door as the others held their breath.

"Angel," Xander whispered bitterly.

Oh, God, maybe he's gone to tell the other vampires we've got the bones, Jenny thought. *Despite all I have been taught about the vampire Angelus being given back his soul, maybe his capacity for evil is still greater than his inherent goodness.*

She cleared her throat and said quietly, "We'd better get these things out of here."

"Indeed," Rupert murmured, as he crept toward the door. She saw that he had a stake in his hand. Slowly, carefully, she bent toward the couch to pick up the crossbow lying there. It was unloaded. She had no idea where the bolts were, nor how to load them.

"But where'd he go?" Xander demanded. "Out for a pack of cigs? 'Cause you know, guys who say that never come back."

Rupert gestured to Jenny. She crept through the shadows toward him. He pulled a ring of keys from his pocket and held them out to her. He smelled good. His light brown hair was shot with gray, but that only made him more appealing, in her eyes. She looked down at his strong hands, the veins in them as he pressed them into her palm, and felt a flutter in her stomach.

If he ever learns who I really am, and why I'm really here . . . She pushed the thought away. For now she was Jenny Calendar, and not Janna, a Kalderash Gypsy. She was a technopagan helping a sorcerer dispose of their common enemy: the world's enemy. Anything else was trivial and irrelevant.

"Right," Rupert breathed. He looked at her. "When you open the trunk, the emanations will probably be stronger. You'd best be prepared."

She nodded. Closing her eyes, she murmured an ancient Gypsy blessing. It brought with it little peace.

She whispered, "Which key?"

"The largest one." He returned his attention to the door. The tension was so thick that Jenny wanted to scream.

"Open the chest, Jenny," he breathed. "I'm going to look outside."

"No," she said urgently. "Rupert, no."

He gave her a smile. "I'll take care."

He slid around the jamb and blended with the night. Jenny heard Willow make a little anxious groan. The two students watched her with large eyes as she crossed back to the trunk and knelt beside it.

As she unlocked all the locks, she could feel the evil of the Master. It was like a bone-chilling ache. The stench of something rotten pervaded the air.

This place has been defiled, she thought.

"So much evil," Willow whispered.

"Of the bad," Xander added softly. "I can feel it now, too."

Jenny opened the trunk.

With sickening dread, she peered in. The arms were folded in on themselves. The hands were positioned palms up. Finger bones had separated and were nestled on either side of the skull, like huge, macabre earrings.

Then the Master's left hand shot straight up and wrapped itself around her throat.

Across the room, Giles burst in, shouting, "Arm yourselves!"

"What?" Willow struggled to pull Jenny free.

Xander pointed at the back window and shouted, "Earth to Alamo! Vampires, dead ahead!"

"Jenny!" Rupert cried.

As Jenny clutched at the bony arm, Rupert grabbed the paper bag of mugwort she had placed on the floor. He ripped it open and sprinkled the mugwort across the bones.

She couldn't breathe. Her vision was blurring, but she saw the window above the trunk splinter as it was yanked from its frame. A vampire charged at the empty space, but was flung backward as if by some unseen force.

"Hah! No invitation, no service!" Xander cried.

The Master's other hand thrust up and wrapped itself around Jenny's throat.

Rupert began the Rite of Cleansing:

> *"Earth, Air, Fire, Water,*
> *Pure Elements, Pure Energy.*
> *All a sign of Purity.*
> *Ashes to ashes,*
> *Of Phoenix born,*
> *Dust to dust,*
> *Cleanse the unclean."*

The skeletal fingers loosened their grip. The bones separated and fell back into the chest, landing inside the rib cage. Jenny collapsed, holding on to the side of the trunk as she spasmed with coughing.

Rupert sprinkled mudwort liberally over each white fragment she could see. His hands were shaking.

At that moment, the pop of a gun gave Giles only brief warning as he was struck. He wasn't even sure where the bullet had lodged as the impact knocked him sideways. He only knew that it hurt, very much.

He landed hard. There were more gunshots; and then something was thrown through the shattered window. It was a Molotov cocktail—a firebomb in a bottle—and it caught the curtains and flashed across the ceiling as if devouring a trail of gunpowder. Flame and smoke erupted in a fireball.

"Oh, my God!" Jenny cried hoarsely. "Rupert!"

"I'm fine," he rasped, though even that effort cost him a great deal. "Bones. Get them," he said.

Things began to get hazy for Giles. He thought he saw Angel dash inside the flat, which was fast becoming an inferno. As the vampire did so, Angel staggered backward and grabbed his chest.

"Angel!" Willow cried.

"Get out of there!" Angel shouted, clenching his teeth. "They're here!"

"We can't let them get the bones," Jenny said to Giles. He nodded. She glanced around the room and picked up a large wooden cross, which had been in the weapons trunk.

"Willow, Xander, go!" Angel shouted, heading for the trunk. "There's too many!"

"Fighting," Willow said bravely. Giles wanted either to hug her or throw her out the front door. *These children are so brave,* he thought. *No wonder the Slayer loves them.*

But there were times for courage, and times for practicality. Heroic as it might be to make a stand and die for it, Giles could not permit them to make that choice.

Pushing himself up with his good arm, he called to them, "Out the door. *Now,*" when they hesitated.

"Giles, no," Willow pleaded. Her eyes widened. "You're hurt!"

Xander looked at Angel, then at Giles, and last at Jenny. Then he wrapped his hand around Willow's forearm and dragged her toward the front door.

The siren of a fire truck screamed in the distance. As Giles listened, it drew nearer.

It was coming to his condo.

There were shouts and cries in the courtyard. A woman screamed, "These poor boys! They've been horribly burned!" He recognized it as Mrs. Potter, the property manager.

"Ma'am, me and my friend here are trying to save the guy who lives there," said a vaguely familiar voice. "Is it okay if we go in there?"

"No, Mrs. Potter," Giles croaked.

"Mr. Giles is in there? Oh, my gracious. Yes, go on in!"

The invitation had been made.

"Angel!" Jenny shouted.

Before Giles knew what was happening, two vampires burst through the door, dashed through the smoke and the heat, and brutally knocked Jenny out of the way. With a grunt she fell to the floor.

Xander and Willow turned on the pair at once. Willow punched at one while Xander took on the other. They were both about to be assaulted when the vampires simultaneously exploded into dust, revealing Angel behind them. He had staked them both with hand-carved stakes Giles had put on his coffee table when loading the trunk with the Master's bones.

There was no time to thank the vampire as he whirled around and took on another vampire, slamming it hard with a brutal roundhouse, then keeping it off-balance with a whipping side-kick. The creature wobbled, and Angel seized the moment to plunge a stake into its unbeating heart. It, too, became dust, which was whipped into the maelstrom of Giles's home.

"Get the bones!" Jenny shouted to Xander.

"Ick," Xander muttered. Then he did as she asked, Willow assisting, gathering up all the little joints and fingers as if they were the playing pieces of an elaborate board game.

Then the two grabbed up the bones in the blanket they had been secured in, and fled through the front door—or rather, where the door once had been. Now it was a gaping maw of fire and burning wood.

"Xander," Giles shouted. "Willow, run."

Through the burning window, he saw the pair fleeing across the yard, only to catch the attention of a pair of vampires who both looked somewhat familiar. *He worked on my car once,* Giles thought, his mind becoming confused with the haze of pain. *Unusual name. Corbel, Cor . . . Corvelle.*

Willow turned and brandished a cross. Xander kicked at the other vampire and disappeared inside a hedge of bushes. The vampire ran in after him. Willow held the other at bay, glancing anxiously over her shoulder.

They're going to die. My fault . . .

"Get out of here," Angel said to Jenny. He was battling yet another vampire.

"No," Jenny whispered. She put both her arms around Giles's chest. "I'm going to move you," she said.

"No," Giles bit off. "Go—"

"Not without you."

Her dark eyes were all he saw as thick smoke swirled around them both.

I love her, he thought. *I cannot let her die.*

Summoning all his strength, he got to his feet. She helped him, and put her arm around him. They half-ran, half-stumbled to the doorway.

Giles turned and saw that Angel was outnumbered. He was surrounded by vampires. Their battle in the orange flames was like a strange shadow-play, the dance of death.

Buffy will be desolate if anything happens to him, Giles thought mournfully.

"Angel," he shouted, reaching out a hand.

Then firefighters in dark rubber suits burst into the room.

Giles was hoisted over a man's shoulder and carried out of his condo. Another firefighter carried Jenny.

Giles was bundled onto a stretcher, half-rising and muttering, "No. Stop." No one listened to him. A paramedic slipped an oxygen mask over his face.

Then he was carried to an ambulance and carted inside. The door slammed shut, and the ambulance spirited him away.

"I'm all right," Jenny assured the firefighter as he set her on the grass.

Just then, Angel appeared. His face was human, and covered with bruises. He shook his head.

She slumped.

Across the street, Willow and Xander emerged from behind a thick hedgerow. As they crept beneath a streetlight, they looked like watery apparitions.

When they saw Jenny looking toward them, they ran across the street to her.

"Miss Calendar?" Willow looked terribly frightened. "They got them. We tried to fight them off, but . . ."

Jenny nodded, defeated. Xander glared at Angel.

"And you were where?"

Angel glowered at Xander. "I was outside, tracking. I smelled them. I went down the road. I was trying to head them off."

"You should have stayed inside. Giles and Miss Calendar almost died," Xander flung at him accusingly.

"No, Xander, he did the right thing," Jenny assured the young man. "If they succeed in resurrecting the Master . . ." She trailed off. *The vampires have the Master's bones. What are we going to do now?*

Then she swallowed hard. "I want to go to the hospital. I need to see if Rupert's all right."

"I'll get you there," Angel said.

"What about the mission?" Xander demanded. "Are we all gonna give up?"

"What do you want to do?" Angel shot back. "Go back down to the lair?"

"At least I'm man enough to," Xander flung at him. "Accent on man, as in human being."

"We can't afford to argue," Jenny said. "I covered the bones with mugwort and I was able to recite an incantation. It might hold for a little while." She took a breath. "*If* it was the right thing to do in the first place."

"It makes sense to check on Giles," Willow offered. "Maybe he can think of some book or something." She made a *moue* of apology. "Thanks for trying to stop them, Angel."

"It's his job, as one of the good guys," Xander said. "Right, Dead Boy?"

Angel said nothing. Miss Calendar said, "I have the keys to Rupert's car. You two go home for now."

"Let's go," Angel said. He turned away without another word.

Jenny walked beside him. As they moved toward the curb, where Giles's car was parked, Willow's voice trailed back at them. "You are so rude to him, Xander."

"He can take it." Xander's voice was hard and cold.

Jenny said, "I can go by myself, Angel. I'm feeling a lot better."

"It's all right." He opened the passenger-side door for her. It squealed on its hinges. "Although I'd rather fight a few more vampires than drive this thing."

She managed a smile. "It's a really terrible car, isn't it."

"It really is."

* * *

Xander's eyes narrowed as he and Willow watched the car disappear into the darkness. "I swear, he planned this," Xander said. He turned on his heel.

"Where are you going?"

"I'm finding me some vampire bones," he told her. "Or die trying. Metaphorically speaking, of course."

She sighed and caught up with him. He smiled at her. "Ready, Girl Wonder?"

"Ready as I'll ever be," she said glumly.

"Me neither."

Grimly, the two walked the walk.

As they ran down the street across from the burning condo, Jay looked at the bundle in his arms with astonishment.

"We did it," he murmured. "We bagged the bones."

Corvelle spit tobacco juice. " 'Course we did."

Jay slowed down and stopped running. Corvelle joined him.

They both made a protective circle around the bundle.

"Hey," Jay said, "where's everybody else?"

They were alone. It looked as if none of the other vampires Absalom had sent on the raiding party had survived.

It took Jay a moment to believe it. Corvelle spit another stream of tobacco, and Jay blurted anxiously, "How long does that crap last, for crying out loud?"

"Huh?"

"Nothing. Nothing." Jay ran his hand through his hair. "What are we going to do, Corvelle?"

"Huh?"

"We've got the bones," Jay said, as if Corvelle was as blind as he was gross. "Everybody else got dusted.

What if we let Absalom think we got dusted, too?" He glanced down at the Master's bones. "Dump these things and head out of town? You can hotwire a car. Hell, you can *build* a car, if it comes to that."

Corvelle considered. Then he shrugged. "Absalom's too smart. They're all too smart." Then he frowned. "How come you told Kevin our secret signal?"

"I didn't. But how come Kevin told us he was the only one who watched the Slayer take out the Master? The only one who knew he wasn't total dust? Because Absalom sure knew."

The bones moved inside the blanket. Jay cried out and dropped the bundle. They landed in the road, beside the storm drain.

"They're alive!" he shouted.

Corvelle shrieked. He turned tail and ran.

Jay had a mind to follow him, until a voice said from the storm drain, "Push them down here."

Jay crept closer to the grate. A pale face stared up at him. With yellow eyes. "Man, they're, like, possessed. They were moving."

"Push them down, Jay," Kevin said calmly.

And Jay was just about to do that when something started burning in the middle of his back.

"Ow!" he shouted, whirling around.

A tall, dark-haired guy was holding a cross. Beside him was Willow Rosenberg. He knew her from the computer lab.

"Jay?" she said, shocked. "You got bitten?"

"What's going on?" Kevin hissed.

"Company," Jay replied uneasily. His back was seared. The guy must have pressed the cross right into his flesh.

"Tell your boyfriend thanks for burning me," he said to Willow.

"He's not my boyfriend," she replied.

"And you're branded like a cow. Ha-ha, Bossy." The guy brandished the cross at him. "Will?"

She pulled a stake from inside the bib of her overalls.

"We'll just take those bones," she said.

Jay made a face. "You don't want them. They're alive."

"Oh, we can probably take care of that," Willow said smugly. "We can do spells and stuff."

"Willow, let's keep our secrets to ourselves," the guy muttered.

Jay said to Willow, "Yeah? You hanging with Miss Calendar these days?"

Willow blinked. "What do you know about her?"

Jay shrugged. "Just what I see in magic shops."

"Jay," Kevin barked. "Come on. Throw me the bones."

Willow firmly clutched the stake. "Do and you're dust."

Jay wanted to lunge at her, but the cross held him at bay. The storm drain was way too small for him to jump down into, but he figured if he ran, he might have a chance at a clean getaway. He wondered where that coward Corvelle had gone to.

"Jay, throw me the bones or else," Kevin said ominously.

Willow set her jaw and raised her chin. "Let's do a series of 'and/or' statements, shall we? We have a cross and a stake. That guy is underground and can't get us before we get you."

Jay stayed silent. She had a point.

"Why do you guys worhsip the Master so much anyway?" Xander asked. "He'd turn on you in a Hellmouth second."

"We don't like him," Jay blurted. "We were trying to make sure he never came back. Then Absalom showed and—"

"Shut *up*," Kevin demanded.

"If you don't want him to ever come back, let us have his bones. We'll put 'em somewhere where the sun don't shine. Or rather, where it does." Willow looked confused.

"What Willow is trying to say," the guy said, "is that we appear to have a common interest. We don't want the Master back, and you don't want the Master back. Now, I don't know what Thing down there wants, but what do you say we make a deal?"

"Kev? He has a point." Jay glanced down at the bundle.

"No!" Kevin shouted, rattling the grate. "Not to humans! Don't give the bones to humans!"

"Why not?" Jay asked.

At that moment, he bent down, grabbed up the bones, and threw them at the human guy. As Jay'd expected, he dropped the cross trying to catch them. But Willow still had her stake, and she lunged forward with a "grrr" as Jay darted out of their way.

He charged down the street, terrified out of his wits, listening as the two humans started arguing about what to do next. Kevin was screaming like a maniac. It finally dawned on Jay that Kevin had been lying about the bones all along—he'd wanted them for himself, before Absalom could locate them. *Why, to raise the Master? Bargain for some power?* Jay didn't suppose it mattered now. All he knew was that everybody was mad at him, Absalom on the one hand and Kevin on the other.

He might as well start singing "Dust in the Wind," and right now.

Then a car squealed up, and the passenger-side door opened.

"Get in, buddy," Corvelle said.

Jay leaped in and slammed the door shut. Corvelle peeled out and nearly took a mailbox out as he screamed around a corner.

"Thanks," Jay said.

Corvelle spat tobacco juice out the window.

"You want to go back and run 'em over?" Corvelle asked.

Jay considered. Then he shook his head. "Naw. Rosenberg was nice to me in school. Didn't hog the equipment in the computer lab. Besides, everybody will be so busy trying to get the bones from her, they might forget about us."

Corvelle grinned. "You're one smart vampire."

"Thanks, Corvelle." He leaned his head back against the seat. "Why'd you come back for me?"

"You might have ratted me out. Told 'em I was still alive. Lied and told 'em I had the bones." He grinned at Jay. "But you didn't, did you?"

"No. I—"

Corvelle lurched the car over to the side of the road. He reached down beneath his seat and pulled out a broken-off bit of a one-by-four. Slammed it into Jay's chest.

"Damn you to hell," Jay said, microseconds before he went there.

* * *

Jenny Calendar walked into the room beside a nurse, who was wheeling in a wheelchair.

"Mr. Giles, you're officially discharged," the nurse said cheerily.

"Thank God. At last," Giles said.

"Are you certain you don't want to wait until morning? Your insurance company has authorized an additional day."

"I'm sure," Giles said.

Jenny took his hand in hers. She smiled at him and said, "Your apartment's almost back to livable, Rupert. You lost a few things, but I found a company that specializes in smoke damage. Not surprisingly, there are a number of them in Sunnydale."

"Not surprisingly," he said.

Angel was waiting for them in Giles's Citroën at the driveway in front of the hospital. As soon as Giles was settled in, Jenny said, "If you can manage it, Willow and Xander are at the graveyard now."

Giles nodded. "You've brought plenty of holy water and wafers, I trust?"

"Lots and lots," Jenny assured him.

"I feel like I'm driving a tanker full of nitroglycerin," Angel said, glancing at her package. Giles liked that the vampire was nervous.

"It was wrong of me to let the Slayer go," Giles said, filled with remorse. "Her friends are going to be in constant jeopardy all summer."

"Willow's been looking forward to computer camp," Jenny murmured wistfully. "And Xander was going on about how he's going to relax and just do nothing."

"Please explain to me how that's different from

what he does in school?" Giles asked. They shared a rueful smile.

"We have to protect them," Jenny said. "If there's slaying to be done, we should do it. Not let them know."

Giles considered. Then he nodded. "Agreed."

Angel raised his head as if to speak, then remained silent.

"They're children," Jenny said.

"Children," Giles concurred.

It was a relatively short drive to their cemetery of choice. Willow and Xander were there, shovels at the ready, the Master's bones back in a trunk. This one was an old steamer Xander's Uncle Rory used to hide his empties in, not realizing, of course, that the entire family knew about his drinking problem.

The moon shone down, no longer full, and Giles emerged painfully from the car. He shuffled like an old man toward the two. Willow waved happily. Giles smiled faintly and waved back.

Xander bobbed his head. Then he gestured to the newly dug grave—practically a pit—and said, "Welcome back, G-ma—Giles."

"Thank you. It's delightful to be back," Giles said. He held out his hand. Willow bent down and produced a Bible.

"I shall be reading the service for the dead," he announced, "while you two and Miss Calendar sanctify the earth."

Angel moved a ways away.

Then he was gone, melting into the night.

"I hate it when he does that," Xander said.

"Please, read fast," Willow begged Giles. "I'm cold and scared and I feel like we're not alone."

We probably aren't, Giles thought. *Who knows what will happen next?*

But he kept his thoughts to himself as he cleared his throat and began to read.

The Anointed One watched from his throne as Kevin knelt before Absalom and said, "I have failed, my brother. The two traitors disobeyed me. They gave the bones to the humans, and ran."

Absalom's hands were folded behind his back. He brought his left hand around and opened his fist. "Not to worry, little brother. They didn't run far enough." Dust trickled to the slick, wet floor of the cave. "But tell me, why did they lose faith in you? How did they know you were secretly serving the Master, rooting out his enemies among his obedient flock?"

Kevin shook his head. "I don't know. I'm not sure they did."

"Nor am I." Absalom smiled gently. "You gave it your all. I know that."

Kevin looked hopeful that he might be spared, despite his failure.

"I gave it my all," he repeated.

"But your all . . . wasn't enough," Absalom said.

He brought his right hand around. In it he held a stake.

Before Kevin could so much as cry out, he was dust.

The Anointed One shifted on the throne and sighed.

"Do not lose patience, my prince," Absalom said soothingly. "I will find a spell to undo the consecrated protection."

He turned to the vampire who had been watching from the shadows. "Which cemetery?" he asked her.

She smiled. "Shady Hill," she replied. "They buried his bones in Shady Hill."

Absalom smiled broadly. His fangs glistened. His eyes glowed.

"Not for long, little sister," he promised. "Praise be, not for long. For I say unto you, before this season dies, our Master will live again."

LOOKS CAN KILL

CAMERON DOKEY

"I don't like this," said Rupert Giles.

"I'll never understand you, Rupert," Jenny Calendar replied lightly, though Giles could hear the nervousness in her voice. It was their first night together on patrol. He figured she was entitled. "It's the middle of the night. We're in a graveyard. What's not to like?"

"And here I was actually afraid I might miss Buffy this summer," Giles remarked.

"Are you comparing me to a teenager?"

"Perish the thought."

"Or not."

But perishing brought Giles right back to his original problem.

I'd really much rather be patrolling on my own.

But with the Slayer gone for the summer, that simply wasn't an option. Giles needed all the help guarding the Hellmouth that he could get. At the moment, that meant patrolling with Jenny Calendar, a thing Giles had definite mixed feelings about.

Jenny was brave. She'd proved that during the fatal encounter with the Master. Fatal to the Master, that is. But she was also inexperienced, not accustomed to the rigors of patrol.

Not only that, being one-on-one with her in a potentially dangerous situation was proving difficult for Giles in a way he hadn't anticipated.

I'm far too old to become a slave to my own hormones.

He did have them. It was true. And, at the moment, they were working overtime.

Because the rest of the truth was that Rupert Giles was having serious feelings for Jenny Calendar. Feelings he was afraid would interfere with his ability to fight effectively when she was by his side. He'd been raised to be a gentleman, as well as a Watcher.

A combination that in this case, he very much feared had the potential to become a fatal double whammy. The urge to protect those for whom he felt responsible was strong.

Carefully, Giles avoided stepping into a gopher hole. Or at least he hoped it was a gopher hole, and not a place where something small, nasty, and underworldly had crawled up to see what was going on. He turned to warn Jenny to be careful.

He was just in time to watch her drop to her knees, a stake in one clenched fist, and sink it full force into the hole. She pulled her arm back out, brushed dirt from the sleeve of her jacket.

"It's all right. It's just a gopher hole," she announced.

Giles felt his stomach lurch, then settle. This was much worse than he had thought.

"Do you suppose you could be a little less precipitous?" he asked, his tone sharp.

Jenny got to her feet, tucking the stake into the back waistband of her pants. She made such a big production of it that Giles knew she was hurt. "I said it was just a gopher hole."

"You had no way of knowing that ahead of time," Giles went on. "You could have been sucked right in by . . . whatever might be down there."

Jenny eyed what was left of the hole a little doubtfully. "I don't think I'd fit through there, Rupert."

"Anything can be made to fit anywhere if sufficient force is exerted," Giles said shortly.

"All right," Jenny challenged with a lift of her chin. "What would you have done?"

"Used my foot," Giles replied.

He moved away, his walk betraying his continued agitation.

"You're doing it again, aren't you?" Jenny asked as she hurried to keep up. "I can always tell."

"I am not."

They walked a few steps in silence.

"What?"

"What?"

"I'm doing what again?" Giles asked. The pace of his walk slowed.

"Wishing I'd be a good little woman and just stay home."

"Are you suggesting I'm a male chauvinist?" Giles said, stopping altogether. "That's degrading to us both."

"That's right, it is," Jenny said, growing heated in her turn. "So I'd appreciate it if you'd just knock it off. I can take care of myself, Rupert. You ought to know that by now."

"It's not your abilities I doubt," Giles snapped. "It's—"

"Get down!"

Without warning, Jenny hurled herself forward, crashing into Giles's chest and knocking them both to the ground. Giles felt the breath shoot from his lungs.

"Miss Calendar—Jenny," he managed to gasp out. "Much as I appreciate your boldness, I hardly think—"

"I saw something," Jenny whispered as she rolled off him. "I'm pretty sure it landed in those trees over there."

She pointed. Giles could see her extended forefinger tremble ever so slightly.

"I don't see anything," he said as he got cautiously to his knees. "But the trees would provide excellent cover."

"What should we do now?" Jenny asked. "I know. We could split up, try to trap it between us."

She boosted herself to her feet, staying low. Before she could take so much as a step, Giles's arm flashed out. He gripped her wrist tightly, halting her forward momentum.

"Absolutely not."

Jenny's head swiveled to face him. *"What?"*

"Absolutely not," Giles said again. "We don't know what it is. There's strength in numbers. We go together, or not at all."

"Well, all right," Jenny said, her tone aggrieved. "If that's the way you want it."

"It is."

Jenny jerked her arm away. "The macho look does not become you."

"I'll take that under advisement." Giles got to his feet in a crouch. "Stay behind me."

He began to lope toward the trees, staying low. As he ran, he reached into the pocket of his jacket and pulled out a stake.

Giles didn't know if what they were facing was a vampire, but it seemed as good a place as any to start. The followers of the recently vanquished Master were scattered, but they were still very much present.

And unless he missed his guess, they had revenge on their minds.

Giles slowed his pace as the trees loomed ahead. *No sense in rushing in blindly,* he thought.

"You're sure you saw something?" he whispered to Jenny.

"I'm sure," she whispered back. "I still think we—"

"Well, well," a voice interrupted. "Look who's come to call. So nice of you to pay a visit. And you've even brought a date along."

Giles stopped cold. So suddenly that Jenny crashed into him, making him stumble. He gestured for Jenny to keep behind him. In the midst of the trees, he thought he could just make out the silhouette of a figure. Tall. Slim.

"Do you see it?"

"I see it," Jenny answered. "But I don't recognize it."

New kid in town?

Giles took a step closer. If Buffy were here, she'd fight first and ask questions later. But that wasn't Giles's style. "I'm afraid you have the advantage of me," he announced.

"In more ways than one," came the reply from the

trees. There was a rustle of sound as the thing launched itself toward him. Giles felt a movement at his back.

"Jenny, no!"

But Jenny was already off and running, angling away from Giles toward the far right of the clump of trees. *Trying to divide and conquer,* Giles thought. He saw their unknown adversary skid to a stop.

Giles hesitated, his body swept by warring instincts. His brain said he should go left, countering Jenny, complementing her action. Trying to put the thing they faced between them.

His gut said he should protect Jenny at all costs.

His brain never even stood a chance.

With an oath, Giles sprinted after Jenny Calendar.

Out of the corner of his eye, he could see the thing from the trees pivot and begin to hurtle toward Jenny at a dead run.

I've got to get there first.

Giles reached Jenny just as they passed under the cover of the trees. His fingers closed around her arm, jerking her back, sharply. He heard a sickening *smack* as she connected with a tree trunk. Jenny tumbled to the ground and lay still.

Dear God, what have I done?

The figure skidded to a stop. He and Giles regarded one another. Quickly, Giles tried to take stock. His adversary was slim, a thing which Giles told himself should work to his own advantage. But he wasn't so sure. Something about his unknown adversary's stance reminded Giles of tightly coiled wire. Dangerous energy barely held in check.

The figure made a movement toward Jenny. Giles stepped to block his way. The figure stepped back.

"Nice going," he commented. "If all the humans I had to deal with were like you, life would be a whole lot easier."

"Can we just dispense with the small talk?" Giles asked, heart pounding.

"Sure. No problem."

How badly is Jenny hurt? Giles wondered. *Did she need a doctor? A trip to the hospital? And just how furious was she going to be when she woke up?*

That was easy. *Plenty.* He'd never hear the end of it, in all likelihood.

The figure glided closer, and Giles shifted position again. The only way this thing was getting to Jenny was over Giles's dead body.

"Just what are you, anyway?" he asked.

"Don't worry. You'll find out sooner or later. Actually, how about right now?"

With a fluid motion, the figure leaped straight toward him. Giles fell backward, stumbling over Jenny's inert form. He landed full length on his back on the damp ground. Before he could begin to rise, strong, supple fingers wrapped around his throat. Giles looked up into a pair of eyes the color of mercury.

Quicksilver, he thought. It was probably a clue, but he seemed to be having a focus problem. Probably due to lack of oxygen.

"I must say, this was much easier than I thought it would be," the thing choking him said in a conversational tone. "Not that I don't appreciate all your help, of course."

Giles bucked. He lifted one arm to try to drive the stake into the creature's back, and found his arm pinned tightly to the ground. The strength of the grip on his throat never faltered.

Giles's breath began to come in gasps. Lights exploded behind his eyes. His chest felt like there were hot bands of iron wrapped around it, squeezing tighter and tighter.

"But it does sort of take the fun out of things," the figure went on. "Still, it pays to be flexible, don't you think? I can cope."

"Try coping with this," said a voice Giles recognized.

Through his dimming vision, he saw two hands descend upon his adversary's shoulder. The pain in Giles's chest ceased abruptly as the thing that had been choking him flew through the air over his head. He heard a *thud* as it hit the ground.

For the first time in his life, Giles found himself grateful to be staring up into the face of a vampire.

"You all right?" Angel asked.

"Ughhh," Giles replied.

Angel shrugged. "If you say so. I'll be right back. Don't go anywhere."

Somehow, I don't think that's going to be a problem.

"What do you think it was?" asked Jenny.

The three night patrollers were gathered at Giles's apartment. Jenny had come to not long after Angel had chased the whatever-it-was away, then resisted all of Giles's attempts to take her to the hospital.

"You've looked after me quite enough for one evening, Rupert," she'd remarked, waspishly.

Deciding that discretion was the better part of valor, for the time being anyway, Giles had retired to the kitchen to make a pot of tea. Now, they were reassembled in his living room, cups of hot liquid steaming on the coffee table.

The vampire. The Watcher. And the pagan.

Even Angel had taken a cup. He sat in one of Giles's overstuffed chairs, cradling it in his hands. Apparently, he was having a let's-fit-in-with-the-humans sort of night.

"What were you doing in the graveyard?" Giles asked now. Jenny cleared her throat, then cocked an eyebrow at him. A signal Giles interpreted as a request to ease up on Angel a bit. After all, this was twice now he'd come to their aid. First he'd helped to rescue the Slayer. Now, her Watcher. Not to mention Jenny, herself.

"Not that I'm not grateful, of course," Giles went on.

Jenny snorted. She took a sip of tea, wincing a little as it burned her tongue.

"That's very good. What kind is it?" she asked.

"Irish Breakfast," Giles replied.

Angel set his cup down on the coffee table. Giles took a sip of tea.

"So—what do you think we're dealing with here?" Jenny asked once more.

"I don't know," Angel replied. "But I don't think he's a local guy. I didn't get a very good look at him, though. Or, not the front of him anyway. He took off as soon as I showed up. Giles is really the only one who got a good look at him. It. Whatever."

"Rupert?" Jenny asked.

"You'll forgive me if I'm a little hazy on the details," Giles said. "I was having the life choked out of me, if you'll recall. Still, there was something—"

He made a face, trying to remember, then shook his head. "I'm sorry, but it seems to be gone. No doubt it will come to me when I least expect it. Probably in the middle of the night."

"It *is* the middle of the night," Jenny reminded him.

"Yes, well, I can't remember anything else right now," Giles said shortly. "But I do know that, whatever it was, it was fast and strong."

"I'll go back out," Angel said, rising to his feet. "Rattle some cages. See what crawls." He moved to the door.

"Take care of yourself," Giles said suddenly.

Angel paused. His dark eyes were unreadable as they stared across the room at the Watcher.

"You're welcome."

The ones who had followed the Master dwelled underground.

Long tunnels sloped deep into the earth. Water seeped slowly, inexorably, from nooks and crannies. The air was close, and bitter. The kind of cold that froze men's souls.

Fortunately nothing that dwelled there had one.

Absalom sat on a chunk of concrete, surveying what was left of the Master's followers, what was left of his kingdom.

There's no place like home.

But this was hardly the time to get sentimental. *The Slayer must be made to pay*, Absalom thought. *She and all those who helped her must be made to wish they had never been born.*

Easy to say, of course. Still, every vampire needed a dream. Something to which he could aspire when the sun went down. The question was, how to accomplish it? How could he assemble the dispirited group around him into an effective fighting force?

A force capable of exacting revenge.

A commotion at the entrance to one of the tunnels

attracted Absalom's attention. The scuffle of foot-steps. Raised voices. The sound of a fist connecting, hard.

Then a figure he'd never seen before shot through the entrance as if shoved roughly from behind. It lost its balance, fell to its knees.

Absalom rose to his feet.

"What's going on here?" he demanded.

Two of the vampires he'd set to patrolling appeared at the tunnel mouth.

"We found this lurking in the upper tunnels," one of them said, moving to the figure who was even now trying to rise to its feet and giving it a shove. It sprawled facedown in the damp earth and lay still.

"Your orders were to bring anything we found snooping around to you, so we . . . encouraged him to come with us."

"Let's have a look at him," Absalom said.

The second vampire moved forward. Together, the two vamps hauled the slim figure to his feet and dragged him forward. They gave it a rough toss, de-positing it facedown at Absalom's feet. Slowly, it rose. Now Absalom could see that the interloper was a slim young man.

He removed a snowy white handkerchief from his pants pocket and wiped the mud from his face. Then he returned the handkerchief to the pocket and straight-ened his clothes. Only then did he address Absalom.

"I meant no disrespect in coming here, I assure you."

"None taken," the ancient vampire replied.

Is this a creature of the Council? he wondered. *Some sort of spy?* Not a particularly happy thought.

He looked young, but then so was the Slayer. And his speech reminded Absalom of the Watcher, clipped and precise. Still, whoever—whatever—this was was presently outnumbered by about twenty to one. Under those circumstances, it was unlikely to pose much of a threat.

Absalom could see the faithful of the Master shifting closer out of the corners of his feral yellow eyes.

"Who are you?" he asked. "What do you want?"

"Actually, I think it's more a matter of what *you* want," the figure replied.

So, Absalom thought. *It was to be a challenge of some kind.* He could kill now, ask questions later. Or he could keep it talking. Stall for time.

"You think you know what that is?" he asked.

"I do."

"And you can get it for me."

"I can," the figure replied.

The vampires around the chamber began to mutter.

"Quiet!" Absalom barked. He got to his feet and circled the figure. *What was this?* he thought. Its form was tall and slim. It held its body easily, power in reserve. *A potentially dangerous adversary,* the vampire thought. *An opponent would never know which way it was going to strike.*

The eyes were strange, like liquid silver.

"You are not human," the vampire stated.

"Not all of the time."

Absalom completed his circuit, returned to stand face to face with the figure once more. He was careful to keep himself at least an arm's length away. There was no sense in being stupid, after all.

"What are you?" he asked.

The figure smiled. "You're evading the real issue," it said. "Why is that, I wonder?"

Absalom puffed his chest out. "Do you think to question my authority?"

"Not in the least," the figure remarked. "I've merely come to offer my services. I believe that I have . . . attributes that you will find useful. That I can do something that you cannot."

Again, a mutter of sound swept through the room. Absalom stared it down.

"And that would be?" he asked.

"I can right a great wrong. Help you avenge the death of the Master."

"How?"

The figure smiled. As if Absalom had finally asked the question for which it had been waiting so patiently.

"I can deliver the Slayer," it replied.

In Jenny Calendar's apartment, the phone rang. Jenny moved to pick it up.

This had better be Rupert, calling to apologize. Being shoved full force into a tree did not go over well. Even now, a full day later, she still had a knot on the back of her head the size of the state of Minnesota.

"Hello?" she said into the phone.

The voice on the other end spoke swiftly, urgently.

"I'm not sure I can," Jenny protested. "It's not the best time right now."

She jerked the portable away from her ear as the voice on the other end rose insistently.

"All right, all right, I'll be there," she said. "There's no need to yell. As soon as I can. Yes. Right."

She hit the "off" button, stood still for a moment as if considering. Then reactivated the phone and punched in a number. A moment later, Giles's voice came over the line.

"Rupert Giles here. Thank you for phoning. I'm sorry I can't speak with you at the moment. Please leave your name and number, and I'll return your call as expeditiously as I can."

Irritated, Jenny hit the "off" button once more and hung up the phone. Then she went into her bedroom. Sliding open the closet door, she grabbed the duffel bag that was always packed and ready to go. Pausing only to get a bottle of water from the fridge, and snatch up her car keys, she headed for the front door.

Giles was probably at the library, she thought. She'd try him there on her way out of town.

Out of town. Just great.

Leaving only Giles and Angel to guard the Hellmouth.

"So you can deliver the Slayer?" Absalom said. He was feeling much better all of a sudden. This thing, whatever it was, would pose no threat. Not as long as Absalom knew things it didn't.

"And just how will you do that?" he inquired. He strode to the chunk of concrete and sat down once more. "Our reports tell us she's left Sunnydale. Her Watcher has bundled her off somewhere, to lick her wounds, no doubt."

The figure made a face. "What a pity," it remarked. "I had hoped—still, you might find me useful. I believe I met the Watcher, in fact. Just last night."

"So?"

"Ah," the figure said. "You're absolutely right. I

have left out an important part. If you'll be so good as to allow me to demonstrate?"

Absalom made a gesture of permission.

And the figure changed before his very eyes. Like an image blurred by a rain-dashed window, the body wavered, lost focus, then began to re-form.

Arms and legs grew shorter. The body, stockier. Face, more square-jawed. Even the clothes changed. Khaki slacks, tweed jacket. Button-down shirt and tie. Wire-rimmed glasses sat on the bridge of his nose.

"I trust I need no further introduction?" he inquired.

"You're a shapeshifter," Absalom said.

"Well done," said Rupert Giles.

"How does it work?" Absalom asked.

The shapeshifter had once again regained its normal, slim form and was alone with Absalom in the cavern. Absalom no longer needed an audience. What he needed was a serious talk with his new ally.

"It's simple enough," the shapeshifter replied. "To acquire a being's form, all I need is physical contact. Then, I can become that being later, at will, in any circumstance I like."

"Can anybody ever tell the difference?"

"There *is* no real difference," the shapeshifter said. "If I assume the form of a vampire—"

Its body performed that strange rippling motion Absalom had observed before, then settled into the form of one of the vampires who had captured it in the tunnels.

"I *am* a vampire," the shapeshifter went on. "I hunt like one. Kill like one."

"And if you assume the shape of a human, you die like one," Absalom put in.

With another ripple, the shapeshifter reassumed its own shape.

"True," it acknowledged. "Though I wasn't actually thinking of killing the Slayer, at least not right off. I was thinking more along the lines of bringing her to you, then assuming her form while you and your gang of ruffians had time to play."

"No," Absalom ground out. "I want her dead."

"And so she will be—eventually," the shapeshifter soothed softly. "But why rush things? Kill her now and you'll only bring another one down on your head in her place."

"I can't kill her at all if she isn't here," Absalom pointed out.

"True," the shapeshifter acknowledged once again. It rose from its seat beside Absalom and began to wander about the room. "Still, we are not without advantages."

"Such as?"

"No wonder your side lost the last round," the shapeshifter muttered under its breath.

"What was that?"

"Nothing. I was just thinking out loud," the shifter said. "I can assume the form of her Watcher, the one responsible for guiding her," it spelled out. "The one she trusts the most. Surely that must work to our advantage. And the Watcher is the direct link to the Council, after all.

"Now that I think about it, the possibilities for mayhem, even with the Slayer temporarily away, are so numerous as to be practically endless. Once we have those close to her, sooner or later, we'll have the Slayer herself."

"I like it," Absalom said.

The shapeshifter smiled. "I rather thought you might," it said. "We're agreed, then? I give you the time you need to get your motley crew in order by distracting those near and dear to the Slayer. And you don't interfere while I play my little games."

"Agreed," Absalom said.

"I'll start with the Watcher first, I think," the shapeshifter continued. "He's the one who controls the others."

"You sound like him already," Absalom muttered.

"Do you really think so? How nice."

"It's the wrong time of year for Girl Scout cookies," Angel said.

He stood framed in the doorway of his apartment while Giles shifted uneasily out in the hall.

"Your feeble attempt at humor is noted," the Watcher said. "Now, may I please come in? There are things we need to discuss."

Angel stepped back, his face unreadable, and gestured Giles across the threshold. "Be my guest," he said. "You'll understand if I don't offer you something to drink."

Giles glanced around the apartment, noticing the books scattered everywhere. The stark drawings adorning the walls. An old armoire. When he realized all he was doing was distracting himself, he removed his glasses and rubbed the bridge of his nose in irritation.

Come on. Get it over with, he urged himself.

He and Angel had worked together before. Sort of. United in their concern over the prophecy predicting the death of the Slayer. And then, as now, it had been the Watcher who'd come to the vampire. That ought to make this easier. But it didn't.

You've done it before, you can do it again.

Giles slid his glasses back into place. "I fear we may have a situation," he informed Angel. "Jenny— Ms. Calendar—has just been called away."

Angel muttered something under his breath.

"What was that?" Giles inquired.

"Nothing," Angel said. "So, that means it's just you and me, doesn't it?"

"It does," Giles confirmed.

"What's the matter, Giles?" Angel asked. "Concerned that, with Buffy gone, I'll revert to my true colors? In case you've forgotten, she was gone the other night and that was still me saving your—"

"Yes, well," Giles broke in, his tone waspish. "I'm sure you'll just have to forgive me if this whole situation is still a tad difficult for me to accept. We're talking about setting aside virtually a whole lifetime's worth of training. I'm sure you're one in a million, Angel, but—"

"Actually, I don't think there are that many of us anymore."

"But it doesn't change the fact that you're a vampire," Giles said.

"Nothing changes that," Angel answered, his voice like the crack of a whip. "I don't need you to pay housecalls to state the obvious, Giles. What do I have to do to prove myself? Stand still and take a stake through the heart?"

The thought had occurred.

"I see," Angel said.

"You don't see anything. I haven't answered the question."

"I think you have," Angel said. "But it doesn't really change anything, does it? With Jenny gone, it's just you, me and the Hellmouth."

"Precisely," Giles said. "I'm willing to . . . work to . . . set aside my . . . natural prejudices, if you are."

"The Council has an Affirmative Action policy? How very PC of them," Angel said.

"If the Council knew I was directly enlisting the aid of a vampire, they'd have my head on a plate," Giles snapped. "I can be replaced, Angel. You might remember that. You may actually stand a chance of convincing me of your good intentions. But you'll never convince the Council, that I can guarantee."

"In other words, we're stuck with each other."

"That's about the size of it," Giles said. He looked at Angel, standing motionless on the far side of the room. "I will *try*. I honestly will."

"That's about all I can hope for then, isn't it?" Angel asked.

"Well, you can just forget about it if you're going to start whining," Giles said.

A faint smile flickered across Angel's features. "Got anything on the whatever-it-is from the other night?"

"Nothing, I'm afraid," Giles said. "Um—you?"

"Not a thing," Angel said. "It's kind of odd, though."

"What is?" Giles asked.

"Ever since that thing showed up, there hasn't been much action. Things are pretty quiet out there."

"That is interesting," Giles commented. "So, I guess we wait for the whatever-it-is to make its next move."

"We could do that," Angel said.

"You have a better suggestion?"

"Well, there's always the direct approach."

"Which is?"

"We hunt it down and kill it," Angel said.

In the shadows, the shapeshifter watched as the Watcher left the vampire's apartment, climbed into a battered car and struggled to get it started.

"Well, well, well," he said. "It seems the unholy alliance is heating up."

The car sputtered to life, and Giles pulled away from the curb. A moment later, the shapeshifter stepped into the pool of illumination cast by the overhead streetlight. The hot white glare reflected off its wire-rimmed glasses.

"Let's just see what I can do to further the cause, shall we?" he murmured.

"I'm bored," Willow Rosenberg said.

She and her longtime good friend, Xander Harris, were sitting at a table at the Bronze, the remnants of a major food event littering the table in front of them.

"It's not boredom," Xander said. "You've had too much sugar. You're in a coma." He picked up an unopened package of cupcakes, then set it down again. "And I think I'm about to join you."

"Come on, you know what I mean," Willow protested. "Ever since we buried the Master's bones things have been so quiet. No supernatural murder and mayhem. No imminent apocalypses. No vampires."

"Explain to me again why this is a bad thing?"

"Well, it isn't, really," Willow acknowledged. "But

you have to admit, things do seem a little flat by comparison. Fighting the powers of darkness does add a certain spice to life."

"I prefer mild," Xander informed her.

"I guess what I'm really saying is—"

"I know, I miss her too."

The two friends sat in silence for a moment, staring at the pile of candy wrappers before them.

"I had a postcard," Willow volunteered. "It said, 'Having a wonderful time. Wish you were here.'"

"How'd she think up something like that?" Xander wondered.

"Well, at least it shows she was thinking about us," Willow said. There was a tiny pause. "She had to look up my address."

"Guess she thinks mine's unlisted."

"Xander, I—"

"Don't sweat it," Xander said. "I mean, really. I save her life, and I don't even rate a tacky postcard? But hey, I can deal. I can be Mr. Stiff Upper Lip."

"Sounds painful."

"You have no idea."

"Let's get out of here," Willow said.

"Good idea."

Together, the two friends slid off their stools and headed for the Bronze's exit.

"I'll walk you home," Xander offered.

"That's okay," Willow said. "I mean, things have been pretty quiet lately. You know, ever since . . ."

"So, you wanna do something tomorrow? Like maybe . . . watch some grass grow?"

Willow nodded. "Definitely. I'll call you. We'll do lunch."

"Please, don't mention food," Xander begged.

The redhead smiled. "See you tomorrow," she said. She turned the corner that would take her toward her house, automatically glancing back over her shoulder from time to time, then grimacing when she realized what she was doing.

I'll probably never again walk the Sunnydale streets at night without looking over my shoulder.

Things had been quiet lately, it was true. But there was still something about knowing that all those things you always feared went bump in the night actually did.

And about half of them were probably following you.

Willow spotted a figure crossing the empty street in front of her.

"Giles?" she called out.

The figure stopped, turned toward her.

"Giles, it's Willow," she said, coming forward into a pool of light. "What are you doing here?"

The figure was silent, staring at her as if he'd never seen her before, his face absolutely expressionless. Willow felt a cold prickle of alarm slide down her spine.

"Giles, is everything all right?" she said.

With a start, Giles snapped out of it. "Willow, of course it's you," he said. "No need for alarm. Just out for an evening stroll. If you see Angel, do be sure and say hello for me, won't you? 'Night now."

Before Willow could get another word in edgewise, the thing that looked like Giles but was acting strange, even for him, strode off down the street and vanished around the nearest corner.

That was definitely more than a little weird.

Willow cocked her head, straining her ears to catch

the faint snatch of sound drifting back from around the corner.

She could have sworn that it was laughter.

"Xander?" a voice behind him said.

Quickly, Xander spun around, then hated himself for backing up a step. "Didn't your mother ever tell you it's not polite to sneak up on people?"

"To tell you the truth, I can't remember," Angel said.

"Well, it would be kind of a long time ago," Xander remarked. "And your brain cells would currently be dead."

Angel's forehead wrinkled. In a perplexed sort of way. "Are you mad at me or something?" he asked. " 'Cause I was thinking maybe we could, you know, hang out."

Okay, now I know I'm in a sugar coma, Xander thought. The last person in the world he'd want to hang out with was Angel. A feeling he'd always taken to be entirely mutual.

Not that Angel actually counted as a person, of course.

"All right, where's the real Angel and what have you done with his body?" he asked.

For a fraction of an instant, the vampire's face went totally blank. In the next, he laughed.

"Good one," he said. "So, was that a 'yes' or a 'no'?"

"I've got a curfew," Xander informed him.

"Too bad," Angel said. "Hey, if you happen to see Giles, tell him I said hello, will you?"

Xander began to feel as if he was in the middle of the pop quiz from Hell. If a guy saw a thing that looked like a vampire named Angel, but didn't sound or act like a vampire named Angel, was it really a vampire named Angel?

"Are we being taped for some kind of vampire *Funniest Home Videos?*" Xander asked.

Angel gave him a slap on the back that sent him staggering. "You are *so* funny!" he said. "How come I never noticed that before?"

"I can't imagine," Xander answered. What he could imagine was getting out of here. Right now. "Are we done yet? 'Cause I'd really like to go inside. You'll understand if I don't invite you to come with me."

"No problem," Angel said. "Catch you next time."

He strode off down the street, long coat flapping.

That's it, Xander thought as he let himself into the house. *I am never eating an entire five-pound bag of M&Ms in one sitting again as long as I live.*

Plainly, it could be hazardous to one's health.

Not a bad evening's work, the shifter thought as he strolled down the street. He was finished with phase one. Planting doubts in the minds of the Slayer's friends. Sowing confusion.

Not that it took much. The look on the boy's face, in particular, had been absolutely priceless.

I should have come to Sunnydale long before now, the shifter thought. It was really the perfect place to exercise his talents. Though, really, playing with the children had been, well, child's play. Too easy. Not entirely satisfying.

He'd just have to make sure phase two made up for that.

In phase two, he got to play with the grown-ups.

"He wanted to *what* with you?" asked Giles.

It was the next day, in the early evening, not quite time for Giles to head out for patrol. Not that he'd informed Xander of this, of course. Giles was keeping to his vow to give Buffy's friends the normal summer they deserved. A summer free from things that did more than go bump in the night.

Giles and Angel had arranged a patrolling schedule. Giles would be out from sundown to midnight. Angel from midnight to dawn. This would provide full nighttime Hellmouth coverage without requiring the two uneasy co-workers to spend more than a few minutes together.

A thing that suited them both just fine.

Giles had been on his way home from the library, after another session of trying to discover what had attacked him and Jenny the other night when he'd encountered Xander.

Make that another unsuccessful *research session,* thought Giles. A thing that was beginning to irritate and frustrate him. He was supposed to be good at this, after all.

The trouble was, *slim build and weird eyes* just wasn't a whole lot to go on. Giles's books and papers provided information on a variety of topics from a variety of sources and in a variety of ways.

Unfortunately, a breakdown by body parts didn't seem to be one of them.

"He wanted to hang out with me," Xander repeated. "Like he wanted us to be best pals. I'm here to tell you, it wasn't normal, even for Angel. I think there's—you know—" His voice dropped. "Something going on."

"Yes, well," Giles said. "Thanks very much for the tip. I'll take the situation under advisement."

"Is that the same as saying you'll check it out?"

"Precisely," Giles said. "Now, if you'll excuse me, Xander, I'm afraid I have to be going now."

Giles moved toward his car, and Xander fell into step beside him, his expression plainly crestfallen.

"You mean that's all? No assignment? I could arrange to meet him again, pump him for information."

The mind boggles, thought Giles.

"That won't be necessary, thank you," he said aloud. "But I appreciate the report. I'll let you know if anything develops."

Giles got into his ancient Citroën and drove off.

Angel wanting to be Xander's best friend? Highly unlikely.

About as unlikely, Giles thought, as an alliance between a Watcher and a vampire.

"He said what?" Angel asked.

"To tell you 'hello,' " Willow answered.

"You're sure we're talking about the same Giles?"

Willow and Angel were standing outside the Bronze. Willow had been on her way to meet Xander when she'd spotted Angel loitering by the door. She'd invited him to join them. He'd declined. But Willow had taken the opportunity to relay the previous night's message from Giles.

"You know, now that I think about it, he did seem kind of funny."

"Giles? A laugh riot?"

"No, I don't mean funny ha-ha," Willow said. "I mean funny, odd. It was like he didn't even know me at first."

"Maybe he was just distracted or something."

"Maybe," Willow acknowledged. "So . . ." she went on, "how's your summer? Anything—you *know*—going on?"

"Not a thing," Angel lied. "Look, Willow, I appreciate you giving me the message, but I've gotta go now. I'll see you around."

"Okay," Willow said. "Hey—have you heard from—"

But Angel was already gone.

"This is taking too long," Absalom snarled.

It was later that same night, and he and the shifter were back in the main chamber of the Master's lair. "The others are growing restless. They wish to hunt."

"Control them," the shapeshifter suggested.

With one sudden movement, Absalom lunged forward and seized the shifter by the throat. "Don't play your games with me," he hissed. "You promised me revenge."

"And you shall have it."

"When?"

The shifter rippled, transforming into Angel. With a snarl, Absalom released him and stepped back. Smiling now, the shapeshifter straightened the lapel of the vampire's black jacket.

"Very soon now."

There's something back there.

Giles moved cautiously along the dark alley, straining his ears for the slightest sound. He was almost certain he was being followed. Had been for several blocks now.

Just keep calm. This was exactly the reason he was out here in the first place, after all.

Slowly, Giles moved his right hand into his jacket pocket. His fist closed around the stake he'd put there earlier.

Try to look normal, he thought. The fact that he was prepared to defend himself was something for him to know, and the thing behind him to find out.

Maybe I should just turn around.

Go on the offensive. Confront the unknown entity head-on. That was almost certainly what Buffy would do. But there were differences between Slayers and Watchers. Not just the age and gender things.

Slayers rushed in. Watchers were more cautious.

Not to mention the fact that Giles had gotten his butt kicked last time around.

So far, whoever, or whatever, it was behind him seemed in no hurry. That being the case, the sensible thing for Giles to do was to simply keep on going. He'd reach his pre-established rendezvous point with Angel in just a few more blocks.

Then the whatever-was-back-there would find the odds were not in its favor. It would be outnumbered two to one.

Giles cocked his head, listening for the sound of the footsteps. Were they coming closer? He picked up his pace, rounded a corner and headed for the only streetlight. The rendezvous point was at the end of the block, in the gap between two warehouses.

Actually, except for the uncomfortable aspect of being followed, Giles considered the events of this evening to be a good thing. It had been awfully quiet since Jenny had left. Too quiet.

Always a bad sign.

Some quiet meant things were under control. Too quiet almost always meant some kind of plan was in the works. Usually of the not-human-friendly variety.

Almost at the rendezvous point now. Giles cast a quick glance over his shoulder. The thing behind him stepped beneath the glow of the streetlight. Giles came to an abrupt and startled stop.

But that looks exactly like—

"You're late," a voice in front of him announced.

Giles jerked his head back around. Angel stood in the shadowy entrance to the space between the two buildings.

"What are you doing *here?*" Giles hissed.

"I'm waiting for you. What do you think I'm doing?" Angel replied. "You're the one who came up with this arrangement, you know. I'm just being a good boy, standing around, waiting to be handed the patrol baton."

"But—" Giles began. "But I could have sworn—"

He swiveled his head back around. The figure behind him was still beneath the streetlight. As Giles watched, it reached into the pocket of its black leather jacket, withdrew a packet of cigarettes and shook out one. He lit it and blew a thin stream of smoke between his lips, then returned the pack of cigarettes to his pocket.

Just some young punk in a black leather jacket, Giles thought.

It wasn't Angel. Had never been Angel. How could it be? Angel was standing right in front of him.

"I apologize," Giles said, turning back around. "I thought I saw—"

"Quiet," Angel hissed suddenly. He stepped back,

out of sight. Giles caught a whiff of cigarette smoke, the sound of footsteps.

"Out kinda late, aren't you, Pops?"

The punk swaggered along the street, stopped in front of Giles and blew a stream of cigarette smoke straight into the Watcher's face. Giles held his breath as long as he could, then began to cough.

"I think there's someplace else you need to be," Angel said, as he stepped out onto the sidewalk behind the kid.

The punk didn't back down an inch. Instead, he flicked his still-burning cigarette into the gutter. "Oh, yeah, where?"

"Anywhere."

The punk laughed suddenly. "Okay," he said. "I can take a hint. No problem."

He sauntered off, whistling between his teeth.

"Follow him," said Giles.

"What?"

"Follow him. I'm pretty sure he's been following me for the last few blocks."

"Giles," Angel said, his tone striving for patience. "There's nothing special about him. Troublemakers like that are a dime a dozen. They're the same in any century."

And you should know.

"Humor me," Giles said shortly. "I just . . . have a feeling there's more to that one than meets the eye."

An idea was growing in the back of the Watcher's mind. One he had to get to the library to confirm.

Angel shrugged. "Okay, if you say so."

"Come to the library tomorrow just after dark; we can compare notes from the rest of tonight."

* * *

Bored much?

Angel had been following the guy Giles *thought* had followed *him* for at least an hour. So far, zippo.

I've seen more action at the Bronze.

There was nothing special about this kid. So far, all he'd done was blow smoke at Giles, and hassle one old drunk. He was just a not very intelligent jerk, out looking for trouble.

And not finding much.

Angel, on the other hand, had had enough.

I've got more important things to do than follow this kid around all night.

It was time to take a swing through the graveyard, he decided. Sooner or later, most things that wanted to cause problems ended up there. That was where the action was. Not following some kid wearing a bad imitation of his own jacket.

Angel spun on his heel and disappeared into the darkness. Behind him, the shifter turned to watch, then smiled.

"Gentlemen, start your engines," he murmured. "It's show time."

"Help! Please, somebody help me!"

Angel spun around. The cry had come from behind him, in the farthest, darkest corner of the graveyard. He sprinted toward the sound and heard a shriek, suddenly cut off. Now he was close enough to see a shadowy figure, stooping over a form on the ground. He heard a sound that sounded like—

Actually, it was probably better not to think about what the sound was.

As if sensing his presence, the figure lifted his

head. Angel caught the wink of glasses in the moonlight as it turned its face toward him.

But that's Giles, he thought.

In the next moment, the figure was loping away, running low to the ground along the fence that bordered the graveyard. It vaulted over and disappeared from sight. Every cell in Angel's body itched to give chase. But he was alone, and there was a victim to attend to.

Angel knelt beside the figure on the ground.

It was the punk he'd been following earlier that night. One side of his face had been smashed in. But he was still alive. He moaned.

"Hang in there," Angel said. "Help is on the way."

He would make sure of that, but he wouldn't stick around to see it arrive. That would only invite questions he didn't care to answer.

Besides, Angel had a few questions of his own.

"Don't tell me you've been here ever since you left me. I saw you in the graveyard!" Angel exploded. He'd gone straight to the library, certain that was where he'd find Giles.

Sure enough, the Watcher was at his desk, surrounded by stacks of research books. He claimed he'd been there since leaving Angel to do his share of the night's patrol.

"Then how do you explain what I saw in the graveyard?" Angel asked. "I'm not stupid, Giles. I don't like being manipulated. Particularly by someone so much younger than I am."

"Just what, exactly, are you accusing me of?" Giles asked. His back was ramrod straight, his tone, brittle with outrage.

"The punk you asked me to follow turns up in the graveyard with his face smashed in and you bending over him. You figure it out," Angel said. "That's what you're supposed to be so good at, isn't it?"

"Why should I?" Giles came back. "You already have all the answers."

"You don't like them, give me some different ones," Angel said through clenched teeth. "I want an explanation. Now."

"I don't care what you want," Giles said. "You have no right to barge in here and accuse me. You, of all people. But then, you're not a person anymore, are you? So maybe you just can't help yourself."

"Last time I checked, I had a conscience, just like you do."

"You're nothing like me."

"Hey, guys. What's going on?" a voice said.

Angel spun around to find Willow standing in the doorway, her face betraying her confusion.

Giles got up from his desk and moved toward her. "It's awfully late. Shouldn't you be at home, Willow?" he asked.

"Well, yeah, maybe," the redhead temporized. "I'm sure my parents are already in bed. But I saw your lights on, and I thought maybe, you know . . ."

Her eyes slid to Angel. "How did you get here so fast?"

"What?"

"I just saw you," Willow said. "Outside the Bronze."

"I've been here for the last fifteen minutes, at least," Angel said.

"Just like I've been here for hours?" Giles muttered.

Angel glared.

"There *is* something going on, isn't there?" Willow asked. "I can help . . . look something up, or something . . ." She came forward into the room.

"Not necessary, thank you, Willow," Giles said. He moved to take Willow by the arm. As he passed by Angel, the two made swift eye contact.

"Actually, Angel was just sort of . . ." Giles's voice faltered.

"Paying a social call," Angel said. He moved to take Willow's other arm. Together, the two hustled her out of the library and down the corridor.

"Giles and I have been trying to, uh—"

"Get to know each other better," Giles filled in.

"Yeah, that's right," Angel said. "You know, so we could—"

"Work together more effectively, when necessary," Giles needled smoothly.

"Right."

From her place between them, Willow's head swiveled back and forth between them like she was following a tennis match.

"Are you sure you guys feel all right?" she asked.

"Perfectly," Giles and Angel answered in unison. The group reached the door to the outside. .

"Thank you for the offer, but I really think you should go home now," Giles said. "I'll call you if I need you. Nice of you to stop by."

He opened the door.

"But—" Willow protested.

Angel scooted her through, out onto the sidewalk. "Sleep tight," he said.

The door closed with a slam.

Together, the Watcher and the vampire walked back

to the library and closed the door. There was a charged silence.

"Okay, I'm ready to listen," Angel said. "How can I be at the Bronze and here at the same time?"

"The same way I can be here and in the graveyard," Giles answered.

"And that way would be?"

"If we were dealing with a shapeshifter," Giles said.

"How do we stop it?" Angel asked without hesitation.

"That depends on the form it's taken," Giles answered. "According to my research," he moved to his desk, picked up a book, and carried it over to the table where Angel had stationed himself, "once a shapeshifter has assumed another, er—"

"Shape," Angel suggested.

"Quite," Giles said. "Once a shapeshifter has assumed a new *identity*, shall we say, it has all that being's attributes. Whatever will destroy the form the shifter takes will destroy the shapeshifter also."

"Sounds straightforward enough," Angel said.

"Not quite," Giles countered. "Once a shapeshifter has taken on another form, it's virtually impossible to tell it from the real thing. You wouldn't be able to tell which was me, and which was the shifter camouflaged as me, even if we were standing side by side. They may be easy to kill in theory. In practice, they're hard to recognize."

"So . . . what then?"

"Not at all," said Giles. "In fact, I feel it is imperative that we discover the whereabouts of this particular shapeshifter and destroy it. Think of the trouble it's already caused. It played us both for fools—"

"Buffy," Angel said suddenly.

"Exactly," said Giles. "I think we have to assume

that the Slayer is the shifter's ultimate target. To acquire her shape, all the shifter needs is one moment of direct contact, and, given the fact that it can now assume either of our shapes, that could be quite straightforward. Our one bit of luck may be the fact that Buffy is out of town."

"So we've got to put an end to this thing before Buffy returns to Sunnydale."

"Exactly."

"And how, exactly, do we do that?"

Giles collapsed into a nearby chair.

"Your guess is as good as mine."

Jenny Calendar hit the turn signal and pulled off the freeway. It was late. It had been a long drive. And she was tired. But before she hit the bed, there was something she had to do.

She went into her apartment, walked straight to the phone and punched in Giles's number.

Be there, Rupert, she thought.

Giles moved quickly through his apartment, stuffing whatever he thought might be useful into a leather shoulder bag. Holy water. Stakes. A flashlight. A large crucifix. The meat cleaver from the kitchen. A can of soda.

He might get thirsty, after all. There was no telling how long he'd be out there.

The longer the shapeshifter went unidentified, the greater the danger. It needed to be neutralized. Yesterday.

I've already let it get far too close to the Slayer, Giles thought.

There was no time for self-flagellation now, however. Wallowing had its uses, but they would simply have to wait.

Giles shouldered the bag, pulled his front door open and hurried down the front walk.

"Rupert Giles here—"

Jenny stood in her apartment, clutching the phone with suddenly sweaty fingers. She'd gotten the machine. Damn.

Was Rupert home and just not picking up? Was he at the library? Out patrolling?

Where?

"Rupert, it's Jenny," she said into the phone as soon as the message beep had ended. "I need you to call me right away. I may have some information about that thing that attacked us the other night."

She heard a click, as if the message she was leaving was being interrupted. "Jenny?" Giles's sleepy voice said.

Jenny felt relief shoot through her tired body. "Rupert, thank goodness you're there," she said. "Listen, I think we've got big trouble. That thing that attacked us the other night may have been—"

"—a shapeshifter," Giles filled in.

"So you know," Jenny said.

"Just figured it out this evening," Giles said. "Are you up for helping, or are you too tired? Did you just get back?"

"Yes, no, and yes. In that order."

"All right then," Giles said. "This is what I want you to do."

Jenny listened intently for a moment, trying to ignore the way her stomach was quietly folding itself into tighter and tighter knots.

"You're sure about this?" she asked.

"Absolutely," Giles's voice said. "It's the thing that

makes the most sense. And it's not as risky as it sounds. I've asked Angel to meet me there."

"If you say so," Jenny finally agreed. "I'll get there as soon as I can."

"Excellent," Giles said. "And Miss Calendar—"

"*Ms.* Calendar."

"I'm glad you're back."

The line went dead. Jenny pressed the "off" button. Closed the mouth she suddenly discovered was hanging wide open.

In that order.

Then she headed for the door, and the rendezvous point Giles had given her.

Standing in Giles's apartment, the shapeshifter smiled as he hung up the phone. He'd come here hoping the apartment might contain information on the whereabouts of the Slayer. If it did, he hadn't found it. But the trip could hardly be considered wasted. Not after what he'd just accomplished.

"*And that,*" he murmured softly, as he flowed back into his own form. "*Is the way we do that.*"

The shifter let himself out of the Watcher's apartment, locking the door carefully behind him.

What on earth am I doing here?

It was a question Giles had been asking himself for at least the last five minutes. Ever since it had become apparent that the most likely place for the shapeshifter to be hiding out was the last place Giles wanted to look.

The Master's lair.

The quick sweep Giles had done of the locations he and Angel had agreed on had turned up nothing. No activity of any kind, not even of the juvenile delinquent variety. Giles was willing to bet Angel was discovering the same phenomenon in the places he'd agreed to check out.

That left just one location. The obvious one. The one right in front of him.

I do not want to go into that tunnel. I don't want to see the place where Buffy lost her life.

And had been brought back because her friends had the courage to follow her, Giles reminded himself. An example he'd do well to emulate.

He could do anything Xander Harris could do. That he wanted to, of course.

Taking a deep breath, Giles started down into the tunnel.

The first thing he noticed was the cold.

The second was the wet. Water seemed to be seeping from everywhere. Weeping like dirty tears down the tunnel's walls. Concrete first. Then, as Giles went lower, dirt.

Perhaps I should have included a snorkel in my bag of tricks, Giles told himself sarcastically.

Something on the floor of the tunnel caught his eye. Giles pulled out the flashlight and snapped it on. On the muddy surface of the tunnel floor before him, he could see a set of footprints, smaller than his own. They looked fresh.

Someone else is down here, he thought. And it didn't look like Angel. Unless there were things Giles had never noticed about the vampire's feet before.

He reached into his coat pocket, pulled out the stake he'd tucked there within easy reach, and continued down.

Not much farther now.

The tunnel widened just ahead. Giles snapped the flashlight off. He didn't really need it. The tunnels seemed to have their own illumination. He didn't really want to think about how. But it did mean his light wouldn't give him away.

Never look a gift stealth in the mouth.

He hesitated for a moment at the entrance to what appeared to be a large chamber, straining his ears for any sound.

Nothing. As in, well here goes.

Giles whipped around the corner. Encountered something solid. Raised the stake high.

"Rupert! No!" he heard a voice cry.

Slowly, Giles lowered the stake, his head swimming. "Jenny?" he asked, his tone incredulous. "When did you get back? What on earth are you doing here?"

"You told me to meet you here."

"I most certainly did not."

"You did, too," Jenny insisted. "Just tonight, over the telephone. I told you there was a shapeshifter. You said you were glad I was back."

"I know that, and I did no such thing," said Giles. "Wait a moment. Let me clarify those statements."

"So you know about the shifter," Jenny interrupted.

Giles nodded. "I just put it together earlier tonight. Jenny, I'm sorry, but I most definitely did not speak with you on the telephone."

"But that would mean—"

"Ms. Calendar," a voice at Giles's elbow said. "When did you get back?"

Giles jumped, then backed into the center of the cavern, pulling Jenny with him.

"Stay back," he warned.

"Oh, for crying out loud, not this again," Angel said.

"I know who I am," Giles said. "But I don't know who you are."

"And I don't know who *you* are," Jenny said, shaking loose Giles's grip on her arm. She put some distance between them. Now the three formed an uneven triangle with Angel as the point. "Either one of you could be the shifter," Jenny remarked.

"In which case, Giles has just acquired the ability to become you," Angel pointed out, indicating her arm.

"I have not."

"Well, naturally you'd *say* that," Angel said.

"This is completely ridiculous."

Angel nodded. "I couldn't agree more. I'd say we've got a stalemate."

"*I* wouldn't say that," said a voice from the far side of the cavern.

A second Angel stepped out into the light.

Instantly, Giles and Jenny moved closer together. *At least that was one problem solved,* Giles thought. *Or . . .*

"I'd say what we have is a trust exercise," the second Angel went on. "Just how much does Giles really trust me?"

"I think you mean *me,*" the first Angel remarked.

"Why doesn't he just give you the signal?" Jenny whispered.

"What signal?" Giles whispered back.

"What do you mean what signal?" Jenny answered, her tone rising slightly. "The one you guys must have worked out. When you knew it was a shifter. You did have a plan, didn't you?"

"My title is Watcher, not Planner," Giles snapped.

But he knew that Jenny was right. He should have thought of this possibility. Should have been prepared for it. And because he hadn't . . .

"Giles," the first Angel spoke up as if he'd overheard the frantically whispered conversation. "How about this? Remember the time—"

"Stop!" Giles cried out. "Don't tell it anything it doesn't already know."

"Very good," Angel Number Two commented. He moved a little farther into the cavern, closing the distance between himself, Jenny and Giles. The two humans stood back to back now, each facing a vampire.

"You knew he wouldn't let you finish, so it was safe to give that a shot."

"If you say so," the first Angel said. "Too bad we'll never really know."

"Visitors, how nice," a new, powerful voice said. One that made Giles's blood run cold.

Absalom?

As if things weren't bad enough.

A vampire strode farther into the cavern until he stood opposite Jenny and Giles. Now the three of them formed a triangle, flanked by the twin Angels. Giles could feel cold sweat snake down into his eyes.

The number odds might still be in Team Slayer's favor, but Absalom had placed himself so that there was no way Giles or Jenny could keep their eyes on Absalom and watch the Angels at the same time. They had to divide their focus.

Divide and conquer.

A tactic that definitely had a way of evening the odds.

"I have a score to settle with the two of you," Absalom said. He took a gliding step forward. Giles swiveled his head to see if the Angel closest to him, Angel Number Two, had changed position. He hadn't. So far.

"Evening it is going to give me a great deal of pleasure," Absalom went on.

"Talk about things I'd rather think about another day," Giles heard Jenny murmur under her breath. He felt a swift burst of emotion. He thought that it was pride. Jenny was actually reminding him of the Slayer, right at that moment. Even when things looked truly desperate, she didn't back down.

"Too bad the Slayer's not here," Absalom continued as he took another step forward. "But her time will come."

Angel Number Two took a sidling step toward Absalom. Giles felt his whole body tense in reaction as a wild thought flashed through his mind.

"Did he move?" he whispered to Jenny.

"What?"

"Your Angel, did he move?"

"He took two steps straight toward me. And he didn't say, Mother, may I?"

"Your time, however," Absalom said. Giles jerked his attention back to the Master's servant. "Is up. Right now."

He lunged.

Instantly, the figures in the cavern became a blur of motion. Absalom dove forward. Angel Number Two lunged straight for him. The two went down in a tumble of arms and legs. Angel Number Two on top. Absalom on the bottom.

Giles had time for just one thought.

I really hope I'm right about this.

"Take her!" he shouted. He whirled and shoved Jenny straight into the arms of Angel Number One, who was already running toward her. He heard Jenny cry out as the vampire's strong arms wrapped around her.

With a cry, Giles raised his stake and rushed forward to where Angel Number Two still grappled with Absalom.

"It's all right, Giles. I've got him," the Angel panted.

"I was thinking more along the lines of I've got you," Giles replied.

He brought his fist down. Hard. Thrusting the stake through the center of Angel Number Two's unprotected back. He threw his head back, face snarling.

This is where we find out if I got it right, Giles thought.

The impaled body of the thing that looked like Angel twisted, then began to change form. Body after body, all the shapes he'd ever assumed, all the beings he had ever been, flowed into existence, then vanished, like a film on fast-forward.

Then, for one split second, Giles was looking down into the shapeshifter's own true face. Those strange, quicksilver eyes stared straight up at him.

"How did you know?" the shifter asked.

Before Giles could answer, the shapeshifter's body crumbled into dust. Giles was left staring down at Absalom.

Quick as lightning, one of the vampire's legs kicked up. His booted toe caught Giles in the wrist and knocked the stake from his hand. Before Giles could step back out of range, Absalom vaulted to his feet, snagged Giles by one arm and twisted it viciously behind him. Then he swung Giles around so that the two faced Angel, Giles like a shield in front of Absalom.

"Now *this* is what I'd call a stalemate," said the ancient vampire. Still holding Giles's arm at a painful angle, he began to ease backward, toward the mouth of the nearest tunnel. "Another time, another place," Absalom said. "You can count on it."

Then he gave Giles a shove that sent him painfully to his knees and sprinted down the tunnel.

"Rupert!" Jenny cried as she hurried to him. "Are you all right?"

Angel silently extended one hand. Giles took it and let the vampire haul him to his feet.

"Let's get out of here," he said shortly.

"How did you know?" Jenny asked.

"I didn't really," Giles admitted. The three were aboveground and moving through the shell of the burned-out church toward Giles's Citroën. "It was just an educated guess."

"Why have I never appreciated the fact that you work in a library before now?" Angel asked.

"But an educated guess based on what, Rupert?" Jenny persisted. "You must have had some basis for making your decision. *Since you didn't have a plan.*"

"Wait a minute. What does she mean we didn't have a plan?" Angel asked. "We had a plan. Hunt the thing down and kill it."

"She's referring to the fact that we should have established a signal," Giles said. "A way of identifying ourselves to one another. In the event that what actually did just happen actually happened."

"Oh, you mean that kind of a plan. So, how *did* you know?"

"Well, for lack of something better, I guess I'd have to call it human nature," Giles explained. "You see, a shapeshifter, no matter what it looks like, is fundamentally a creature of darkness, a thing without a soul. It's actually quite breathtakingly evil, in fact."

"But it attacked Absalom," Jenny said.

"Exactly," Giles said. "It *attacked*. That's all it knew to do, all its—consciousness, if you will—would allow it to do. Absalom was the logical target, given those parameters."

"Because it would make it appear as if the shapeshifter was on our side," Jenny broke in.

Giles nodded. "But the real Angel could do something else," he said. "He could—" Without warning he broke off, staring at the tops of his muddy shoes. "He could do what I would have done," he finished finally.

"Try to protect me," Jenny said.

Giles nodded. "It takes more than consciousness to do that. It takes *conscience*."

"I knew it!" Willow's voice called out.

The trio turned to see Xander and Willow hurrying toward them. They arrived out of breath.

"I knew there was something going on," Willow gasped. "It just didn't make sense. Oh, hi, Ms. Calendar."

"Hello, Willow, Xander," Jenny said.

"So, what's the plan, and where are the bad guys?"

"There isn't one, and there aren't any," Giles said.

"What didn't make sense?" Angel asked.

"The way you two were talking all funny in the library," Willow answered, her tone triumphant.

"Don't forget about the door thing," Xander muttered.

"And then there was the door thing," Willow said. "You scooted me out."

"I never scooted." Angel looked at Giles. "Did you scoot?"

"Not in this lifetime," Giles answered.

"Well, okay, but how about the fact that it was really late?" Willow asked. "Anything could have happened to me, and you didn't even pay attention."

"Nothing can happen to you if there isn't anything going on," Giles said.

"All right," Xander spoke up. "Then answer me this one, *Jeopardy* fans. If nothing's going on, what are the three of you doing standing above the Master's lair in the middle of the night?"

There was a tiny beat of silence.

"We were—" Giles began

"Taking a walk," Jenny quickly filled in.

"Yeah, that's right," Angel said.

"Jenny and I were—" Giles continued.

"Walking," Jenny said. "Because I just got back to town and—"

"I found them and then we all walked together," Angel finished with a flourish.

"To the entrance to the Master's lair," Willow said.

Angel looked around, as if noticing his location for the very first time. "Is that where we are?" he asked.

Willow and Xander exchanged glances.

"I have an idea," Giles suddenly said. "How about, seeing as how we're all together, we go back to my place for some lovely hot cocoa?"

Willow and Xander exchanged glances once again.

"Well, you are kind of right," Willow said.

"Thank you," Giles answered. "About what, exactly?"

"It is pretty late. We should probably get going. If there really isn't anything you need our help with."

"There really isn't," Giles said, suppressing a smile.

"I'll give you guys a lift," Jenny offered.

"Thanks, Ms. Calendar. That would be great," Xander said.

"See you at your place in a few, Rupert," Jenny said.

"What? Oh, yes, right," Giles answered.

"My car's over here," Jenny told Xander and Willow. The three moved off, leaving Giles and Angel standing by the Citroën.

"Can I give you a lift?" Giles asked.

There was a quick beat of silence. Then Angel stepped back.

"No, thanks. I'll walk. I think it will be faster."

"Not you, too," Giles said.

A swift smile flickered across Angel's features. "Next time, we make a better plan," he said.

"We do," Giles concurred.

Angel turned, began to move away.

"Thank you," Giles said.

Angel didn't stop. Didn't look back. But Giles heard his voice, floating back on the still night air.

"Don't mention it," Angel said.

NO PLACE LIKE . . .

CAMERON DOKEY

I'm going to die. And there's nothing I can do.

Buffy Summers struggled, and felt the strong arms that held her clamp down, tighter. *It's hopeless,* she thought. Her eyesight had begun to dim. She couldn't feel her legs anymore.

Blood, she thought. *I've lost too much blood. I've—*

"What's the matter, Slayer?" she heard the voice of the Master taunt in her ear. "Afraid to wake up dead?"

No!

Heart pounding, Buffy sat straight up in bed. Sunlight streamed through the window of the spare bedroom of her father's L.A. apartment.

It's all right, she thought. *It's over. This is L. A., not Sunnydale. I'm here, with Dad.*

She was awake, and very definitely not dead.

Buffy threw back the covers and eyed the digital clock on the nightstand. Ten A.M., the red numbers glowed.

Great. Another morning of missing her father because she'd overslept. At the rate things were going, she'd spend the rest of the summer in L.A. and only see her dad on the drive back to Sunnydale.

She thrust her feet into her favorite pair of bunny slippers and headed for the kitchen.

And the drive here was certainly a big success, now wasn't it?

Hank Summers had tried to make conversation with his daughter all the way from Sunnydale. Tried to explain about the new woman in his life. *And what did I do? Turn into Ms. Neanderthal.* The best Buffy had been able to manage was a grunt now and then.

Of course, the fact that she'd had a lump in her throat the size of Nebraska hadn't exactly helped at the time.

I didn't want to touch him, Buffy thought. All she'd wanted to do was to feel safe. From those visions.

She opened the fridge and sloshed orange juice into a glass. Since then, things had gotten better between them. Her father had asked an awful lot of questions since then. What on earth was she supposed to have said?

"How was the end of your school year, honey?"

"Just fine, Dad. Except for those couple of minutes in there where I died."

Oh, yeah.

But now her father's job was occupying him round the clock. And the girlfriend—after a few stilted dinners in character-less restaurants—had moved on. "We didn't mesh," Hank Summers had said. But Buffy suspected Wendy was in search of a man without a teenage daughter.

Now Hank was virtually gone, too. And Buffy's old friends were scarce.

But memories were plentiful.

I will not break down.

It was the same vow Buffy had made every day since she'd opened her eyes to see Xander's worried face hovering above her. The day she'd discovered that she wasn't invincible.

That prophecies could come true after all.

The day her battle with the vampire so old and powerful he was known simply as the Master had left her facedown in a pool of water.

The day she'd gotten dead.

Buffy drank half the glass of orange juice in three huge gulps, wincing as the cold of the liquid penetrated her sinuses.

Those things that dead girls didn't have.

That would be right before you got back up and kicked the Master's ass, she told herself. She slammed the refrigerator door.

She was alive. The Master was dust.

He'd lost. She had won.

That's all that matters. All that counts.

Buffy finished the glass of juice, set it in the sink, then turned back to the fridge. On the door of the freezer was a *Cathy* notepad, the top page covered with her father's scrawl.

The Slayer shuddered.

Cathy. So not her favorite way to start the morning.

But she was willing to bet her dad had put a lot of thought into the selection of that notepad.

He probably thinks she's a good role model, or something.

Cathy might have more neuroses than even Freud could handle, but she'd never burned anything down. Or not to the best of Buffy's knowledge.

She tore the top page off, then scuffed her way into the living room.

Let's see what the absentee Dad-lord has to say this morning.

Since the face-to-face approach plainly hadn't worked, and since Hank's work schedule was full, notes and voice mail had become Buffy's primary means of communication with her father. Every single morning when she got up, it was to discover her dad had left her a note on the fridge.

Their tone was deliberately upbeat, as if Hank Summers had taken a course entitled, "How to Communicate with your Troubled Teenage Daughter."

It had been a correspondence course. Obviously.

Good morning, lazybones, this morning's note said.

Buffy made a face. Just what she needed. A reference to bones.

"Big meeting this afternoon, but I should be home in plenty of time to take my favorite daughter out to dinner. Put your party clothes on. I'll call from the cell when I leave the office. If you go out to the pool, don't forget to put on lots of sunblock."

For the first time that morning, Buffy felt her lips quirk up in a smile. That remark ranked fairly high on the cuteometer, she thought. At least her father was worried about something that might happen to her during the daytime.

"Have a good day, honey. See you tonight."

Buffy felt her spirits begin to lift. *Things are definitely looking up,* she decided. Not only was her dad doing his best to give her another shot at quality togetherness time, he hadn't drawn a smiley face on the bottom of this note like he had on the last one.

She set the note beside her on the couch and

propped her feet up on the coffee table, angling her toes together so that the bunnies looked like they were talking to one another.

Tonight's dinner with her father could be a second chance. *I've got to get it right, this time,* she decided. She could tell him what she'd been doing in Sunnydale.

Selectively, of course.

Buffy tapped the bunny heads together, deep in thought. There was all the time she spent in the library, for instance. That ought to perk her father up.

As long as she left out the part about the way the library sat right on top of a Hellmouth.

Well, then, there was Willow, her new best friend. Buffy's dad had always wanted her to be a better student. Maybe she could get some mileage out of talking up the way Willow carried a 4.0.

As long as she didn't mention the way Will's brainy loneliness had made her an easy target for Moloch, the demon masquerading as a sensitive chatroom guy.

Oh, I give up.

She could tell her father exactly the same thing she told her mother. Nothing. Zip. Zilch. *Nada.*

The dinner tonight was going to be just like the drive. A disaster from start to finish.

I've got to get out of here, the Slayer thought.

She'd come to L.A. to heal, to forget.

And you're just doing a dandy job so far.

That's enough! she told herself. If there was one thing she hated, it was a whiner.

So what if she was having a little trouble settling in? If the real reason she slept so late was because she hardly slept at all. If she still felt edgy and off-balance.

She'd died. She was entitled.

It was just taking her a little longer than she'd thought to catch her breath, that's all.

Catch my breath. Ha ha. Very funny.

Buffy pushed herself up from the couch. Thinking was plainly getting her nowhere in a hurry. *So stop thinking,* she told herself. Frontal-lobe activity was Willow's department, after all. Buffy was more of the action-figure type.

She strode purposefully toward the bathroom, heading for the shower. It was time to stop sitting around. Time to be moving. Be bold.

Get over yourself.

There was one thing guaranteed to do that more effectively than any other.

It was time to shop.

"Will you buy some cactus candy, senorita?"

Buffy looked down. In front of her stood a young boy carrying a tray full of small white bags filled with translucent slices of candy.

Sure, she thought. *Why not?*

She'd come here to do something different, hadn't she? Eating candy made from a plant that could double as a lethal weapon seemed like a pretty good place to start.

Buffy's quest for shopping had ended in Olvera Street, the oldest street in L.A. The last place she'd intended to go when she'd set out. But every time she pictured herself going to the Beverly Center, Buffy'd suddenly felt like she was right back in her dad's apartment.

Same old. Same old.

There were no surprises at the mall. No life.

And Buffy was beginning to discover that what she wanted was to feel like what she was.

Alive.

And what better way to prove it than by making myself sick? she thought. She bought a bag of cactus candy and began to eat it as she strolled along.

It was hot on Olvera Street, something else that made it different from the mall. Buffy knew the street catered primarily to tourists, but it still felt more real than the mall, somehow.

She could smell the scent of food wafting out the door of a nearby restaurant to mingle with the dusty smell of hot asphalt. She could feel the heat of the day radiating up through the thin soles of her sandals. Feel it beat down on top of her unprotected head.

Guess Dad was right about that sunblock.

But the best thing was the sense of anonymity Buffy felt. Nobody here knew she was the Slayer. Nobody cared that she was the Chosen One. Nobody here needed rescuing, or, if they did, it wasn't the sort only she could provide.

Slowly, amazed to find herself relaxing for the first time in weeks, Buffy worked her way down one side of the street, and started up the other, not even minding the endless jostling of the crowd.

She inspected terra-cotta pots and silver jewelry. Admired braids of bright peppers. Red. Orange. Green. Yellow. She looked at baskets. Embroidered dresses and tablecloths. Resisted a wild impulse to buy Giles a fringed sombrero. A Watcher in fringe. Now there was a scary thought.

The only shop she avoided was the one with the fortuneteller sitting out in front.

The fortuneteller was an old woman sitting behind

a folding card table, a big umbrella shielding her from the sun. Her eyes were dark and bright in a face as wrinkled as an apple doll's.

"Tell your fortune, senorita?" she asked.

Not likely, Buffy thought. *I've had enough of prophecies, thank you very much.*

Besides, she didn't want to be responsible for this woman's demise. Buffy had to figure anything the fortuneteller might see in her future would scare the old woman half to death. And it still wouldn't tell the Slayer anything she didn't already know.

She shook her head, sidling silently by the table, trying to ignore the feel of the old woman's eyes. The way they followed her, focused as a laser, hard and black as shiny jet buttons.

Stop looking at me, Buffy thought. *I'm nothing special. I'm just a tourist like everybody else.*

Yeah. Right.

"Dennis Michael Jones, you come back here this instant!" Buffy heard a voice cry out. A moment later, something small, sticky, and hot careened into the back of her legs, moving full force, knocking the Slayer to one side. She reached to brace herself, caught the edge of the card table, and felt something close around her wrist, tight as a vise.

Fingers.

Buffy jerked back, but the fingers held on. She turned, instinctively raising her other hand to strike out, and found herself looking down into the fortuneteller's eyes.

She could see herself reflected in them. Her blond hair disheveled, her own eyes startled, wide.

Is that what I really look like? she thought.

"So you have come," the fortuneteller said, her

voice like the whisper of thin paper in one of Giles's oldest reference books. The sound of it raised goose-bumps on the Slayer's skin, even with the sun beating down. "She's been waiting for you. It's about time."

Who's been waiting for me?

Scratch that. I don't want to know.

The last time somebody'd waited for her, she'd ended up making a quick trip to the afterlife.

"I'm waiting for you," the Master had said as he'd taunted her, playing hide and seek. *"I want this moment to last."*

"I don't," the Slayer had answered. Right before his strong arms had closed around her, disarming and imprisoning her.

"I understand."

No! Buffy thought. *I'm not going back there!*

Her stomach lurched, like she'd taken a fist straight to the solar plexus. The cactus candy roiled, then threatened a sudden return to the light of day. Buffy jerked her hand back, out of the fortuneteller's grasp.

She heard a grunt of breath as the fortuneteller fell forward against the table. Doubled over, hands folded across her stomach, Buffy lurched through the doorway of the nearest shop.

It was hot, close, dark. *Away.*

"What is the matter, senorita?" she heard a woman's voice exclaim. "Are you ill? I have a chair in the back. Please, you must come and sit down."

Buffy felt a second set of fingers close around her elbow. Soft. Gentle. Persuading. Still fighting nausea, she let herself be led forward into the shop. After the bright, hot light of the street, the shop seemed pitch dark, save for a strange glow at the back.

"Sit here," the woman's voice said. Buffy let herself

be eased down. She felt the backs of her legs connect with the cool metal of a folding chair. "Close your eyes," the woman said. "Put your head down. I will get you a drink of water."

Buffy complied with the woman's instructions, heard the soft rustle of her garments as she moved away. Head down, eyes closed, Buffy pulled in one deep breath, then another. Slowly, she felt the candy stop its spinning as her pulse rate returned to normal.

Way to go, ace. Could she have possibly been more stupid? She'd let that fortuneteller spook her like she was some kid at a Halloween carnival. *"She's been waiting for you."*

Give me a break.

That had to be about the oldest line in the book. Right after, I see a tall, dark, handsome man in your future.

Does he occasionally have yellow eyes and really bad dental work?

Buffy sat up, scrubbing her hands across her face. She opened her eyes. And found herself staring at the flickering light of dozens and dozens of votive candles.

What on earth?

At the back of the shop was another card table, this one spread with a brightly colored embroidered tablecloth. A photograph of a young girl in a silver frame stood in the very center, surrounded by the candles.

Intrigued in spite of herself, Buffy stood up and moved closer.

A child's rag doll leaned against one side of the frame. On the other side, someone had draped a length of skipping rope. Jars filled with bright orange marigolds lined the back of the table. Petals were scattered across the surface of the tablecloth. Buffy could smell the peppery scent of the flowers in the still, hot air.

It's a shrine, she thought.

In front of the picture sat a bag of cactus candy. There were tiny square cakes in paper holders, each cake decorated with pale pink frosting.

Directly above the center of the table hung another image of the young girl, this one cut from delicate tissue paper. She was sitting in a swing, legs extended into the air, head thrown back, braids streaming out behind her. A figure Buffy assumed was her mother stood behind her, pushing the swing.

The images reminded Buffy of the cutout paper snowflakes she and her cousin Celia had made as girls and taped to the front windows of the Summers' house at Christmastime. After Celia had died, Buffy had never made one again.

Celia, she thought. The girl in the papercut even looked a little bit like her. In the heavy air at the back of the shop, the image cut from the thin tissue was absolutely motionless.

"Ah, you are feeling better?" a voice behind her asked. Buffy jumped. She'd been so engrossed in looking at the shrine, she hadn't heard the shopkeeper's return.

"Yes, I am," she acknowledged. Talk about embarrassed. Buffy felt like she'd been caught eavesdropping. "Thank you for letting me sit down."

The woman shook her head, as if dismissing her own kindness. She held a glass out toward Buffy.

"Here is your water."

"Thanks," Buffy said, feeling a little awkward. She

took the glass, took a sip of water, holding the cool liquid in her mouth for a moment or two before she swallowed.

How old is this woman? she wondered. Her skin was mostly smooth, but her hair was bone-white. Not as old as the fortuneteller outside, but older than Giles or her mother, Buffy decided. The shopkeeper's eyes were old and dark and sad.

"You have been looking at the papercut?" she asked.

Buffy caught a strange thread of eagerness running through the other woman's voice. She nodded.

"You know about *Los Dias de Muertos,* the Days of the Dead?"

Once more, Buffy nodded. Giles had given her the basic info during one of their early "Things Every Slayer Should Know" sessions. Because the lecture had coincided with a display of papercuts Joyce was doing in the gallery at the time, Buffy had actually retained some of it.

Los Dias de Muertos was the festival celebrating the return of the dead. But didn't it happen in October? At pretty much the same time as Halloween, in fact, if Buffy was remembering Giles's lecture rightly. The night the spirits of dead children were supposed to return was October 31, All Hallow's Eve.

What's all this still doing up in July? Buffy wondered.

"I made it myself," the shopkeeper explained. "For my daughter."

The papercuts were a part of the festival decorations, but they also served another function. When the cutouts moved, it was considered a sign that the spirits were present.

"What was your daughter's name?" Buffy asked. Then she could have kicked herself. She didn't want to know any more about this woman's personal life than she already did. She had her own to worry about.

"Cecelia," the shopkeeper answered.

Buffy felt the room give a sudden swoop around her. She stared up at the papercut, still hanging perfectly still.

I should have known better than to ask, she told herself. The girl had already reminded her way too much of Celia for comfort. She didn't need to know they had almost the same name, too.

"She was just seven years old," the shopkeeper went on softly.

Not an exact match, Buffy thought. Only close enough to make her scalp tingle, her hair threaten to stand straight up on end. Only way too close to be a coincidence. Her cousin Celia had been eight when she had died. In a hospital. Alone.

And you've never even been to her grave.

"All these years, I have waited," the old woman whispered. Silently, she moved to stand beside Buffy. "I have waited for her spirit, watched for it, prayed. Never has she returned to me. Not once."

That explains the shrine, Buffy thought. The woman must be trying to draw her daughter's spirit to her, no matter what the time of year.

"So you put the two of you together in the papercut?"

The old woman's head jerked toward Buffy as if pulled by a string. "You think that is me with my daughter? You do not look carefully enough. That is not me. It is the thing that keeps her from me. It is the witch. It is the *bruja.*"

Buffy stared back at the papercut again. At first glance, the scene seemed joyful. Just a young girl being pushed on a swing. But now that Buffy was looking more closely, she noticed things she hadn't before.

The girl's head was thrown back, braids streaming out, but now Buffy could see that what she'd taken as an expression of joy on the girl's face was actually one of pain. Her mouth was open not in a cry of delight, but in a scream. The ends of her braids didn't fly free. They were tangled in the hands of the figure that stood behind her.

Buffy looked into its face. And found herself looking at something she'd never seen before, but knew she'd recognize anywhere.

Evil.

Let her go! Buffy thought. *All she wants is to be with her mother. It's not fair!*

Without realizing it, she took a step forward.

And the papercut moved in the still air.

Drifting back as if to gather momentum, then swaying straight toward Buffy. It arced out over her head, a soft rustle of thin paper, then settled into place once more, motionless as always.

"Aiee!" the shopkeeper wailed. She fell to her knees on the cement floor before the card table. "They are true, the words of the fortuneteller. You have come at last. You are the one. The warrior who will free my daughter."

Abruptly, Buffy felt cold in the hot, close air at the back of the shop.

I don't want this! she thought. She didn't want one more person telling her what to do, what her duty was. She didn't want one more person to need her.

She wanted to be anonymous, to be left alone. And she definitely didn't want to be responsible for saving anybody's daughter.

I wouldn't be any good at it anyway. I couldn't even save myself.

She set her glass beneath the table. *I've got to get out of here.* But she couldn't just leave this woman kneeling on the floor.

"Please," she said, as she knelt down beside the shopkeeper. "Please, get up. I'm sorry, but there's been some sort of mistake. Are you hurt? Should I get some help?"

"No, no," the shopkeeper murmured as she let Buffy help her up and lead her to the folding chair. "You are all the help I need. You are the one the fortuneteller told me of. You have come at last. You will fight for my Cecelia."

Ready for the release of the CD anytime now, Buffy thought. This woman was starting to sound like a broken record.

"I'm *not* the one," Buffy said, her voice more forceful this time. She battled back a spurt of guilt. Oh no? She was the Chosen One. *And you're the Slayer, not a Ghostbuster.*

"I'm sorry, but I can't help you."

The old woman looked up at her, her face confused. "But the papercut, it moved," she protested softly. "It showed my daughter's spirit was present, if only for a moment. She was here, in this room."

To Buffy's dismay, the shopkeeper's eyes began to fill with tears. "Never, not in all the years since my Cecelia's death, has such a thing occurred," the woman went on. "She could not come to me, but she has come to you. Because you are—"

"A *tourist*," Buffy broke in.

"I will go, tonight, to visit my daughter's grave," the shopkeeper said eagerly, riding right over Buffy's interruption. "You will see where she is buried. You will know how to free her spirit."

"No," Buffy said. "No, I won't." *What do I have to do to get through to this woman?* she wondered. All of a sudden, she felt like Giles. "Look—I really appreciate you helping me when I didn't feel well, but I'm not who you think I am, and I have to go now."

The shopkeeper fell silent, her dark eyes searching Buffy's face, her lips parted ever so slightly. Then she closed them firmly, plucked a handkerchief from a pocket on the front of her dress, and rose to her feet.

"As you wish, senorita," she said briskly. She wiped her eyes, then turned and led the way toward the front of the shop.

What did mothers do, take special classes in making people feel guilty? Buffy wondered as she followed.

She was on vacation. She'd said thank you for the help. Beginning, middle, and end of story. It wasn't her fault if it had been a short one.

She snatched several votive candles from a shelf at the front of the shop. "I'd like to buy these," she said as she thrust them onto the cash register counter.

"As you wish," the shopkeeper said again. She rang up Buffy's purchases and slipped them into a paper bag, automatically adding a book of matches. As she handed the bag across the counter to Buffy, their fingers met. Buffy felt the shopkeeper's tremble.

"Please, senorita, I . . . I will be here until eight o'clock," she burst out as if she couldn't help herself.

"If you change your mind, you can come back. You can still come with me."

"No, I can't," Buffy said. But by then she'd realized she had a real excuse. "I'm supposed to spend time tonight with my father."

Telling him all the things she hadn't been doing.

"I'm sorry about your daughter, honestly I am. But I won't be back. I can't help you."

Before the shopkeeper could say anything more, Buffy stepped out of the shop into the late afternoon glare to find the fortuneteller blocking her path.

"You cannot escape," the old woman challenged.

I knew it was coming sooner or later, Buffy thought. The good old you-cannot-escape clause. She stepped around the fortuneteller.

"Excuse me," she said. She was finished spending time explaining her actions. Or their absence.

"You cannot escape. It is your destiny," the fortuneteller called after her.

Buffy felt something threaten to give way inside her.

"Destinies can be changed," she snapped over her shoulder. If anybody ought to know, she should. She walked briskly toward the end of Olvera Street. She was almost to the end before she heard the fortuneteller's parting shot.

"You'll be back."

"Only if you promise to hold your breath."

He isn't home.

Buffy stepped into the silence of her father's apartment. She could tell at once that the rooms were empty. The apartment had a different feel when her dad was home.

Maybe he got caught in traffic, just like I did. Buffy

worried she'd be late for dinner all the way home. She crossed the living room, heading for the answering machine's blinking red light.

Please, just say you're on your way home, Dad.

She hit the playback button. Her father's voice filled the living room.

"Hey, sport," he said. *He sounds tired,* Buffy thought. She could feel her head start to pound. She was almost certain she knew what was coming next.

"Listen, I . . . I'm really sorry, but something's come up and I have to stay late at the office, so I can't make dinner tonight, after all. But we'll go some other night soon, okay? I . . . I think there's a pizza in the freezer or something. Geez—don't tell your mother I was a flake about feeding you. I'll never hear the end of it."

Buffy could almost feel her father's frustration.

"I'm not sure how late I'll be, so don't wait up or anything. I'm sorry, honey. I'll—what?" Buffy could hear a voice, talking in the background. "I have to go now, sweetheart," her father said. "I'll see you, soon. I—all right, all right, I'm coming."

The line went dead.

Well, that's that. So much for getting a second chance.

Except I did get one, she thought suddenly.

She wasn't dead.

Slowly, not stopping to think about what she was doing, Buffy walked down the hall to her father's bedroom, pushed the door open and went to stand in front of his dresser. It was there, just the way she'd known it would be.

The last picture of Buffy and Celia together.

It was Celia's birthday, and she was wearing a frilly party dress. Buffy was dressed as Power Girl. Her dad had taken the picture himself, kneeling down on the floor of the Summers' living room. The two girls were looking straight into the eye-level camera, their arms around each other. Both faces lit up by ear-splitting grins.

The photograph had been displayed on the mantel, until Celia had died. After that, because anything to do with her cousin only seemed to upset Buffy, her parents had moved the picture to their bedroom. Buffy knew her mother still had a copy of her own, on her dresser. This photo was one of the few things her parents still shared.

How would they feel if they knew that she'd been dead?

How would they feel if she'd never come home from that night she'd faced the Master? A thing they hadn't known about. Could never know about.

This would be all they'd have.

Memories. Photographs. And no explanations for their daughter's early death. Just a hole where she had been.

This is a shrine, too, Buffy thought.

My little hero.

It was what her father always called her when she wore her Power Girl outfit.

If I'm such a hero, why couldn't I save Celia? Buffy wondered. *Why couldn't I save myself, Dad?*

Her friends had done that. Risking themselves. Following her when she hadn't asked them to. Right into the jaws of death.

And if she was such a hero, what was she doing standing here doing nothing?

She couldn't come to me, but she came to you, the shopkeeper had said.

Buffy wasn't sure she believed it, but she was beginning to realize it might not matter what she believed. What was important was that this mother needed her. What was important was that, just maybe, she could give this woman what Xander and Angel had given her.

A second chance.

Buffy pivoted on one heel and headed for her own bedroom. *There's no fighting it,* she thought. Maybe the fortuneteller had been right after all. Maybe helping this woman and her daughter was a part of Buffy's destiny. Not just because she was the Slayer. But because she had been given her own second chance.

L. A. is starting to seem a whole lot like Sunnydale, Buffy thought. Nowhere to run. Nowhere to hide.

And another night spent in a graveyard.

"No one comes here anymore," said Mrs. Aragon.

Buffy and the shopkeeper were driving east, into the hills outside the city. Buffy had been surprised to find herself all but in the country as the car began to climb. It was **easy to** forget there were places like this so close to the city, and that L.A. was surrounded by mountains. Usually, you couldn't see them because of the smog.

The two hadn't spoken much on the drive from Olvera Street, though they had introduced themselves. Buffy now knew that the shopkeeper was Mrs. Theresa Aragon. After that, they'd fallen silent as Mrs. Aragon negotiated first the freeway, then side streets, as the sun slipped closer and closer to the horizon.

By the time we get to the graveyard, it will be nearly dark, Buffy thought.

Par for the course.

Mrs. Aragon turned left at the base of a steep hill. "Not much farther now."

Almost show time, Buffy thought. The trouble was, she didn't know which program she was watching. What should she expect?

She curved her fingers around the strap of her shoulder bag. Buffy had tried to come prepared. A good Slayer was pretty much like a Girl Scout in that respect. Except for that thing where you had to sell cookies.

Mrs. Aragon made a hairpin turn, the car skidding as the pavement ended, and the back tires fought to find purchase on the steep dirt road. Billows of dust rose up around the car. Buffy rolled up her window. The shopkeeper drove to the top of the hill and parked beside an old adobe church.

"We are here," said Mrs. Aragon. "The graveyard is over there." She pointed in front of them. In the fading light, Buffy could see tilting gravestones at the edge of the hill. They vanished over the side. A chain-link fence separated the graveyard from the rest of the hilltop.

"They stopped burying here not long after my Cecelia died. The hillside can be treacherous when it rains."

Together, Buffy and Mrs. Aragon got out of the car. Buffy followed the shopkeeper to the gate. Its hinges screeched as she pulled it open.

"Wait a minute," Buffy said. Mrs. Aragon paused. She looked back at Buffy, her expression expectant.

Now what? Buffy thought.

"I just wanted to say . . . I'll do my best . . . but . . . We don't know quite what we're dealing with here," she finished somewhat lamely. "So, don't get your hopes up."

Very smooth, Summers, she thought. Not to mention sensitive. She'd probably get some sort of Slayer Humanitarian of the Year award.

"Are you finished?" the shopkeeper asked. Buffy nodded. "Then come," said Mrs. Aragon. She passed through the gate and held it open.

Buffy followed her into the graveyard.

She tripped over a clump of crabgrass almost at once. *This is a far cry from the tidy suburban graves of Sunnydale.* Buffy'd seen pet cemeteries kept up better than this. And at least they were level. One false step and she was likely to go tumbling down the hillside.

She followed Mrs. Aragon down the slope, picking her way carefully. The graveyard occupied one wide shelf, a terrace to the dead across the face of the hillside. The end of the chain-link fence looked like it extended right out into open air.

No wonder nobody comes here, the Slayer thought.

Mrs. Aragon stopped, then knelt. Buffy moved to stand beside her. In front of them was a round-topped gravestone. Plain. Unadorned.

Cecelia Micaela Aragon the gravestone said. *Beloved Daughter.*

What do I do now? Buffy wondered. *Knock on the stone and say "Let my people go?"*

Somehow, she didn't think so.

Buffy looked at the dates that showed the brief span of Cecelia's life. 1952–1959. Cecelia Aragon had died more than twenty years before Buffy had been born.

And all this time, her mother has been searching for her spirit. Waiting for a sign.

Buffy felt a strange feeling rise within her: a combination of rage and sorrow. *It isn't right,* she thought.

Cecelia and her mother belonged together, even if it was only for the few days of *Los Dias de Muertos.*

And I'm going to make it happen.

The question was, how?

Buffy was completely on her own here. No backup. No Willow or Giles. She had to make her own rules, her own plan, at least for the moment.

In the meantime, standing still was beginning to make her crazy.

Maybe I'll learn something from scouting around.

Mrs. Aragon was bowed forward, her face in her hands. Quietly, Buffy slipped from her side. She began to make her way horizontally across the graveyard, lower and lower, moving through the rows of headstones. The lower she went, the older the dates on the headstones became, and the taller the grass. Behind her, the sun went down like a fireball.

So many women and children, Buffy thought. Sadness seemed to hang in the dusty air. High in the trees, cicadas whined.

Buffy stumbled. The vanishing light was beginning to make exploring treacherous. *Wait a minute,* she thought. She dropped to her knees and let her shoulder bag fall to the ground beside her. A moment later, Buffy had what she was looking for. The votive candles she'd purchased from Mrs. Aragon. The shopkeeper had even tucked a book of matches into the sack, if Buffy remembered right.

She struck a match, lit a candle, then caught a flash of white out of the corner of her eye. The sudden flare of the match had spooked a bird. It streaked through the air, its wings flashing black and white, then alighted on something just outside the fence.

It looks like another grave, the Slayer thought.

Who was buried outside the graveyard?

Sheltering the flame of her candle with one hand, Buffy moved to the chain-link fence and vaulted over. Spooked again, the bird flew off, but now Buffy could see the worn edge of a gravestone barely protruding from the tall grass. Slowly, careful of her footing, Buffy walked toward it.

The name on the stone was completely obscured. Buffy reached down and pulled a handful of grass away. Still, she could see nothing. Irritated now, she set the candle on top of the headstone and reached for the grass with both hands.

The burst of frigid air knocked her over.

Buffy smashed face first into the headstone as a wild wailing filled the air around her. She struggled to turn around, bracing herself against the headstone, one arm flung up to protect her face from the wind.

And saw the *bruja,* floating in the air before the stone. Hair, wild. Face, distorted. She raised a hand, the finger pointing at the Slayer.

And then she swooped straight toward her.

Buffy launched herself around the edge of the headstone in an effort to put something solid between her and the *bruja.* But she'd forgotten about the steep slope of the hill.

Too much! Too fast! she thought. Wasn't Giles always telling her not to get carried away?

Too late. She was already rolling down the hillside.

Long grass whipped against her face as Buffy desperately tried to slow herself down. Slithering. Rolling, she tried to keep herself on her stomach. Her fingers scrabbled for purchase against the hard-packed ground.

If she didn't stop her momentum somehow, she'd roll right off the face of the hill. The only thing between Buffy and disaster was . . .

The chain-link fence around the graveyard.

Frantically, Buffy twisted herself to the left. She flailed out with her arm, her fingers seeking the links of the fence. Her fingers scraped painfully along the metal, then caught. Buffy's legs flew out into space as she stopped with a wrench so sudden it all but jerked her arm from its socket. She lay against the fence for a moment, fighting for breath.

Don't just lie there. Do something, she thought. *There's a* bruja *to fight.* No Slayer'd ever been taken out by a roll down the hill, and Buffy Summers didn't intend to be the first.

She pulled herself into a sitting position, then got to her feet. She didn't have her shoulder bag. Just wonderful. It looked like things were going to be hand-to-hand. Not that that was going to be a problem.

Buffy felt a second blast of air as the *bruja* materialized in front of her once more. One hand on the fence for balance, Buffy aimed a kick, high—and pulled up short.

There were children all around the *bruja.* Insubstantial. Ghostly. Dozens of them, more than Buffy could count. All of them girls, their mouths open in wails of pain.

"Cecelia!" Buffy heard Mrs. Aragon cry.

The girl closest to Buffy started forward, then jerked back, as if held by invisible chains.

"Mama! Mama!"

Buffy eyed the *bruja.* "Let her go," she said.

Tears streamed down the *bruja*'s face. *Wait a minute,* Buffy thought. Since when did witches cry?

"I cannot," the *bruja* choked out. "They are bound to me until—"

"Please," Buffy heard Mrs. Aragon sob as she ran toward her. "My daughter is here! You must save her! Do something!"

At the sight of her mother, Cecelia Aragon began to wail, her cry infecting the children around her. As if their cries made her own pain worse, the *bruja* whipped her head from side to side. Tears flew from her face like a spangle of stars.

Something definitely doesn't add up here, Buffy thought.

The *bruja* raised one arm and pointed her index finger straight at Buffy. Then, as abruptly as she'd appeared, she vanished, taking the children with her. Their cries shivered in the air, then faded away. Behind her, Buffy could hear Mrs. Aragon sobbing, harshly.

"I believed in you," the shopkeeper gasped. "I believed in you. Why did you do nothing?"

She turned, clinging to the fence, and began to make her way back to the entrance of the graveyard. Her whole body aching, Buffy vaulted the fence and prepared to follow.

The ride home is not going to be a happy one, she thought.

She took two steps, and fell right over a headstone.

Buffy lay for a minute in the rough grass. *What I did on my summer vacation, by Buffy Summers.*

And the fun wasn't over yet. Not by a long shot. Buffy couldn't leave things the way they were.

I started this. I'm going to finish it.

I'll be back, she thought as she hauled herself to her feet and went in search of her shoulder bag.

In the daytime. When she could see where she was going.

"You did what?" said Giles.

Buffy rolled her eyes. Just one time, she wanted Giles to say, "By Jove, Buffy, that's absolutely brilliant." Then they could both expire of surprise.

"It's called the right thing, Giles. You remember—that thing you're always telling me I should do more of?"

A brief silence filled the phone connection.

"Strive to forgive me," Giles said, his voice bone dry. "But I tend to say the first thing that comes into my head when awakened by the phone in the middle of the night. I can't imagine why."

"Is there a time difference between L. A. and Sunnydale?" Buffy sweetly inquired. To her surprise, she was actually enjoying herself. The truth was, it was good to hear Giles's voice. It made her feel less alone, somehow.

It was also true that he could be infuriating and dense at times. And he was way too attached to going by the rules. But Buffy pretty much figured he couldn't help it. He was a grown-up, after all.

"Because it's not even midnight here," she went on. "Don't try and tell me you were asleep. You're probably in bed reading *Dusty Tome Illustrated* and eating scones."

"Soda crackers, actually," Giles came back. "They make such lovely crumbs."

"Feel free to spare me the details, Giles."

"Am I to take it this is not a social call?"

"Does this mean we're going right to the Giles helps Buffy portion of our program?"

Instantly, Giles's tone became all business. "Tell me what you've got."

Quickly, Buffy filled him in. "I know it's not my usual Slayer gig, but something about this just doesn't feel right, Giles. I mean, I know I may not be up on the latest *bruja* lore, but I just don't think that's what we're dealing with here. She was *crying.*"

"Based on what you've told me, I think you may very well be right," Giles said.

"I don't suppose you'd care to put that in writing."

"There are a couple of avenues to explore here, I think," Giles went on. "I'll do some research and call you back in the morning. You, meantime, will get a good night's sleep. We don't know what you're facing here, so it's safest to assume you'll need all your strength."

"Okay, Dad," Buffy said, her tone joking.

"Speaking of which, how is your father?" Giles inquired.

"Fine," Buffy said shortly. *Well, it's true,* she thought. Her dad *was* fine. She was the one who was experiencing family-togetherness technical problems.

"Well, right then," Giles went on. "Speak to you in the morning. And Buffy—I agree with you, by the way. You did do the right thing."

Buffy heard the *click* that meant Giles had hung up, then, after a moment, the dial tone.

"Thanks," she said.

Then she hit the "off" button and put her father's portable phone back in the recharger.

She got ready for bed, fell asleep, and dreamed of a pair of ruby slippers and a girl's voice saying, over and over, "There's no place like home."

* * *

"Right," Giles said the next morning. "I'll try to be brief."

That'll be a switch, Buffy thought. She took a sip of coffee, wincing as it scalded her tongue. Not one of her better mornings. She'd awakened to find no sign of her father save a pot of cold coffee and another note on the fridge.

She hadn't even bothered to read it. She'd simply stuffed it down the garbage disposal along with the coffee grinds. Then she'd poured herself a cup of coffee and zapped it in the microwave while she waited for the call from Giles.

"I think you're right to doubt that what you encountered was a *bruja*," Giles said now. "Or, actually, anything with supernatural powers of its own. I think it's most likely that the woman you saw is a spirit herself. Obviously, a very disturbed one. You did say you placed a candle on top of the headstone?"

"Right before all heck broke loose," Buffy confirmed.

"That would seem to make sense," Giles went on. "Unknowingly, you performed a ritual that is part of *Los Dias de Muertos.* Placing candles atop a grave is supposed to help guide a spirit back to earth. It would appear that your action of placing the candle on the gravestone during a time when spirits don't usually walk the earth served as a direct summons."

"So I called up whoever's buried in that grave?"

"That's the most likely explanation," agreed Giles. "I was able to do fairly extensive research on the Days of the Dead. The festival has its roots in the rituals of the ancient Aztecs.

"The Aztecs believed that what a person experienced in the afterlife would be determined by the manner of their death. That being the case, I'd say that discovering who is buried in that grave and how she died should be your first priority. Unfortunately, that's not something I can help with from here."

"There's a church," Buffy said. "Right beside the graveyard. They might have records there."

"Good thought," said Giles. "Once you've determined how the woman died, you'll know how to confront her. My sources don't provide a lot of detail, but they all confirm a tormented spirit such as this one must be made to face the way she died. Doing this should free her."

"What about the children?" Buffy asked.

"I think that freeing her should release them also," Giles said. "It's likely the reason she's holding on to their spirits is also related to her past. Knowing more about who she and how she died should provide the answers that you need. Only, Buffy—"

I knew there was going to be a catch. "What?"

"You did say that grave was *outside* the grave-yard?"

"Just outside the fence," Buffy confirmed. "That means something special, doesn't it?"

"It does," said Giles. "Being buried outside of holy ground was usually a fate reserved for suicides. Confronting this woman with the means of her death could be very dangerous."

"I'll watch myself," the Slayer promised.

"You might want to—" Giles began.

"Giles," Buffy interrupted. "I'll be careful. I promise."

"This was supposed to be your vacation, you know," Giles remarked.

Buffy sighed. "Tell me about it."

* * *

"You want to see what?"

Buffy stood just inside the doorway of the old adobe church, facing the church's young caretaker.

How come there are never any easy parts?

Buffy'd already had a phone consultation with Giles, a face-to-face meeting with Mrs. Aragon, followed by the trip to the graveyard. Then she'd done some on-sight reconnaissance to determine who the graves she'd discovered last night belonged to.

The grave outside the fence belonged to a young woman. The one she'd taken a header over in the far corner of the graveyard, to a child.

Both had died in the year 1889.

And they both had the same name: Josefina Maria Alonzo.

A mother and daughter? Buffy wondered.

The church records would be the best way to find out. Not to mention the best way of discovering why the older Josefina had been buried where she had been.

If Buffy was back home in Sunnydale, this would be the part where Giles and Willow would take over. They'd paw through Giles's musty tomes and produce the answer.

But Buffy wasn't in Sunnydale. And she didn't have Will and Giles. All she had was herself. And the clueless caretaker.

It's just me and juvenile-delinquency boy.

"I'm doing some research on the graveyard," she said again, being careful to speak slowly. "I need to see the church's burial records—"

"What are you, some kind of freak or something?"

You have no idea. "Do you know where they are, or don't you?"

"Yeah, yeah, I know. No need to get all bent about it. They're in there." He gestured with his thumb toward a small room at the back of the church. "Don't expect me to baby-sit you, or nothing. I got work to do, you know."

Right, Buffy thought. *And I'm Santa Claus.* "Don't let me stop you."

She turned and walked into the room the caretaker had indicated. It was like everywhere else in the church that Buffy had seen so far.

Dusty.

But there were bookshelves, with actual books on them. Big leather ones. And a table and chair in one corner. Buffy pulled out several volumes and carried them to the table, sending clouds of dust flying. Then she leafed through them until she found 1889. Inside, the book was covered with spidery handwriting.

Buffy felt her spirits sink.

Just her luck. The one time she had to do the research herself and it was before the invention of the word processor.

In the very back of the book, she found an entry.

This day have buried Josefina Maria, only child of Rafael Alonzo. At her father's insistence, the grave is far removed from the others, marked only by a small, plain headstone. Rafael Alonzo attended the ceremony alone. He would permit no other mourners.

Not even his child's mother? Buffy wondered.

The dates on the headstones said simply "1889." How long between the deaths of the two Josefina Maria Alonzos?

Buffy turned the page.

Nothing.

Great, she thought. *A dead end. My favorite part.*

She went back through the book again. Maybe she'd missed the entry for Josefina's mother the first time around.

She hadn't.

I'll never take Giles and Will for granted again.

Compared to researching, slaying was starting to look pretty straightforward. Get hit, hit back harder. Kill, or be killed. Not all that complicated. And at least you tended to know what to do next at all times.

What was she supposed to do now? Go through every single volume on the shelf? Not very likely.

If this were a movie, now's the time when I'd discover the secret diary, she thought. She turned the last page over and ran her fingers over the inside of the book's back cover.

You've got to be joking.

There was something there. No two ways about it.

Buffy dug the Swiss army knife she always carried out of her shoulder bag and slit the back cover. She pulled out several sheets of thin paper, unfolding them to reveal the same spidery handwriting.

What, no treasure map? she thought.

He made me bury her outside the holy ground.

Now we're getting somewhere, Buffy thought. She leaned closer, squinting at the faded writing.

Be it known that I, Father Paolo Hernandez, do here set down the true story of Josefina Maria Alonzo, whom I have greatly wronged this day.

I have condemned her soul to eternal unrest by committing her body to unholy ground, though I believe her death was innocent. In this, I have let my will be overcome by that of her husband, Rafael Alonzo, whose wealth supplies my living and the bounty of this church.

Perhaps if I had not—but it is no matter. I confess my weakness and my wrong to the Holy Father.

May He have mercy on all our souls.

If I had not—what? Buffy wondered. She leafed through the pages, trying to find more. The pages seemed to ramble, filled with Father Hernandez's tortured thoughts. Whatever had happened, it seemed plain that the priest viewed himself as at least partially responsible for the fate of the elder Josefina.

If only I had not married them. The words seemed to leap at Buffy from the page. *If I had counseled her to follow her heart, and not the desires of her family. But that is not our way. The will of the daughter is subject to the father, as the wife's is to her husband. And the husband Josefina's father wished for her was Rafael Alonzo.*

Sometimes, I think her fate was sealed upon her wedding day.

It's like a soap opera, Buffy thought. But it had been played out with real live characters, who'd suffered deadly consequences.

As the sun sank lower and lower in the sky, the Slayer read the history of Josefina Maria Alonzo. When she was finished, she sat back.

It wasn't very much to go on, but it just might be enough. At least she knew who all the players were now. The two Josefinas were, indeed, mother and daughter.

Josefina Sanchez had been forced by her family to marry wealthy Rafael Alonzo, even though she'd loved someone else. Their only child had been a daughter, also called Josefina.

The girl buried in the corner of the graveyard, Buffy thought.

Miserable in her marriage, the older Josefina had taken as her lover the man she'd wished to marry, the one she'd loved all along. They'd planned to run away together, taking young Josefina, a plan that was foiled when they were caught by Rafael Alonzo.

Rafael had given his wife an ultimatum. Leave her daughter behind, or he would shoot her lover in front of her. When a desperate Josefina agreed, Rafael shot and killed the lover anyway. The only thing that had enabled Josefina to escape had been her daughter's hysterics.

She'd feared her father would shoot her mother also.

The young Josefina never truly recovered from the events she had witnessed. Not long after, she contracted a fatal fever. With her dying words, she called out for her mother.

When Josefina learned of this, she was beside herself with grief. No longer fearing what Rafael might do to her, she left her hiding place and set out for the graveyard.

She never got there.

It had been a spring full of sudden, violent rainstorms, sending flash floods sweeping down the hillsides. On her way to the graveyard, Josefina was caught in a sudden onslaught of water.

Determined to keep mother and daughter apart even in death, Rafael Alonzo insisted his wife be buried in unconsecrated ground, her death treated as a suicide. He claimed his wife had taken her own life, blaming herself for what had happened to their daughter.

Although the priest resisted, Rafael's wealth carried the day. The elder Josefina was buried outside the graveyard. Her daughter, in its farthest corner. Alone. Forgotten.

Buffy sat back, drumming her fingers on the table top.

Looks like a family reunion is in order.

What was it Giles had said? To free the spirit Buffy would have to confront her with the manner of her death.

Buffy folded Father Hernandez's confession and slipped it into her shoulder bag. She might need to refer to it again. On the off chance the plan that was forming in the back of her mind turned out to be totally hopeless.

She had votive candles. She had matches. There was just one thing left.

She found the caretaker, out front, having a smoke break.

"What do you want now?" he asked, his tone and expression surly.

Buffy gave him her nicest smile. "Could you show me where I can fill up my water bottle?" she asked.

"I hate to say this," Buffy said. "But I need you to understand that—"

"I know—no promises," Mrs. Aragon interrupted.

The two women stood just outside the church, watching the sun go down. The caretaker was long gone. As Buffy had promised earlier in the day, she'd waited until the shopkeeper arrived to put her plan into action. It was almost time now.

Quickly, Buffy checked her supplies. Candles. Matches. Bottle of water. Check. Check. Check.

"Well," she said. "I guess it's time to get this show on the—"

"Wait!" Mrs. Aragon blurted out as Buffy moved forward. The Slayer stopped, surprised. "I want to apologize," Mrs. Aragon went on, her tone halting. "For . . . the . . . things I said last night. I should not have spoken so."

"It's all right. I think I understand," Buffy said softly. It was how she felt about Angel, in a way. So close, and yet so far. "I just don't think this is something we have to fight," Buffy went on.

"We'll know soon enough," Mrs. Aragon said.

You got that right, Buffy thought.

"Are you ready?" she asked.

The shopkeeper nodded.

"Then let's do it," Buffy said. Together, the two women walked toward the graveyard.

Mrs. Aragon got into position to await Buffy's signal. The Slayer halted just outside the fence, at the grave of the elder Josefina Maria Alonzo. As she had the night before, she set a votive candle atop the gravestone. Then she tucked her refilled bottle of water under her arm and pulled out the book of matches.

"Are you ready?" she called.

"I am ready," Mrs. Aragon called back.

Well, here goes nothing, the Slayer thought.

She struck a match and lit the votive candle.

Almost at once, she felt the blast of icy air. Josefina Alonzo exploded into being before her, her mouth open in a mournful wail.

"Why do you torment me?" she cried out. "Why do you summon me if you will give me no peace?"

The children around Josefina cried and clung to her skirts, as if infected by her pain.

Quickly, Buffy took the cap off the bottle of water.

Was she supposed to say something? she wondered. *Perform some sort of ritual?*

"Josefina Maria Alonzo, I confront you with the manner of your death."

Buffy raised the bottle and pushed down hard in the very center, sending a spray of water straight at the spirit.

A wild shriek split the night air. As Buffy watched, Josefina's form began to bleed and blur around the edges, like a chalk sidewalk painting being slowly washed away by the rain.

Bingo! she thought.

"Why have you done this to me?" the spirit wailed. "All I wanted was to find my child, my Josefina. Without this form, I will lose that chance. I will be confined to the realm of the shapeless ones, forever. Even if I find her now, she will never know me. I will fail."

"You won't," the Slayer said. "I know where she is. But you have to promise to let the others go."

"My child! You have seen my child?" the spirit asked.

"No, but I know where to find her," Buffy said. "But you have to let the others go. It's not right for you to hold them."

"All I wanted was to find my daughter," Josefina said. "I never meant to hold so many others. But once I had called them, they were bound to me. I could not bear to release them until I had found my daughter. If you show me my Josefina, I will release the others. I swear it."

Good enough for me, Buffy thought.

"Now!" she shouted.

In the far corner of the graveyard, a single match

flared. For one split second, Buffy saw the face of Mrs. Aragon, outlined in the sudden glare. Then the shopkeeper touched the match to another votive candle. The one resting on top of the young Josefina's grave. The candle sputtered, then sprang to life.

And a child materialized above the long-neglected grave.

Her dark hair tumbled to her shoulders. She was dressed in a plain white nightdress.

"Mama," she cried out. "Mama, where are you? I am frightened."

"Josefina!" her mother said.

With a cry, the young girl launched herself forward. The spirit of her mother met her halfway. The mother reached out and enfolded the daughter into her arms.

"My child. My daughter. I have found you at last." Buffy heard her say.

She put her hands on the chain-link fence and vaulted over, moving quickly to Cecelia Aragon's grave. Mrs. Aragon was already there. As soon as she'd lit the candle for the young Josefina, she'd made her way to the grave of her own daughter, as she and Buffy had planned.

"Remember your promise," Buffy called out to the spirit.

Josefina lifted her head. "My little ones, I release you," she said. "Go to your rest. Wait for the day when your true mothers will call you home."

The spirits of the children rose up into the air. For just a moment, they clung together. Then they burst apart, flying in every direction. Their glad cries filled the night air. Then, one by one, they vanished. There would be lots of happy reunions during the next festival, Buffy thought.

"Are you ready?" she asked.

"I am ready," Mrs. Aragon answered. Carefully, Buffy struck one final match, and lit the candle she and Mrs. Aragon had placed earlier on Cecelia's grave. The candle that would finally guide the young girl's spirit to her mother.

"It's time to come home, Cecelia," Buffy murmured.

Time for your second chance.

"Hi, honey," Buffy's father said.

It was late when Buffy let herself into her dad's apartment. The living room lights were blazing, the TV on low. A tantalizing smell filled the air, one that made Buffy's mouth water.

"Hey, Dad," she said. "Do I smell popcorn?"

Her father poked his head in from the kitchen. "Got it in one," he said. He hesitated, as if uncertain how to handle the next moment. "How was your evening?" he asked.

"Fine," Buffy answered. Before heading out to the graveyard, she'd left a message for her father on the *Cathy* notepad, saying she was going out with old friends. And she'd given *Cathy* a handlebar mustache.

"I was thinking I'd watch a late movie. Care to join me?" her father asked.

"Can we watch a Bugs Bunny tape first?" Buffy asked.

Her father's face lit up in a surprised and delighted grin. Watching Bugs together on Saturday morning had once been one of their most cherished family rituals.

"You know it," Hank Summers said. "Pick one that has a couple Wile E. Coyotes on it, will you?"

"Sure thing," Buffy said. "I'm just gonna go dump my stuff."

"I'll finish putting way too much butter and salt on the popcorn," her father said.

Buffy went into her bedroom, shed her shoulder bag and jacket. Then she took off her boots and put her bunny slippers on. Finally, she stopped in the bathroom to splash some water on her face. She looked at her face in the mirror.

Not a bad evening, all in all, she told her reflection. Even if it wasn't her usual Slayer-type event. Buffy had reunited two sets of mothers and daughters. And she hadn't had to kill anything. Not even something that was already dead.

Buffy had given Father Hernandez's confession to Mrs. Aragon on the ride home. The shopkeeper had promised to see to it that the older Josefina's grave was moved, inside the cemetery this time. And close to her daughter, so they would never be parted again. It had taken almost a hundred years, but the evil caused by Rafael Alonzo would finally be undone.

Josefina and her daughter, too, would have a second chance.

Buffy toweled her face, headed for the living room. Her father was crouched in front of the VCR, pawing through his movie collection. A huge bowl of popcorn sat in the center of the coffee table.

"I wasn't sure if you'd be home, so I didn't rent anything," Hank Summers said. "I don't think I have any—what do they call them—chick flicks."

"Good use of the lingo," Buffy praised. "Have you been studying again?"

Her father laughed.

Suddenly happier than she'd been in weeks, Buffy knelt beside him to study the movie collection. "What about this one?" she asked.

It, too, had been a tradition when she'd been growing up, though she didn't think they'd ever watched it in the summertime.

"You want to watch *It's a Wonderful Life?*" her father asked, his tone surprised.

"Yeah," the Slayer said.

Her father reached out and ruffled her hair, just like he'd done when Buffy was a little girl.

"Okay, hero," he said. "You're on."

UNCLE DEAD AND THE FOURTH OF JULY

YVONNE NAVARRO

beg your pardon?"

Jenny Calendar tapped a fingernail on the colorful flyer she'd just slid across the library counter in front of Rupert Giles. "Come on, Rupert. It'll be fun."

Giles squinted down at the red, white and blue piece of paper. Curved across the top, in screamingly bright red, three-dimensional block letters, were the words JOIN OUR UNCLE SAM CELEBRATION!!! " 'It'll be fun,' " he repeated. "Why do I always cringe when I hear that phrase?"

Jenny tilted her head. "It *will*," she insisted. She folded her arms and gave him a stern look. "Plus it will get you out of this musty old library. It's summer, remember? The birds are singing, the sun is shining—"

"Yes," he interrupted. "And there are biting mosquitoes and sunburns to be had by one and all. Must we share in the experience?"

"We must," she said. "Besides, it's about time you learned to appreciate this holiday. It's all about tradition."

"I'm quite well informed in my history," he said huffily.

"I'm sure you know the British version very well," Jenny shot back. "But you live *here* now. You need to be imbued with the American spirit."

He gave her a dark look. "Thank you, but such as things are around Sunnydale, I'd prefer to avoid being imbued with anything. Spiritual or otherwise."

A corner of Jenny's mouth lifted in a pretty smile, and despite himself, Giles felt his resolve weakening. "Point taken, but really, Rupert—lighten up. I just can't let you spend the best months of the year tucked away in the library and hiding behind the excuse of a handful of summer-school students." She pointed again at the flyer. "Besides, it's on a Saturday."

Blast it. "The Fourth of July is . . . Saturday?" He felt his last excuse slip away.

She nodded. "Yes, Rupert. And that would be tomorrow. Amazing how the calendar sometimes arranges that. Tuesday comes after Monday, Saturday comes after Friday—"

"Yes," he cut in. "I believe I get it." He shivered as the air conditioning suddenly kicked on and a cool draft skittered across the back of his neck, too much skin exposed by the casual summer shirt. He much preferred the formal shirt, vest, and tweed jacket that was his usual attire the rest of the year, but Jenny had pointed out that he was standing out among the summer faculty and students like a green cabbage in a petunia bed. He was sure that somewhere behind that observation was a gentle bit of mockery, but he couldn't pinpoint it enough to defend himself.

"So I'll pick you up at three?"

Giles blinked and mentally searched his schedule, desperately trying to find something—*anything*—that would rescue him. "Well, I—"

"Great," Jenny said brightly. "I'll see you tomorrow then." She turned and strode briskly away.

"Wait," Giles said. "What about, er, tonight . . . ?"

Jenny paused and looked at him inquisitively. "Tonight? Oh, no. Last night was a new moon. I have an on-line chat with my Wiccan group that starts at dusk. We probably won't be finished until after midnight."

Giles nodded. "An on-line chat. Of course. I'll call you, then?"

"Tomorrow morning," she reminded him. "The phone will be tied up tonight." She gave him a cheerful good-bye smile. "Have a great evening."

"Right."

"And Giles?"

He looked up. "Yes?"

"Please try to get out of this stuffy old library. There's a big, beautiful country out there, just waiting for you to encounter it."

Giles only nodded as another wave of damp air inexplicably caressed the back of his neck.

It had taken Patrick Beverly a long time to come home.

Of course, the home he'd thought he was headed for had things like air conditioning, overstuffed furniture in the living room, a waterbed in his room, his pipe-smoking Dad watching Sunday basketball while his Mom baked—cookies, dark fudge brownies or sometimes a cherry pie—for her Monday evening Bridge Club. It had a cranky old cat named, courtesy of his own less than creative mind at eight years old, Hisser. It had heat in the winter, electric lights at night, and sunlight streaming through his Mom's handmade lace curtains.

Yeah, most of all, it had *sunlight*.

Scowling, Patrick looked around his new, and hopefully, temporary abode. It had a window, true, and someone had thoughtfully put a pattern of dark stained glass in it, some patron saint or another instead of a cross, thank you very much. It also had mildewed concrete walls, a cold floor, and six tombs in it. One of them was his, and oh, joy—there was his bed now: nice oak wood, the equivalent of satin sheets and a pillow. Too bad it was a coffin instead of a four-poster.

He scuffed his shoes along the floor—nice, dirty concrete there, too—and sulked. Some rest of his life this had turned out to be. Join the Army and serve your country and look what had happened—they'd shipped him over to Bosnia and he hadn't even had the honor of getting shot down by an enemy sniper, or blown up by a rocket. Oh no, Private Patrick Beverly had sucked in one too many lungfuls of sooty, frigid air (after being repeatedly reminded by his C.O. to wear his filter mask) and had come down with pneumonia.

A grueling, fever-filled airplane ride had gotten him home and then into the V.A. Medical Center in Washington, D.C. To make matters worse, his weakened lungs invited in a new visitor—imagine, *him,* a guy barely nineteen, with TB! He'd thought it was an old person's disease, not something for the twenty-first century. For crying out loud, his *grandmother* had endured it in the 1920s and won. Why was he having such a hard time with it now?

The crud in his lungs, that's why—smoke from the barrel fires he and his buddies had built to warm their hands over, drifting ash and soot from bombed-out buildings, all settling deeply into tissue he'd never considered could be so fragile. Months had passed, too many to count, while he lay in a blood-tinged fog, isolated from all but masked doctors, nurses and aides who washed his wasting body like he was an infant. But he was getting better, his body slowly fighting off the TB while his lungs struggled to clear themselves of the black sludge embedded in the tissues. He'd been too ill—nearly comatose—to know how much time had passed, but his parents had finally gotten the go-ahead to transfer him back home to Sunnydale. Another month or two as they waited for a bed to open up, then voilá—he was as close to home as he'd seen since the break between boot camp and his assignment to Fort Stewart in Georgia. A nice, sun-filled room at the back corner of the V.A. medical facility right here in his hometown, another couple of months and hey, he could actually *walk* again instead of being trundled around in a wheelchair. Rehab then, and he'd been . . . what? A week, maybe two, away from finally, *finally* going home, when he'd met the girl.

The hell of it was, he couldn't even remember her name, or what she'd been doing there, or . . . anything beyond the fact that two nights after she'd introduced herself, she had slipped into his room and made herself a nice dinner out of the side of his neck. Who knew why she'd turned him—amusement perhaps, maybe even a misplaced sense of guilt out of chowing down on a good ol' American service boy pulled back from the brink of death and about to finally go home.

Well, she'd sent him "home" all right.

Patrick didn't like this being a vampire business. In fact, it *sucked*. He couldn't go out in the daylight, he was dirty, this place smelled like dust, old rat droppings, and mummified flesh, he was hungry all the time, and all he wanted to do was bite people. What was the deal with this sudden craving for blood, when a few days ago all he could think about was that he was only hours away from being able to sit down to his mom's homemade corned beef and cabbage?

He felt like a runaway kid: lonely, dirty, and stuck in a hiding place instead of being able to go out and play. And even the hiding place had its tiers of importance. His was at the bottom in the back, the last slot. It had taken him a while to get it, but then he realized his parents had put his body in a long, unused family spot in Sunnydale Cemetery, one originally intended for his war hero grandfather. Grandpa, however, had come back from World War II and met himself a grand old matron from Seattle. He'd moved there and married her when Patrick was little, and the now-deceased couple were moldering happily away in a dual plot in the rain-soaked ground of the Northwest.

So here was Patrick Beverly, turned nineteen right before he left the Washington V.A. center, buried with a bunch of dead World War II fogies. Ugh.

Bored, restless, Patrick poked around the inside of the small mausoleum, reading the inscriptions on the other tombs. There wasn't a single inscription for anyone younger than seventy except for him—it figured he would be the only young person in here. And what was with this uniform his parents had buried him in, anyway? Dull, dull, dull, and besides, he'd had more than enough of the military when he'd been alive, and look at what it had gotten him.

Say . . . maybe one of these old farts had something a little brighter.

He peered at the inscriptions again. What was this one . . . General Samson Murray. He vaguely remembered hearing about this guy, some fanatical war hero who was housed in another part of the same V.A. Medical Center in Sunnydale that had kept Patrick himself until a few days ago. In fact, it looked like it hadn't been that long for General Murray, either—he'd died only a couple of weeks back.

Hey, Patrick thought, maybe the good old General was wearing something a bit more interesting than the green army uniform adorning his own somewhat skinny form.

With something to finally occupy his time and mind, Patrick grinned and started working at the mortared edges of the faceplate to General Murray's tomb. It didn't take long to get it open—one of few pluses about being a vampire was the increased strength, and once he found a couple of chinks in the seams, he just dug around in there until he could wiggle it side to side; eventually, it toppled off and shattered, barely missing his foot when he hopped backward. *Can vampires get broken bones?* He had no idea.

The smell that drifted out of the chamber he'd opened up was ripe and, by his old human standards, unpleasant. Now it didn't bother Patrick, and he squinted in the low light, trying to see inside. He finally gave up and just yanked the casket out of the hole in the wall, letting it fall to the floor. No cheapie box here: the General's bed was made of rich, dark mahogany with plenty of decorative carving on all sides, and it gave Patrick hope that the old fart inside might be wearing something worthy of confiscation.

A good hard wrench and the lid fell victim to his enhanced strength. Then he was staring down at the earthly remains of General Samson Murray.

Thanks to modern-day preservatives, the elderly war hero didn't look half bad. Prune-wrinkled, of course, and his closed eyes were all sunk in, as was his nose, the area under his cheekbones, and the ends of his fingertips—everything looked pretty much fat-free. More important, he was wearing a nifty looking uniform, nice dark blue with a whole bevy of medals pinned to it, and the clothes looked like they just might fit him. Patrick recognized most of the glitz on the old man's chest, but one oddball medal stood out, a big, oval-shaped opal rimmed in ornate gold and pinned above his heart. The stone was shot through with dark fire, and when he reached to touch it, it pulsed with hot light.

Patrick drew his hand back. What was this, some kind of occult magic? A week ago he would've rolled his eyes, but, *Hey, Ma—look at me now!* His brain might be dead, but it was suddenly open to all sorts of new and intriguing possibilities. What would happen to him if he stripped the dead guy down and put on his clothes? Probably nothing. Then again . . .

Curious, Patrick decided to check the pockets of the uniform jacket, all the while keeping his hand carefully out of range of the weirded-out opal. He'd almost given up and called himself an idiot, when just for grins he stuck a couple of fingers into the breast pocket on the inside of the jacket and something rattled.

Bingo.

But what he pulled free of Murray's pocket turned out to be nothing more exciting than a piece of paper with indecipherable scribbles on it. They looked vaguely familiar, like they ought to be letters but were backward or something, and they made no sense. Then he turned the paper over and was gratified to find that at least this side was written in good old American English. It was . . . well, a spell or something, and while it took a little bit of focus, he began to realize that hidden within the words were the instructions for working it, not very complicated at all. Again, where he once would have crumpled up the parchment and tossed it away in derision, now his mind whispered that he could do something he'd never dreamed was possible. It was a spell, all right.

To raise the dead.

Patrick Beverly read the incantation, then read it again, just to make sure he understood.

And he smiled.

"Oh, Rupert, look!" Jenny tugged on his arm and pointed. "They've even decorated the roof of the gazebo." Giles turned obediently, and Jenny tried not to laugh out loud—he was trying so *hard*. If cooperation were as visible as perspiration, any moment now Rupert was going to start dripping. When he did, perhaps she'd hand him a red, white and blue hankie, just to stay in the spirit of things.

Meanwhile, he was studying the colorful ribbons twined around the posts and amid the latticework of the large gazebo that marked the center of Weatherly

Park. The Park District really had outdone themselves on this year's Uncle Sam Celebration, and not just in that tiny section. Their efforts were everywhere, from the traditional tricolored balloons tied to any available bench or lamppost to the lightweight Uncle Sam banners that fluttered gaily between the tree trunks. Each time she turned she saw vendors and Park District employees dressed in period costumes, some selling hot dogs and extra-snazzy balloons and noisemakers, others simply walking around and making fanciful animal creatures out of long, skinny balloons. A tall, gangly teenager grinned at them as he strolled past and shoved yet another red, white and blue pamphlet into Giles's hands, and Jenny glimpsed a heading that read "GENERAL SAMSON MURRAY: SUNNYDALE'S OWN WAR HERO." Noise filled the air—kids screaming with laughter while adults called out to them, dogs barking, speakers blaring out tinny renditions of "The Star-Spangled Banner" and, to Rupert's obvious continued discomfort, "Yankee Doodle Dandy."

"Come on," Jenny said enthusiastically. "They've set up the picnic area on the other side of the gazebo. I'm starved. You can buy us hot dogs."

Giles looked decidedly shocked, and she wanted to laugh at him all over again. "Hot dogs? Good Lord! Do you have any idea what's in those things? Can't we just go somewhere and have a nice turkey sandwich—"

Jenny gave him a severe glance . . . well, not *that* severe. "Hot dogs and apple pie, Rupert. These are essential parts of the American spirit. Plus we need to eat now. Then we can join in on some of the games. Remember, the parade's supposed to start at six o'clock."

She couldn't decide if the expression on Giles's face was dismay or frustration. He glanced down at the pamphlet still clutched in his hand and sighed. "At least this—" he waved the pamphlet in the air "—has more of an historical bent to it. Look at how foolish everyone is acting. For God's sake, the British uniforms aren't even accurate. A country's independence should not be celebrated with hot dogs made of unspeakable contents, screaming children, atrocious band music and—" He stopped momentarily, staring. "What on earth are they doing?"

"What?" Jenny squinted against the late afternoon sunlight, trying to see where Giles was focusing. "Oh—those are potato-sack races."

She had to giggle at his wide, frightened eyes. "Good heavens, Jenny. You don't expect me to stick my leg into one of those, do you?"

She laughed and tucked her hand into the crook of his elbow. "Let's just start with one of those unspeakable hot dogs and some chips, then see where those lead."

"Straight on to food poisoning, no doubt," Giles muttered. Cranky he might be, but Jenny saw that he still couldn't hide his happiness at spending the day with her.

"It's almost six-thirty," Jenny said. "The parade should have started by now—they're running late." She craned her head over the shoulder of the person in front of her in the crowd.

Giles looked up from where he'd been reading the pamphlet on General Murray. "Hmmm? Yes—the parade." He bent his head back to the pamphlet, then jumped as Jenny poked him playfully in the side.

"C'mon, share," she said. "What's so interesting?"

"What? Well, I suppose you'll find it boring, but

it's this pamphlet." He frowned at it, as if his stern expression could do something to make sense out of what he was reading. "Quite a bit of creative writing, I suspect. I remember reading something recently about this General Murray—it wasn't so long ago that he passed on, you know. Only a few weeks."

Jenny nodded and looked at him expectantly. For a moment Giles didn't say anything. He was so accustomed to dealing with Buffy and her friends, to seeing that constant glazed look in their eyes when he tried to tell them about something he thought particularly interesting, that he always felt surprised that Jenny was actually attentive to what he had to say. She was just so . . . *delightful* that sometimes he actually became speechless.

"And?" she prompted gently.

"Well," he said, then finally managed to pick up the thread of his thoughts again, "if memory serves me correctly, the General wasn't the hero that the events committee in our fair town portrays him to be in this." He tapped the glossy pamphlet on which was a photograph of a distinguished-looking older man with a white buzz cut. Below the stiff brim of a military hat, Samson Murray's eyes were small and brown, without a trace of warmth. "I recall reading several articles on him. I believe his military career included an abundance of . . . shall we say, less than savory activities."

"Really?" Jenny's eyes lit up with curiosity. "Like what?"

Giles frowned and swatted at a mosquito that had landed on his neck. *Little flying vampires, that's what the bloody things are. Don't we have enough of those in Sunnydale already?* "I'm a bit foggy on the details, I'm afraid. Something about a couple of court martials, but he was acquitted because of questions regarding his mental stability. He spent his last years at the V.A. Medical Center on the edge of town." Giles raised an eyebrow. "They have a psychiatric wing there, don't they?"

Jenny shrugged. "Call me clueless. I never heard of him before today."

"Yes, well." Giles held up the history brochure. "This artful piece of work neglects to mention the one thing I do recall—that the late, great General was never at all convinced that World War II was over. He spent his last years raving about counter-attacking enemy forces he insisted were spreading through Sunnydale." The librarian shook his head in disbelief. "Despite all that, apparently he's still quite the celebrity around here."

Jenny smiled lightly. "At least for today." Something over his shoulder caught her eye. "Oh, look—finally!"

Giles twisted his head around. "What is it?"

"The start of the parade. Good thing, too. It's supposed to be pretty long. They're going to have a hard time getting it all in before sunset. We've got, what—"

"Sunset tonight is at 8:09 P.M.," Giles said absently. "I keep track of it—professional need and all." He squinted over the heat waves, trying to see the float at the front of the procession, then wishing he hadn't had the privilege. It was a huge caricature of Uncle Sam, bobbing and weaving on some sort of spring contraption that reminded him more of the movement of paper dragons in a Chinese New Year's parade. He thought it was utterly hideous.

"I suppose it's okay that they delayed the start," Jenny said at his side and nudged him closer to the front of the growing crowd. *Marvelous,* Giles thought sourly. The line of floats, dancing clowns, baton twirlers, and the first of the school bands already looked endless; to make matters more burdensome, they seemed determined to go no faster than the pace of a very old tortoise. "It really should be full dark before the fireworks start."

"I really can't wait," Giles said.

"Don't be such a stick in the mud, Rupert." She caught him off guard by leaning over and kissing him on the cheek, then she shook out the red gingham blanket she'd been carrying over one arm and spread it on the ground. "This is the perfect spot for both the parade and the fireworks. Look, you can even see City Hall from here. Sit here with me and enjoy it. We'll have a grand old time, you'll see. Before this evening is over, I guarantee you'll look at American patriotism like you never have before."

"Peek-a-boo," Patrick whispered. Feeling a bit averse to the notion of getting his eyeballs fried out of his skull, the newbie vampire gave the heavy door to the tomb a solid kick, hard enough to crack the lock but not quite there on opening power. If his heart had been working, he was sure it'd be pounding, but that little side effect of fear was lost to him. That didn't mean he was fear*less,* though. When he finally shoved the door wide, Patrick leaped backward like a puppy that had just discovered fire via the tender tip of its nose.

It was twilight, or damned close—the sun wasn't quite down, but it had gone far enough below the line of trees on the western edge of Sunnydale Cemetery to cast comforting gray shadows over everything. A sunburn-free zone . . . nice.

Still, caution was always a good thing, so Patrick scoped out the area around the mausoleum carefully before he stepped outside with the paper he'd lifted from General Murray's suit pocket. Deserted, although he could tell from the plentiful arrangements of fresh flowers placed here and there around the cemetery that there had been a fair share of Independence Day visitors—he was just lucky no one had decided to pop in on his little piece o' the dead realm. Patrick shook his head, disgusted at himself. Idiot that he was, he had never even considered that.

As final resting places went, this was a nice-looking spot, he decided. Lush and green, lots of leafy trees and bordered with pretty flowers for which he didn't have a name. He was new to the vampire world, but Patrick could already appreciate his heightened senses: insects buzzed everywhere but didn't land on him; in the high branches of the trees above him birds sang their final songs of the evening. Farther away, he could hear the strains of "Yankee Doodle Dandy" being hammered out by a less than proficient band, probably one of the junior-high attempts. To his over-sensitive hearing, it sounded like a bunch of people beating on pots and pans with wooden spoons.

"Okay," Patrick said, then jumped at the sound of his own voice, the way it seemed overly loud in the silent cemetery. Boy, he just hated this being-alone business—you'd think there'd be like a vampire social group, something to bring newborns like him into the fold and teach them. But since there wasn't, he'd just have to make his own company.

He'd crumpled up the parchment a bit, and now he held it up and tried to smooth it out so he could read the words in the deepening dusk. "Okay," he said, and realized his voice was raspy. Would it make a difference? He cleared his throat and tried again. "Here goes."

> I call to powers from afar,
> here beneath the moon and stars,
> On the fields of battle, and in the halls of war,
> Gone on to his dark glory,
> this leader's meant for more.
> With the power of the Opal,
> the key to all Unlife,
> We bring him back among the living,
> awake to walk this Night.
> And if he chooses, let him call,
> to others of his kind.
> They to follow, one and all,
> the orders of his mind.

Patrick didn't really know what to expect—a pause, a crack of thunder—shoot, even a sudden rainstorm with lightning and gale-force winds, just like in the movies. For a few overlong moments he thought nothing at all had happened, and he simply stood there, feeling as stupid as a twelve-year-old who'd still believed in Santa Claus but had finally gotten the department store clue.

Then he heard the scrabbling from inside the tomb.

Patrick turned and scampered back through the door, the parchment paper crushed in his suddenly nerveless fingers. What he found made a cold grin stretch across his face.

General Samson Murray was very much alive.

Well . . . he was *moving,* anyway. Whether that meant he was alive or unalive made no difference to Patrick. That opal medal, obviously the stone referred to in the spell, was glowing something fierce, spitting streaks of hot pink, yellow, blue and white light all over the inside of the small chamber. The old man was pulling himself to a sitting position in his casket, his still-withered hands sure and strong where they gripped the sides.

"Excellent!" Patrick exclaimed. He tossed the parchment aside and offered a hand to the General. No warm flesh here, so Patrick knew he'd zapped up a zombie, but that was cool. He didn't care, so long as it could walk the walk and talk the talk. He started to say "Welcome back to Sunnydale," but the words froze in his throat when General Murray fixed him with a hellish stare.

"Attention, solider!"

Uh-oh.

Boot-camp-instilled habits died hard, even when they'd been interrupted by a long illness. Patrick's spine snapped straight, and his arms slapped hard to his sides, shoulders back and eyes forward. His mind, though, it was still his, and wasn't that a big old question—

What the hell have I gotten myself into?

—bouncing off the insides of his brain like an electrified Superball?

"Follow me out, soldier, and watch your step!" The General's voice was rough around the edges, as though it was full of dirt. There was something in it that made disobedience unthinkable, and if Patrick had thought he'd forgotten what fear, the real deal, felt like, he'd been very, very wrong.

"Yes, *sir!*" Patrick snapped right back.

And just like when he was in the army, Patrick had no choice but to follow the General out of the mausoleum and into the night.

And, as it turned out, there'd clearly been a lot more to the spell on that little piece of paper than what had sunk into Patrick's limited-capacity brain. Marching behind General Samson Murray like the good little soldier he was, Patrick could only watch with wide and marveling eyes as the military man went from grave to grave and, by nothing more than force of will, sheer *presence,* raised himself up a full-blown, unified army of the dead.

"I don't believe I've ever watched a parade this long," Giles grumbled. He slapped at his arm. "For God's sake, Jenny, we're getting eaten alive by mosquitoes!"

"Must be that British blood of yours," she said cheerfully. "I haven't been bitten once."

"I hardly think it matters what my heritage is," he said huffily. "A parasite is a parasite, and—"

"They're patriotic, you know."

He peered at her over the top of his glasses. "Excuse me?"

"The mosquitoes," she explained. "They're singling you out because you're a foreigner."

"I feel fairly certain that it has nothing to do with nationality," Giles retorted.

"Well, the parade's almost over," she said in a soothing voice. "The fireworks will start, and then maybe the smell of the powder will drive them off."

"Yes," he said, still cranky. "The scent of burning sulphur always chases *me* away. I most certainly—" He stopped and frowned at her. "Jenny?"

Next to him on the blanket, she was suddenly sitting up very straight. "Giles, what's that? There, at the tail end of the procession?"

Baffled, Giles craned his neck and tried to see where Jenny was indicating. When he found it, what he was seeing didn't quite sink in: gray faces, blank eyes and blackened lips, the jerky movement of flesh and bone that didn't function well anymore. Was it . . . could it be . . .

He was on his feet instantly, pulling her up with him. "Jenny, those are *zombies!*"

But when he would have looked for an escape route, she paused. "Wait, Giles. Look, there's something odd about them. They aren't attacking. . . . I think they're *marching.*"

Every instinct screamed at him that they should run, but his curiosity was undeniably aroused. "Marching?" he asked. "As in, together?"

"Exactly." She squeezed his hand. "Come on, let's get closer and find out what's going on."

He wanted to say no, yet he couldn't. Even with Buffy gone to L.A. for the summer, Cordelia off on vacation, and Xander and Willow gone for the evening to some dreadful rock-'n'-roll concert in a neighboring town, he was still a Watcher, still charged with a measure of responsibility toward this tiny metropolis. As long as the creatures weren't actively munching down on the residents—

"All right," he said. "But we need to be careful. Whatever's keeping them civilized could change at any moment. Remember that." Gripping her by the hand, he began to zigzag through the crowd, moving steadily to close the distance between their original spot and the newcomers. The people around him had grown suddenly quiet and still, their disbelieving gazes fixing on the mass of undead lined up in neat rows at the front entrance of City Hall.

"Oh, I think caution's high on the brain's forefront," Jenny said with forced lightness as she kept pace with him.

Since no one else seemed particularly inclined to get too close, it wasn't hard for them to end up nearly at the front of the crowd. The rest of the spectators had lapsed into a nervous silence and now stood and watched the parade's ending, unsure of what to make of the macabre appearance of the soldiers. The view was anything but pleasant, but at least Jenny and Giles could see what was going on.

"My God," Jenny breathed. "It's like a—"

"An army troop," Giles finished for her. It was hard for him to accept that statement, but the proof was certainly in front of him—there were at least fifteen rows of soldiers, with each row containing eight men and a few women. Almost all of them were in uniform, and he'd bet that the ones who weren't had still been, in one way or another, involved with the military when they'd been among the living. From the looks of it, most hadn't been . . . *aboveground* in a while.

Except, perhaps, for their leader.

"Look," Giles said to Jenny in a stage whisper and drew the now well-read pamphlet from his pocket. "The man at the front—see the dress military uniform? It's General Samson Murray."

She nodded. "I recognized him," she said back,

keeping her voice low. "Well . . . sort of. He's a little, uh, ripe around the edges. Wait—he's saying something. Is that Allan Finch, the Deputy Mayor, he's talking to?"

Yes, it sure was and, being careful not to draw too much attention to themselves, he and Jenny inched closer. At about fifteen feet away, now they were mingling with the apprehensive people at the very front of the crowd, others like themselves who were perhaps a bit too curious for their own well-being. Cautiously, he and Jenny pressed even closer, until they were at the very fringe of Murray's detachment.

Dead or not, Samson Murray presented an imposing figure, and his voice boomed over the crowd and the thin, cowering form of the Deputy Mayor. "Who's in charge here? Step forward and account for yourself!"

"Rupert," Jenny said under her breath, "did you notice his little military group is armed?"

And indeed they were. The ranks of soldiers stood at well-ordered attention, every one of them clutching, in military fashion, some implement or another. Most seemed to be carrying gardening tools—shovels, hoes, axes and miscellaneous—no doubt picked up along their trek from whatever grave had formerly been their home. Others, however, had somehow managed to acquire actual weapons such as rifles and bayonets. It might be that these men had been buried with them, and Giles could only hope that if that was the case, the families and funeral directors hadn't thought it appropriate to include ammunition.

With great reluctance, the timorous Allan Finch stumbled forward; in fact, it looked very much like someone had given him a little push to get him going.

"I-I-I'm in ch-charge," he stammered. "Wh-what can I d-d-do for you?"

"My, doesn't he just inspire confidence?" Jenny murmured, her expression never changing.

General Murray glared at Finch. "Where is Mayor Wilkins?" he rumbled.

"On vacation," offered a man standing to the right of the Deputy Mayor. "He can't be reached. I'm the Chief of Po—"

The General cut him off with a wave of one slightly blackened hand. "You are inconsequential." He fixed his gaze on the Deputy Mayor again, eyes burning redly from sockets sunken deep into his skull. "Then I must deal with you." He stepped closer and Finch obligingly backed up. "I am General Samson Murray of the United States Army. I know this town has been infiltrated with the enemy, and I demand that you surrender it to me immediately or face the consequences."

Giles inhaled. "Oh, my heavens."

Finch's eyes widened. "Surrender the t-t-town? What do you m-mean—"

General Murray thrust his head forward, putting his nearly sunken nose almost up to Finch's. "You speak English, don't you? If not, go look it up."

Allan Finch frowned uncertainly, the dilemma making him, finally, forget to stammer. "Of course I know what it means." He hesitated, then looked at the Chief of Police and the other officers who had stepped up to stand close to him. Their hands were on the butts of their revolvers, and their faces were mistrustful and full of disgust as they surveyed the battalion in front of them. "And . . . if we don't surrender?"

The General's mouth stretched into a terrible rictus

of a grin, showing yellowed teeth rimmed with brown. "Then of course we will attack, young man. I will order my troop to eliminate the enemy."

The parade had wisely kept going, and Deputy Mayor Finch eyed the stiff-looking men waiting below, then the crowd gathered around them. His face took on a sly, slightly belligerent expression that Giles remembered well, because he'd seen it on the faces of hundreds of secretly rebellious students throughout his career.

"I do believe Mr. Deputy Mayor is going to tell the General to go scratch," Giles said, slightly awed.

"I remember you," Allan Finch said. "And you're supposed to be dead. Mayor Wilkins isn't around, so he doesn't know about this. It's some kind of hoax, right? A joke. I bet you and these so-called soldiers of yours are wearing Halloween make-up." He shook his head, and even from where Giles and Jenny stood, there was no mistaking the stubborn, inarguable aura he projected when he folded his arms and lifted his chin. Foolish, perhaps, but Giles had to admire the way he'd gone from stammering idiot to complete self-assurance. Of course, that was going to evaporate soon enough. "So, *General,* I don't think we're going to—"

"Perhaps I can be of some assistance here," Giles interrupted, cutting off the rest of Finch's sentence before the man allowed his mouth to get in the way of common sense.

Samson Murray whirled and glared at him. "And you are?"

"Giles," the librarian said, with as much exaggerated British inflection as he could manage. "Uh . . . Commander Giles, of the Allied Forces."

"Why are you humoring him?" Finch demanded. "He—"

"One would think diplomacy is the best course of action in this instance," Giles said hastily. He gave the Deputy Mayor a sharp glance. "In view of the safety of the townspeople."

Finch scowled but wisely kept silent as the General paced toward Giles. "This is wartime. Why are you out of uniform?" he growled.

"I was on . . . a short holiday," Giles improvised. "In any event, perhaps we can discuss matters—"

"I don't discuss military matters with civilians," Murray grated. Behind him, Giles saw the Chief of Police doing a fast fade into the depths of the building with Allan Finch, and no doubt many of the onlookers were being quietly ushered away by parade security. "I'll give you a half-hour to return here properly attired, *Commander*. If you're really who you say you are, that should pose no problem. If you don't return, I shall assume I must instruct my army to take Sunnydale by force."

They were disheveled and sweaty, but Giles was satisfied that at least they'd managed to keep the area in front of City Hall from being instantly turned into a mini-battleground. The police, no doubt, would have soon learned their bullets were useless against men who were already dead; it was damned difficult to kill an attacker who neither felt pain nor feared for his life. Most of the onlookers had managed to leave but some of the more unlucky ones had been rounded up by the General's rotting soldiers and were now prisoners of war, held at bay by a handful of expressionless dead soldiers who would show no mercy to anyone.

"I can grab a uniform from the costume shop," Giles told Jenny as they hurried into the library. "But first perhaps we can find something in one of my books that will tell us how this happened—"

"Try this."

Both Giles and Jenny jumped as Angel stepped from the shadowed area by one of the bookcases. "I saw the esteemed General leaving his tomb. Apparently he was raised up by one of my less brain-empowered brethren," the tall vampire said, sounding disgusted. "I followed him for a bit and saw him gathering his little army, so I decided to double-back and check out where he'd been buried." He held up a rumpled piece of heavy parchment paper. "Take a look at this."

Giles took the parchment and studied it. "A resurrection spell," he said. "Marvelous. It couldn't have happened to a nicer man. Jenny—"

"I'm already on it," she said from behind him, and when he turned he saw her busily typing away at the computer keyboard. "Let's see what we can find out about General Samson Murray that they might have left out of their glitzy Uncle Sam pamphlet." After a second, she sat back, looking surprised. "Well."

"What is it?" Giles asked as he and Angel came over to join her. "What did you find?"

"It seems he really was quite the war hero as the booklet said," Jenny told them. "But you were right, too—he also had a *very* controversial military career. It seemed he was constantly being accused of cruel and inhumane treatment of prisoners and brutal disciplinary action toward soldiers. There was always some scandal or another going on."

"Not the type one would consider a suitable dictator for our happy little town," Giles commented.

"Precisely," said Jenny. "Especially since you were also right about him spending the last years of his life in the psychiatric ward of the V.A. Center."

Giles grimaced and rubbed his forehead as he examined the parchment again, then realized there was something on the back. "What's this?"

Angel looked over his shoulder. "I can't read that."

Giles frowned at the strangely familiar markings, then his eyebrows raised. "Of course you can—anyone could! They're backward, meant to be read using a mirror."

Angel's expression never wavered. "Guess I missed that. Mirrors not being my thing."

Giles blinked. "Oh—of course." He hurried behind the counter and rummaged around for a minute, then came up with a small, square mirror. "Let me—excellent!" The librarian beamed at the other two. "It's a reversal spell, meant to return to their graves the General and those he, in turn, brought back."

"Really?" Jenny looked doubtful. "Why does this sound far too easy?"

Angel looked pointedly at Giles. "Because he's making it sound that way. Reversal spells are pretty common, aren't they, Giles?" He folded his arms. "But they usually call for some pretty specific procedures."

Giles squinted at the small mirror, trying to read the rest of the spell. His expression soured. "Always a catch, isn't there? Damn."

Jenny looked at him impatiently. "Anytime, Rupert."

"Angel is correct," he admitted when he finally

looked up from the words. "This spell will indeed send them all back to their graves, but of course the words must be read directly from here to do so. It also refers to something called the 'Opal of Unlife,' and crushing it, no doubt immediately following the recitation of this spell. Oh, and a small detail—it appears that this must all be done on the *same* day he initially came back to life."

"Fine," Angel said. "Then we do it tonight. All we need to zap army-guy back to the Big Beyond is to find this opal thing and smash it right after we read the spell. So where is it?"

Giles gave Jenny a knowing look, then turned back to Angel. "I'm afraid that the esteemed General Samson Murray . . . is wearing it."

"You want to me to do *what?*"

"Carry this," Jenny said and handed Angel the smaller replica of the Sunnydale school flag that she'd retrieved from the gymnasium. "You'll look like 'Commander' Giles's second-in-command and announce his arrival. It will make everything more convincing."

Angel started to laugh, then tried to disguise it by coughing instead. "Sorry," he managed. "Just, uh, clearing my throat." He pressed his lips together momentarily, then found control. *Commander* Giles? "What, uh, what do I say?"

"Being the courageous man he is," Jenny said, "the Deputy Mayor has no doubt gone into hiding. Rupert pointed out that General Murray died still believing World War II was in full force, so there'll be no one to contradict you if you reinforce the idea that as a representative of the town—"

"That would be you, Commander," Angel put in. He smirked.

"—Giles intends to discuss the terms of Sunnydale's surrender," Jenny finished.

Giles gave Angel a dark look. "Laugh all you want, but *you* certainly can't act the part. You seem to lack the requisite heartbeat to represent the living in other than a supporting capacity."

Angel shrugged. "Touché."

"We need to get as close as possible," Jenny said. "Draw him out into the open."

"The best scenario would be to just snatch the medal and run," Giles put in. "We've *got* to get that medal and read the spell before midnight. If the clock ticks so much as a single second beyond the hour of twelve, it's quite likely that the General and all the members of his nasty little army will remain as they are—animated dead—forever."

"Why can't we just rush him?" Angel demanded.

"We all know that zombies are nearly indestructible to begin with," Giles said impatiently. "The General is an expert at killing and survival tactics—this makes him even more challenging to eliminate. We need to get closer to him than it would be possible for someone just appearing out of the blue. This is the only way."

"Great. I just hope he doesn't decide to kill the messenger." He looked at the mini-flagpole dubiously. "Are you sure about this?"

"Don't worry," Jenny said sweetly. "The General wants the town, and he's already indicated he'll talk. A quick stop at the costume shop to meet the General's expectations and we're set." She turned a cheerful grin on Giles. "Just think, Rupert. You get to play the part of a loyal American army man!"

"Don't be ridiculous," Jenny said. "Of course I'm going with you two."

"Oh, no," Giles protested. "You should go back and watch the library—"

"Watch it what?" she demanded. "In case you haven't noticed, you and Angel really don't have much of a plan beyond grabbing that opal and taking off. You need all the help you can get."

"But—"

"She's right, Giles," Angel cut in. "If you grab the opal and get caught, I can try to get you out. She's even more backup."

Irritated, Giles tried again to button the too-tight collar of this abominable general's uniform. He finally got it, but he felt like he was being slowly throttled. "I suppose you'll have to accompany me," he told the vampire. "As my second-in-command."

Angel grimaced. "I'm not high on the idea since there are way too many pointy objects surrounding Murray, but I can see the need. After the intro, I'll back off but try to stay only a few feet away." He glanced at Jenny. "I think our best bet to work the spell is the roof, don't you?"

She nodded. "Then I'll head straight there and wait for you."

Not much left to argue about, was there? With the last of the geegaws and gilded ropes in place, the librarian finally looked down at himself. "I've never felt so conspicuous in my life."

"Don't be ridiculous," Jenny said. "You look quite handsome."

Giles started to retort, but something in her tone stopped him. When he glanced at her, he saw her eyes shining with pride. "I . . . well, thank you," he finally managed.

"No one but you could pull this off, you know." She eyed him. "Here," she said then, and stepped quickly in front of him. "Take this, for luck." Unexpectedly she leaned forward and gave him a healthy kiss on the lips. For a moment, Giles forgot about General Samson and his undead army, Sunnydale, and everyone else.

Angel cleared his throat and they broke apart. "If you two are through with your patriotic farewells, I think we'd better get going." He shot a glance at the library clock. "Midnight, remember?"

"Jenny, I still don't like the notion of you coming with us," Giles said a little breathlessly.

"Nonsense," she said. "What happens if I don't go, and one of you gets caught . . . or worse? Who's going to perform the ritual then? In this instance, three isn't a crowd—it's safety."

God help him, Giles just couldn't find a good answer for that.

The stare that General Samson Murray fixed on him was red and hot and hellish, and reminded Angel of a whole lot of things he really didn't want to think about.

"You are not among the living," the dead man grated. "Why would you stand as their second-in-command?"

Angel fought the urge to shrug, knowing the military man would see it as an insult. "Just call me Diplomat Guy," he answered. "Somebody has to do it. Do you want to meet Commander Giles or not?" As he waited for Murray's answer, Angel let his gaze skim to the zombies guarding him. Fixed right there

214

on the breast of the General's uniform, the Opal of Unlife was impossible to miss . . . so close, and yet so far. He'd hoped to go with Giles's original scenario—snatch and grab—but there was just no way. The army leader had far too many dead soldiers strategically positioned between Angel and himself, and those same unfriendly zombies were wielding enough pointy-ended weapons to keep him, so to speak, on edge.

Samson Murray stared at Angel long and hard, as though he could somehow read his mind. Angel waited, knowing he couldn't and hoping the dead old guy wasn't going to just get peeved and order one of his ghouls to poke him with a bayonet. Finally, though, the military man's blackened lips drew back. "So be it, though trusting a turncoat vampire is risky business. Have your Commander step forward."

"Well," Angel began, "we were hoping we could discuss this in private—"

"Are you still talking?" the General asked icily.

Angel winced as a couple of zombies moved toward him, brandishing rifles at the ends of which were affixed U.S.M.C. KA-BARS. "No. No." He cleared his throat and stepped to the side, surreptitiously working his way backward as Giles moved in place and stood, stiff and ramrod straight, in front of General Murray.

Angel shuddered inwardly as he watched the two men face each other. He didn't know if it was the fact that Murray was a zombie or as crazy as a bat in the sunshine, but he really didn't think this was going to go well.

"I've come to discuss the terms of the surrender of Sunnydale," Giles declared as formally as he could. Bluff and bluster, he decided, would have to make up for what he lacked in true military training. And yes, he knew it was all in the plan, but wasn't it still a horrifying experience to be this close to a walking, talking dead man . . . who, by the way, smelled about as awful as his mold-mottled skin appeared?

When General Murray's laughter came, it was harsh and loud. "You fool," he wheezed. The skin of the animated cadaver's neck rippled unpleasantly above the collar of his uniform. "Did you really think I'd give you *terms?* Look around!" He waved jerkily at the small knots of terrified human onlookers, and Giles realized that most had been herded into groups at gunpoint; a few unlucky resisters were either lying wounded in the street or being stalked by the zombies patrolling the perimeter of the park. "You call yourself a Commander of the Allied troops? This town is *infested* with the enemy, and I am not deceived by their attempts to masquerade as townspeople. I don't know what your connection is here, but I strongly suspect you're a spy. Thus there is only one *term*—surrender the town or everyone in it dies!"

"But General Murray," Giles protested. "There are civilians here. Women and children, the elderly—"

"Casualties in war are a fact of life." The zombie's voice was frigid.

For a moment Giles didn't know what to say. He'd been so certain he could play for time, perhaps haggle back and forth, all the while building up a sense of false camaraderie. This put an entirely different spin on things. With the lives of everyone in town resting on his shoulders, time was short and the weight of responsibility was heavy. "And if I agree?" he asked cautiously. "What then?"

The General looked down the remains of his nose. "Then you, and they, become prisoners of war and live. At least until I decide otherwise."

Giles nodded, trying to appear thoughtful. "All right," he finally said, and held out his hand expectantly.

The General stared from Giles to his outstretched hand and said nothing.

"If we don't publicly shake on it," Giles said with exaggerated patience, "the residents . . . those you believe are opposing forces, will suspect the decision was forced and they may resist. Wouldn't it be simpler to present a unified front?"

General Murray's heavy gray eyebrows drew together in a fierce scowl. Nevertheless, he stepped toward Giles and reached out a rotting right hand to take Giles's own.

The librarian masquerading as a Commander leaned forward—

—and yanked the Opal of Unlife from the General's jacket.

Samson Murray howled with fury, and Giles was instantly surrounded. With nowhere else to go, he leaped upward, hanging in the air for a fraction of a second like a basketball player aiming for the net. Somewhere in the scope of his vision he caught a glimpse of Angel's hand waving frantically at him, and with a spit and a prayer, Giles tossed the Opal of Unlife up—

—and away.

Leaning over the stone railing on the roof, Jenny saw Angel's arm snake up and snatch something white from the air, then the whole crowd of people, dead and undead, seemed to go up for grabs.

The handsome vampire was damned quick—she had to give him that. One second he was only a few feet from Giles, the next he was ten feet away and fleeing. Still, the General and his zombies knew what had happened—a good number of Murray's undead army immediately went slathering after him. She saw frightened people and confused zombies as the soldiers who had been among the crowd tried to control "prisoners" now stumbling in front of them. Angel went through them all like a stiff-armed football player who couldn't be bothered with worrying about whether he thundered over his own teammates or the opposition—zombies and humans alike were knocked in every direction.

She wanted to cry out a warning as she saw a knot of cadaverish soldiers rounding the corner at the far end of the building, but she didn't dare call attention to herself. Their movements were lurching and awkward as they stumbled toward Angel, but they were still frighteningly quick . . . as capable and unrelenting as the ones coming up from behind. Angel was trapped.

Jenny leaned farther out and saw the vampire duck into a doorway almost directly below her. When she ran back to the entry door to the roof and strained to hear, she was rewarded by the sound of the lock giving way down on the first floor. She heard furniture grate across the floor and knew he was bracing the door, and a few seconds later fists began hammering against the metal barrier. It wouldn't hold them back for long. Should she go meet him? It would save time . . . but no. The original resurrection spell had specified that it be read beneath the moon and stars— the reversal spell would no doubt have to be performed the same way.

Jenny backed away as she heard the metal give and noisy zombies begin piling through the door downstairs. Where was Angel? He should have been here by now. What would she do if he'd been captured, or even killed?

Then the door crashed open and rebounded off the wall, making her jump and clap a hand over her own mouth to stop a scream as she waited to see who—or what—would come lurching through.

"If I do not get my medal back, you will find, Commander, that you have made a *fatal* mistake."

Giles lifted his chin and stared defiantly at General Samson Murray. "Yes, well, life is not without its annoyances."

Murray laughed, and the sound was like stiff cardboard being torn, grating and unpleasant. Still, there was a hint of something else beneath it . . . panic, perhaps? "In an orderly existence," the military man said, "there should be no annoyances." He held out his hand and one of his corpse soldiers stepped forward and dropped a bullhorn onto his palm, no doubt pilfered from a supply room in the city administration building. General Murray raised it to his lips and his voice, horrible and gravelly, boomed out over the street and the people once again being held prisoner by his troop. Giles saw most of the humans visibly wince at the awful sound.

"*Attention—I demand your immediate attention. If the medal which was just taken from me is not returned within five minutes—FIVE MINUTES—I will have my troops begin executing civilians. If necessary, I will exterminate each and every person in this town. You will all suffer a horrible fate. RETURN MY PROPERTY!*"

The last of it came out as more of a scream and Giles would have clapped his hands over his ears if a nearby zombie hadn't glowered at him when he started to move. "I realize you need that opal, but really," he said. "Losing your temper won't accomplish anything."

"Oh, *yes* it will." The General pushed his face up to Giles's, close enough for the librarian to see the way the dead man intentionally pulled in air so he could talk. "It will make me feel *better!*"

What if someone besides Angel had caught the Opal of Unlife, and what if, in mistakenly thinking they were doing right, they came forward with it? This small town in America, his home for the past year, would pay dearly—every man, woman and child would become a prisoner of this insane zombie. General Murray spun and stomped away, and Giles let him get about as far as he thought he would go before the dead man would do an about-face and return. Then Giles let his own voice rise above the forced knot of onlookers. "Don't do it!" he shouted, his words tumbling out as quickly as he could make them. "Don't trust him! He'll kill you all anywa—"

Pain exploded across the right side of his face as the dead General, his movements much faster than Giles would have expected, sprang in front of him and hit him. "Another word from you and it will be your last," he snarled. "Are you ready to die?"

Blood splattered from his lip, and Giles looked down and saw it drip on his nice, clean uniform. A pity—beyond the fact that the mess meant he would lose his deposit on the costume, for a Brit he'd really made quite the honorable picture in this getup. He found himself glaring at Murray as loyalty blossomed in him. "Die? I'd do it *twice* before I'd see you turn this town into a mass graveyard!"

General Murray grinned dreadfully. "Quite the patriot, aren't you? Well, don't worry, Commander Giles." He glanced around, then plucked a bayonet-tipped rifle from the hands of a nearby zombie private. "In three more minutes, perhaps I'll personally start the festivities." His terrible smile widened. "And I'm sure I'll get around to you eventually."

"Angel!" Jenny gasped as he scrambled through the doorway. For a long second, her heart was pounding so hard she couldn't say anything else. Then she hurried to meet him. "We have to do this quickly! Did you hear that? Murray's going to start killing the townspeople!"

"I heard it," Angel said grimly. "Loud and clear." Off to the side was a small pile of short steel supports and cinder blocks, construction materials for some unfinished city project, perhaps a roof storage area. Angel grabbed a steel support and dragged it to the front of the door, then positioned it along the roof so that one end acted as a door stop while the other was braced against one of the roof vents. "There," he said. "That'll hold 'em—for maybe five minutes before the top door hinge breaks."

Jenny's voice was panicked. "And we only have three before someone dies! Come *on!*"

He ran to her side, then stopped and pulled out the Opal of Unlife. "What now?"

"Here." She thrust the spell paper Giles had given her earlier into his hands, then took the medal from him, dropped it on the roof, and stood with one foot poised over it. "You read, I'll shatter."

Angel fumbled with the parchment, then looked from it to her helplessly. "Jenny, I have no idea what this says—I can't read backward!"

"Oh, for Pete's sake!" She seized the paper, then stared at it. No, he couldn't . . . and neither could she. Her purse—she'd put her little mirror somewhere in there, hadn't she? On the verge of hysterics, she dug roughly into the small, drawstring bag she'd used for today, just big enough for the bare essentials—

Bodies crashed against the other side of the rooftop door.

"Jenny—"

Now even Angel sounded alarmed, and that made their situation all the more terrifying. Something screeched over by the iron bar, the top hinge of the door protesting as the weight of the zombies on the other side began to bend it.

At the bottom of the bag, her fingers closed around something tiny and heart-shaped. Without looking, she kicked the medal toward Angel and brought out the antique fold-up mirror, such a small thing and barely big enough to use to freshen her lipstick.

It would have to do.

Another screech from the door hinge, a little louder and more threatening. Jenny ignored it and held up the tiny mirror, running it back and forth across the paper as she stumbled hastily through the backward words:

Those among the living are through with this dark soldier,
His time of battle finally done,

his words and deeds grown colder.
So heed this incantation,
its spell cuts like a knife,
To still the soul of this dead man,
and those he brought to life.
Return to the dead from whence you came,
no more to walk the land,
With the crushing of the Opal,
by someone else's hand.
On this the same day of his birth,
nevermore to walk the earth.

Just as the word "earth" left her lips, the door caved in and at least a dozen, semi-rotting zombies rushed through. They were only a few feet away when the heel of Angel's shoe slammed down on the Opal of Unlife that lay glowing on the dark surface of the roof.

Crraaaackkkk!!!!

Blue-white light, like an explosion of lightning, swept over everything.

Jenny instinctively threw her arms over her eyes but still saw both the zombies and Angel collapse before a pseudo-snowstorm clouded her vision. Were Giles and the townsfolk safe? Had they completed the spell in time? And was Angel still alive? The words of the spell—

Angel groaned, and she rubbed her eyes and flailed at the darkness, gratified to see shadows and shape returning as her eyes readjusted themselves. She stumbled forward, and her hands closed over his arm, his flesh unnervingly cool beneath her touch.

"Whew," Angel said. He sounded vaguely stunned. "I thought for a second that 'return to the dead from whence you came' part was gonna do it for me . . . but I guess I'm already there."

Glad he was all right, Jenny squeezed his arm, then rose and ran to the edge of the roof. Nearly too frightened to look, dreading what she might find, she made herself lean forward anyway.

And there, at the edge of the steps below her and amid a crowd of collapsed zombies, stood a slightly bewildered-looking Giles. A few feet away from him, clearly as confused as the librarian, was a young man dressed in a private's green uniform.

"Bummer," Patrick Beverly said.

Just a second ago he'd been getting a good chewing out by General Murray for leaving that piece of parchment back at the mausoleum. Murray had been telling him to double-time it back to the cemetery and retrieve it, but now everyone around him, including the old fart General himself, had done a face-first concrete dive.

Well, except for the dude with the British accent who was dressed up like an Allied commander and standing only about three feet away.

And picking up a bayonet rifle.

Why did he get the feeling he was suddenly in enemy territory? Patrick's mouth made an *O* of surprise that unfortunately did nothing to hide his vampire teeth, and he said the only thing that came to mind.

"Oops."

* * *

"You!" Giles snapped. "Blast it all, you're the one Angel told me about—the one who started this whole absurd mess!"

The young vampire, hardly more than a teenager but obviously capable of all sorts of evil mischief, gave a self-conscious shrug. Before he could turn that movement into fleeing, Giles swung the end of his rifle to bear and jammed its wooden-handled bayonet dead center and all the way to the hilt into the bloodsucker's chest.

Dust.

"Well," Giles said. "That was certainly bracing. Willow and Xander will be sorry they missed the excitement."

They were nearly back to the library and somewhere behind them one of the church bells tolled, marking the midnight hour. They'd barely made it.

"Look at them," Jenny said in awe as they passed a young couple stoically rolling one of the zombie bodies into a blanket as a police officer stood by and filled out a report. As they watched, the officer handed them a copy of it, then the couple hefted their load and marched off in the direction of Sunnydale Cemetery. "They're just . . . claiming the bodies, I suppose to reinter them. Don't they even think this is strange?"

Giles sighed. "I suppose they do, but it's fairly obvious that only those cadavers with, shall we say . . . still *viable* parts—the ability to move around well on their own—came back to life." He was silent for a moment, trying to work through something in his mind. Finally, he continued.

"You see, one of the things I recall reading about that V.A. Center some time ago was that a new administrator discovered evidence that many of the patients had been sedated with a compound that quite often induced a coma deep enough to be mistaken for death. Apparently this went on literally for years until it was discovered."

Jenny's face was white in the shadows. "Oh, Giles—that's horrible!"

The librarian nodded. "And finding it out was nearly as bad as the crime, because they realized that for decades many patients had been prematurely interred. Many were subjected to autopsies, obviously killed during the procedure by unknowing doctors. Others were veterans without families, buried without autopsies or the benefit of embalming. Their fate— waking within sealed coffins—was, perhaps, worse. These could be the soldiers we saw reanimated tonight, resurrected by the spell and grasping at the rest of lives they were wrongfully denied."

Angel made a strangled sound in his throat. "Buried alive? Too close to personal experience for me."

"Oh my," Jenny said. Her expression was filled with sadness as they watched two more men, older, carry a fallen comrade into the shadows at the edge of the cemetery. "It's yet another instance where the residents of Sunnydale manage to look the other way in the face of what really happened . . . in more ways than one. How sad."

"Well," Giles said, "that does seem to be a habit with Americans." He couldn't keep the disdain out of his voice. "I always thought that's probably what happened in 1776."

Angel cleared his throat. "Actually, I knew some people who were there and they said—"

"Never mind," Giles interrupted.

"Rupert, don't you want to know the truth?" Jenny asked sweetly.

"Spare me," Giles said, raising his chin. He'd never admit it, of course, but despite the unexpected excitement of the day, he still felt quite tall and proud in his military uniform. "A man needs to hold on to his fantasies."

"Really," Angel said. His dark gaze cut from Giles to Jenny, and he smiled slightly, just before he faded into the darkness at the side of the school building and left the two of them standing there.

"Maybe yours need to be updated. . . ."

THE SHOW MUST
GO ON

PAUL RUDITIS

*"**L**ife . . . commandment . . . death . . . bloody . . . view . . . "*

"He's talking gibberish," Jenny said, cradling the man in her arms.

"carnal . . . unnatural . . . slaughters . . . mistook . . . heads . . . "

"I'm not surprised," Giles said, "after witnessing this massacre."

"voice . . . wild . . . plots . . . "

The man's words made little sense to Jenny. But then, neither did the slaughter surrounding them. It seemed heartless to say that they found *only* four bodies in the Sixteenth-Century Hall of the Sunnydale Museum. But, after the scenes of horror arranged by the Master and the summer that they had already shared, *only* four bodies made for a minor murder scene. It was not the body count that was horrific. It was how the bodies were arranged. This was not some random vampire feeding, it was thought out and planned.

"Can't we do something for him?" Jenny asked, and wordlessly added *Please*.

The man had been blinded by his attackers. He was left stumbling through the room, bleeding, unable to find the exit. Unable to do anything but scream the same few words that Jenny had heard, that had brought them into this section of the museum.

They had been visiting the latest traveling exhibit at the museum, an Ancient Greek display of the artistic renderings of mythological figures. The event was being held during the museum's Midnight Madness Summer Hours, which were a thinly veiled ploy to get in some more summer dollars. It didn't seem to be working because only a handful of people showed up for the non-event. *In retrospect*, she thought, *this was the one good point since it meant less people to stumble over.*

"There is little that we can do to ease the pain," Giles said, wishing that he had another reply. "Surely others have heard the commotion and will be coming soon. We have to find out as much as we can before the scene is disturbed."

That line sounded as cold and callous as the thought of *only* four bodies. But it was those four bodies that they needed to focus on. They needed to know who they were and what the deaths signified to ensure that there would not be more. While Giles's training prepared him for this sort of carnage, Jenny's lifestyle was not one that included experiences in this category. When Jenny released the man from her arms, the volume died down to a strained whimper of despair. This was far worse than listening to the screams.

"Where do we begin?" she asked.

It was obviously the work of vampires as the bodies had been drained through the telltale two puncture wounds per neck. But it was like no vampire attack Giles had ever witnessed before. The bodies weren't simply bled, they were arranged in some ritualistic fashion that Giles could not identify. One woman lay beside a chalice with the remnants of what appeared to be wine. *Did she drink it,* he wondered, *or is it for show?* After debating the best way to preserve the liquid so that it could be tested, Giles decided that he may as well just take the chalice. Technically it was illegal to remove evidence from a crime scene, but his type of investigation would surely come up with more accurate results than anything the police would be looking for. He would also be able to research the chalice itself. In general, a chalice had many meanings in ritualistic lore. Most of them were positive, but this was far from a positive scene.

After covering the chalice with a handkerchief to keep the wine from spilling out, he switched his investigation to the three men in the middle of the room. Between them were two foils, the type of weapons used in fencing. While there were numerous references to ritualistic swords, Giles could not recall any mention of the use of foils in his studies. By its very nature, a foil was not a ceremonial weapon related to the magicks. It was a dueling device, used for sport or battle in only the most chivalrous of circles. Even more confusing was the fact that the three men had each been cut by the swords, but the little scratches were not deadly. The cause of death was obviously the draining by the vampires.

Giles handed Jenny a pen and his copy of the museum's brochure for lack of anything better to write on. He instructed her to take down the ravings of the madman. The words may have just been a reaction to what he had seen and not actually mean anything, but they would not rule that out until every possible angle had been reviewed. *Of the words,* he noted, *most are in reference to death and carnage.* It was the two that were not, "mistook" and "plots," that intrigued him the most. *What kind of mistake or plot could the man be referring too, if, in fact, he is referring to anything at all?*

While Jenny took her morbid dictation, Giles checked the bodies for identification. According to their licenses, three of the four victims had the same last name and address. *Father, mother and adult son?* he wondered. *Jenny can run their names through her computer to see how they were related.* The other body bore a different last name, which gave no indication of relationship whatsoever. After Jenny recorded the names for him, Giles attempted to go for the identification on the lone survivor, but he had grown fidgety and would not let the Watcher near him. As Giles tried to get closer to the man, he heard the echo of footsteps growing louder over the sounds of his whimpering.

"We'd best be going," Giles said. "Lest we be delayed by the police for interviews."

Jenny could not help but take one last look at the man in agony. She did not want to leave him to the

Sunnydale authorities, but knew that she could do more good for the other residents of Sunnydale if she did.

Giles, however, could not bring himself to look at the man again. He knew that he would not be able to sleep for days. And it was not just because of the researching he had ahead of him.

The next afternoon, Giles was still in the Sunnydale High School library. He had sent Jenny home a few hours earlier after apologizing for work getting in the way of the evening. Naturally, she had said that she understood and promised to come back and help after getting some rest. Giles hoped that he would have some information to tell her when she came back. It was beginning to look like he would have to bring in Angel to do the hunting while he and Jenny did the reading.

One thing was working in the Watcher's favor. He did not have to fear any interruptions from Willow and Xander. The pair had gotten temporary jobs on the backstage crew of the Shakespeare Players, a traveling theater troupe that went from town to town over the course of the summer performing various Shakespearean plays. In every town, they would fill out their cast and crew of mostly college-age students with local teens and have an intense two-week rehearsal period culminating in three nightly performances of the chosen play. The jobs made Giles's life easier as he had two weeks in which he did not have to worry about the summer of slayage encroaching on Willow and Xander's lives. In addition to barely seeing Willow, Giles was happily aware of the fact that he had not seen Xander at all during the time. It's not that he didn't like Xander, but it was much easier to do his Watcherly duties without the young man around.

Noting the time, Giles picked up the chalice and left the library with it. He had waited for the summer-school students and teachers to clear out before moving to this next stage of research. While he did have a ready-made explanation if anyone asked what he, the librarian, would be doing at the school in the middle of summer, he didn't have any good lies prepared to explain what he was about to do. Naturally, this was the point when he turned a corner and ran right into the one person he did not want to see.

"Principal Snyder!"

"Let's cut the chit-chat. What are you doing here?"

"Restocking the library," Giles responded with his prepared answer while deftly hiding the chalice behind his back. The chalice itself was not the concern, but the remaining wine would lead to too many difficult questions, and possible suspension from his job.

"Oh, yes," the surly principal said. "I still don't understand how that earthquake managed to destroy the library and not touch the rest of the school."

That was the weak cover story he and Buffy had concocted to explain the destruction resulting from the opening of the Hellmouth. With the exception of this one mention, it was a sufficient explanation for a town where most odd occurrences were overlooked.

"It was strange, wasn't it?" the Watcher replied.

"No more strange than anything else that happens in this school," the principal said, looking as agitated as he usually did. "I promise you, next semester things will be different."

"Under your guidance, I'm sure that they will be." Giles did his best kissing-up in the hopes that it would end the conversation.

"Lock up before you leave," Snyder complied with the Watcher's silent wish. "I don't want any more vandals getting into the school. We've had enough of that this year."

As he watched Snyder continue on his merry little way, Giles brought the chalice from behind him, careful not to spill the remains of the wine. He still had the handkerchief covering the top. It had soaked up some of the wine, but there was still enough in the chalice for the tests he needed to run.

In the science lab, he put the chalice down on one of the lab tables before going through the chemical closet. Naturally, the closet had been locked, but that was of little concern due to the fact that earlier in the year he had made a duplicate of the school master key. As the librarian, there was no reason for him to have a copy of the key, but in his role of Watcher, it was quite helpful. Once he found the jar holding the right chemical, he returned to the table.

From the shelves before him, Giles took an eyedropper and the glass slide from a microscope. He placed the slide on the table and used the dropper to extract a small amount of the wine.

Now let's see if my suspicions are correct.

Placing a drop of wine on the slide, he repeated the action with the chemical he had taken from the closet. The result was instantaneous and as he had expected. The mixture began to bubble. The wine had been poisoned.

His satisfaction from the findings was short-lived. He now had new questions to add to his growing list pertaining to this mystery.

Why would vampires use poison on their victims and then drain their blood? Wouldn't the blood be tainted?

Angel was pondering that same thought hours later as he patrolled the cemetery. Since Giles had clued him in on the events of the previous night, Angel offered to fill in for the vacationing Slayer and go on patrol so that Giles and Jenny could continue researching. Nothing the Watcher had told him made any sense, and he had many years of experience in the area of death.

A commotion brought him out of his thoughts, but by the time he reached the area of the cemetery from where the noises had come, they were replaced by an unsettling silence. Commotion was easy to handle, but silence required additional stealth. Carefully, Angel crept up to a clearing to watch from behind some bushes.

What he saw raised even more questions in his mind. Twelve dead bodies along with five undead ones. He arrived just in time to watch the last body fall from the lips of one of the vampires. It was too late for Angel to save anyone. Since taking on five unknown vampires alone was too much of a risk, Angel remained where he was and continued to watch as the scene played itself out.

The five vampires, all dressed in black, moved to a pile of metal folding chairs. One by one, they opened the chairs and placed each on top of a gravesite in three rows of four chairs each. Then they propped each of the bodies on the chairs. They seemed to be taking special care with one of the victims. The body of a woman was posed in a variety of positions before they decided that having her with head tilted down was the best. The vampires then took a moment to admire their handiwork before leaving.

Things have just gotten stranger.

Once Angel felt it was safe to proceed, he came out from his hiding spot to examine the scene. He started with the body of the girl since she had received the most attention from the vampires. Upon closer examination, he found nothing out of the ordinary about her. Two bite marks appeared on her neck, but she was otherwise untouched. He did notice that she was atop the gravesite of a woman named Emily. Just to make sure that the genders being the same was not a coincidence, Angel checked the rest of the bodies and found that each of them matched the gender of the person in the grave. The victims had been selected based on the layout of the graves.

This is a new one to me.

As Angel was examining the last headstone, he noticed a clipboard lying on the ground behind it. He picked it up and found the layout of the graves, each with a name written on the gravesites. With the exception of Emily, none of the graves matched the names on the sheet. Angel was trying to figure out this latest clue when a fist slammed into the back of his head, knocking him down and the clipboard out of his hand.

"I believe that is mine," the voice that owned the fist said.

When Angel looked up to the speaker, it was with his vampire face in full bloom.

The other vampire was roughly Angel's height but with a more gangly build. His dyed black hair was in stark contrast to his pale face.

"Well, this is certainly an interesting development," the vampire said.

"Not as interesting as what you've been up to," Angel said as he launched himself up at the vampire, knocking him over one of the bodies. One dead and two undead fell to the ground.

The vampire pushed Angel off him and jumped to his feet. Likewise, Angel ended his roll standing up.

The vampire threw a fist, which Angel blocked with his arm. Shifting from defense to offense, Angel grabbed the vampire's fist and used it to flip the vampire end over end.

As before, the vampire used his balance to land on his feet.

"Correct me if I'm wrong," the vampire said. "But shouldn't we be on the same side?"

"You mean the maniacs-who-like-to-play-with-the-dead side?" Angel slammed his fist into the vampire's head. "I don't play that g—"

Swinging around, the vampire slammed his foot into Angel's chest, knocking him back ten feet and into Emily's lap. The metal chair buckled from the impact.

The vampire snatched up his clipboard and fled.

The following afternoon, Giles was back at the research table after having gone home to get some rest in a proper bed and to change clothes. In his mind he went over the facts of the latest plague to Sunnydale, incorporating the details Angel had supplied from the previous night. Generally, vampire behavior was simple to follow. They would attack, eat, and kill. There was usually little variation on that theme, unless they were siring new vampires. Very rarely did they use sketched-out attacks with predetermined results unless there was some greater plan. It was that greater plan that Giles feared.

Until the Watcher could figure out that plan, there were plenty of contradictory clues to keep his mind occupied. The man left sightless on the first night was obviously meant to bear witness to the act, but they left none of the victims alive on the night of the second attack. On the first night, three of the bodies had been cut by swords before dying. Last night there were no visible signs of attack besides the puncture wounds on their necks. Then there were the foils, which paled in comparison to the metal chairs that Giles was sure were never used in any ritual in history.

It was two hours to sunset, and he could feel the time running out. The minutes grew even more precious because he had promised Willow that he would come to the final performance of the play that evening. While he knew that she would understand that he had to back out due to Watcher duties, he had no intention of telling her what really was going on if he could help it. He had hardly seen her in the past two weeks but knew that she was enjoying herself at the theater. There was no way that he intended to spoil it by introducing demons to her summer.

As if on cue, the library doors swung open on Willow's entrance.

"I knew we'd find you here," she said as she came in with a young woman whom Giles did not recognize.

"Sad but true." He closed the book he was reading, lest Willow think that there was researching to be done. "I was just trying to catch up—"

"Oh, you don't have to explain," the unidentified young woman said. "Willow told me all about everything."

"She did?" He performed the appropriate raising of the eyebrow, wondering what exactly Willow had told this stranger.

"And I think it's great that you're going to summer school to get your teaching certificate. Going after a new career at your age and all."

Giles was thrown off by her comment, but did manage a glance at Willow to show that he was proud of her forethought in explaining why he was in the library over summer vacation. This elicited a little smile from the student.

Wait a minute! At my age? he thought.

Willow took his silence as the opening for introductions. "Giles, this is Elisabeth, one of the actresses in the show I'm working on. She plays Lady Macbeth."

"Very nice to meet you," he said, shaking her hand. "If you don't mind my saying so, you seem rather young for such a role." *Take that.*

"We're a young cast," she replied easily. "Mostly college kids, but you'd be surprised how much life experience we've had."

"I can't believe the amount of experiences we've had in the last two weeks," Willow said.

"I must say how impressed I am that you took on this job, Willow," Giles's spoken praise caused her to smile even more. "Especially considering how uncomfortable you were working on the talent show."

"I'm only behind the scenes," Willow said, hopping up on the counter. "As long as I don't have to go *on* stage, I don't have to worry about the stage fright that manifests itself as temporary paralysis."

"Don't believe her," Elisabeth added. "She also understudies some of the roles and she's been fabulous."

"Really?"

"I wouldn't say *fabulous*," Willow said. "Let's just say that I haven't tripped and fallen off the stage into the orchestra pit yet."

"Well, compared to the untalented townies we hired for the smaller roles, you've managed to hold your own."

"And how is Xander doing?"

Giles's question was met with an uncomfortable silence.

"I take that to mean that he's not enjoying himself?"

"He isn't," Willow confirmed. "He's . . . had a few accidents."

"A few?" Elisabeth added sarcastically.

"He just needs a little confidence," Willow hastily defended her friend. "It doesn't help that we're on two different schedules. We took the jobs so that we could work together, but I had to work all the rehearsals and the crew didn't come in until after they were over. We hardly saw each other while the show was in rehearsal."

"Well, it will all be over tonight," Giles said.

"Speaking of tonight," Willow removed something from her pocket. "I have your tickets for the show. There's also a cast party afterward."

"You have to come," Elisabeth added. "It'll be a blast."

"Thank you, I'll think about it."

"I notice you asked for two tickets," Willow said. "Will you be bringing someone of the Ms. Calendar variety?"

"As a matter of fact, Ms. Calendar will be accompanying me," he confirmed, pocketing the tickets. "We thought it would be a nice show of support for our students."

"How romantic," Elisabeth added dryly. "On that note, we should be going."

"We need to get Elisabeth a new pair of shoes for the show," Willow said as she slid off the counter. "Her other pair was lost last night."

"The costumer was ready to kill Xander for losing them," Elisabeth said. "That is, until Willow, the peacemaker, offered to go with me to get new shoes."

"Well, it's been nice meeting you, Elisabeth," Giles said, shaking her hand. "Break a leg tonight."

"Thank you," she said. "But you can wish me luck. I don't believe in theater superstition. I mean, we're performing one of the most cursed plays in theater history and, Xander's screw-ups aside, nothing bad has happened."

The concept of cursed plays sent Giles's mind into overdrive. He barely managed to say good-bye to Willow before racing back to the stacks. It took him a few minutes to find what he had been looking for because, since Buffy had arrived in Sunnydale a few months earlier, he rarely spent any time in the section of the library actually devoted to school books.

* * *

When Jenny arrived an hour later, she found Giles exactly where she had left him, at the research table. However, this time he was not reading books that were written centuries before. These books looked more modern, like regular library books.

"Listen to this," he said as he opened one of the books. "Had it the ability of *life* to thank you: He never gave *commandment* for their *death.* But since, so jump upon this *bloody* question."

As Giles's voice trailed off, Jenny filled in the blanks, excited by the fact that they had their first real clue. "The words that the man was repeating!"

"They are from *Hamlet!*" Giles explained, handing her the book. "From Horatio's final lines. The man who was left to bear witness to the killings at the end of the play."

"The murders were taken from plays?" she asked as she quickly scanned the text.

"The poisoned woman represented Hamlet's mother. The three men who had been cut by the foils were Hamlet, Laertes, and the King." Giles was rubbing his creased brow, mentally berating himself for not being more thorough. "If we had taken the foils, we probably would have found that one of them had been dipped in the same poison that was in the chalice."

"And last night?"

"The final scenes of *Our Town,*" Giles explained, as if it should have been obvious all along. "The *entire* third act centers around the dead in a cemetery. They are seated on twelve chairs in three rows. I don't know how I missed it!"

"This isn't normal behavior for vampires though," she said, closing the book and putting it down on the table among the pile of other plays.

"Ah, but history is littered with stories of theater troupes bringing death with them as they travel from town to town."

"The same was said of murderous Gypsy bands or strong women who were called witches," she countered as she took a seat beside him. "It was just a reflection of ignorant times in which townspeople were afraid of anything different."

"True," Giles agreed. "And I am rarely one to put so much faith in baseless folklore, but the killings do coincide with the nights of the performances."

"And you think it's the cast?"

"No," Giles said slowly, sounding it out. "Willow just came over with the lead actress this afternoon. But it has to be someone associated with the show. It's too large of a coincidence for it not to be. . . ." He trailed off in thought, absently chewing on the arm of his glasses. "It could be the backstage crew. They don't report to work until after the rehearsals, so they don't have to be out during the day."

"Vampires with secret identities," she said. "How Clark Kent of them."

"Tonight is closing night of the show. Willow said that there's going to be a big cast party afterward. I'm afraid to think what could happen."

"Before we jump to conclusions based on coincidence, let's do some more research of the modern variety."

Jenny moved over to the computer and warmed up the search engine on the Shakespeare Players. Conveniently the troupe had a website listing their summer tour. From there, it was only a matter of cross referencing the newspapers of the towns in which they had performed. She had their answers printed out in less than a half-hour.

"Okay," she said. Her voice brought Giles back from the stacks where he had been pulling other plays for potential research. "The company has performed in three other towns this summer. In each of the towns there were several unsolved murders during the time the company was there."

"Murder scenes?" Giles asked, placing his new pile of books on the table.

Scanning the pages, Jenny read a few off. "Two young brothers. Their mother is missing and, as far as I can tell, has not turned up yet . . ."

"Medea."

"A young couple found in a crypt, one stabbed, the other by a vial of poison . . ."

"Romeo and Juliet."

"A crucifixion scene . . ."

Giles looked through his new pile of books. "Obviously a play about Christ."

"Jesus Christ Superstar?" Jenny guessed. "There are other murders too."

"I think we've proven our point," Giles said with satisfaction. "Someone associated with the theater is responsible for these killings."

"Not just that." She handed him the printed pages. "I meant there are a *lot* of other murders. The scenes aren't just contained to the nights of the performances. They occurred nearly every night that the troupe was in the towns."

"What could be different about Sunnydale?" Giles wondered as he browsed the information. "If anything, this town would be the one most likely to see the worst of the murders. Historically speaking, of course."

"We'll have to find that out tonight," Jenny said.

"We can watch the first act from our seats and get a read on the theater. Nothing should happen until after the show. I'll go ask Angel to watch the backstage once the sun sets in case he recognizes the guy from last night. In the meantime, you really should warn Willow and Xander."

"I know," he said. "But I don't want them to be involved if they don't have to be."

"If you're right, then they're already involved."

There's no way I can do this.

Willow was pacing outside the theater in a truly agitated state. Her breath was short, her mind racing. She could not believe what she had just been told. It shouldn't have come as a surprise, but it did catch her off guard.

Everything had been going so well . . .

She had been enjoying her summer job until moments ago.

In the midst of her hysterics, she saw Giles. Before he could reach her, she found herself running to the Watcher, the shock showing on her face.

"Willow, what's wrong?" he asked as she reached him.

"It's horrible," she cried.

"Vampires?"

"No," she said. "Kirsti didn't show up. She plays one of the three witches. We've been calling, but can't find her anywhere."

"And you think she's been—"

"Oh, no," Willow said, barely registering the significance of his question. "She's been flaky for the past two weeks, always late to rehearsal, never knew her lines." Then it hit her and she shifted gears. "Why would you think something happened to her? Nothing evil has happened since Buffy left."

Giles decided to ignore that last part. "But that doesn't explain why you are so upset."

Why isn't he getting it? "I have to go on in her place!"

The Watcher relaxed slightly. "Well, that explains why you are wearing so much make-up. Willow, you'll be fine. I have total faith in you."

"I'm glad someone does," she said. "Giles, how can I do this? You remember the talent show."

"That was different."

"How?"

Giles was at a loss. "Um, it wasn't a paying audience?"

"This isn't one of your better pep talks."

"Willow, listen to me," he said calmly. "You've been preparing for this for the past two weeks. You knew that it was possible that you would have to go on stage."

"But I never thought—"

"You told me yourself how much fun you've been having. When you're on the stage, you'll be surrounded by the friends you've made at the theater. Ms. Calendar and I will be out front watching you. You have nothing to fear."

"But I'm—"

"Going to be fine." He placed his hands on her shoulders in a fatherly manner. "You're going to be just fine."

His calming voice had an effect on her. It wasn't enough to make the nerves go away, but it was sufficient to get her to remember her responsibilities.

"I have to call places," Then she realized, "And I have to get *into* place. I'm in the first scene!"

Without another word, she ran to the stage door, unlocked it and disappeared inside, leaving Giles behind to contemplate what he had not told her.

There was a small crowd in front of the theater for the last show.

"I told Angel we'd meet him backstage during the intermission," Jenny said to a preoccupied Giles as they went inside. "He's going to be hiding back there during the first act. Apparently one of the many tunnels under Sunnydale has an opening in the alleyway behind the theater. He may already be in place."

"Which explains how they have been getting in and out of the theater during the day."

"Did you tell Willow and Xander?" she asked.

"I . . . didn't see Xander."

"Willow?"

"There was a slight change of plans."

"How slight!"

"One of the actresses has gone missing, and Willow has to go on in her place. She was a nervous wreck. I didn't think that it was a good idea to make things worse."

After a pause, Jenny eased his conscience. "You made the right call."

"Thank you."

They had come to their row. An usher handed them each a program. After they took their seats, Jenny began to read over her program looking for clues, while Giles's thoughts shifted from Willow and Xander to the theater full of unsuspecting innocents.

How many people do they intend to kill tonight? the

Watcher thought. *And how do we stop them before they enact their plan?*

"I think I've found something." Jenny's comment put an end to his musings.

"What?" he whispered, cognizant of the fact that they were surrounded by audience members who were easily within earshot.

"There seven people on the stage crew," she said, also in a whisper. "Subtract Willow and Xander and that leaves five. The same number of . . . people . . . Angel saw last night."

"I guess that's the final confirmation," he said. "It's the whole crew."

The house lights began to dim.

"We have to get back there and tell Angel," she whispered more urgently.

"They won't do anything while the show is on. They'll wait until after the curtain call."

"How can you be so sure?"

"This is theater. They won't let anything get in the way of the show."

The curtain opened, and Willow had the first line of the play. Giles not only saw, but actually felt her fear from where he sat. She was frozen on the stage, and the play would not start until she spoke her lines.

During the silence, a loud crash was heard from backstage. Giles wasn't sure if it was a sound effect or an accident. The noise, while scaring half the audience, managed to jar Willow into speech.

"Wh-When shall we th-th-three meet again? In thunder, l-l-lightning, or in rain?"

Having snuck in through a window after sunset, Angel found himself a place to hide in the catwalks thirty feet above the stage. The first act seemed perfectly fine from Angel's vantage point. When they weren't on stage, the cast stayed in either the greenroom or their dressing rooms. The only people walking around were the stage crew.

He could not help but notice that the crew was all dressed in black just like the vampires from the previous evening. Although that was probably normal for people working backstage, what was abnormal was the sense of death associated with them. Angel knew when he was in the presence of other vampires, and the air felt as if he'd stumbled into their nest. The darkness of the backstage area normally would not affect his surveillance, but that in combination with the natural havoc of backstage during a performance and the height from which he was perched, kept him from getting a true read on the situation. Every now and then he would see Willow and Xander scurrying about and, though they were not looking in his direction, he was careful not to be seen by them.

As the intermission was nearing, Angel decided that it was time to do some looking around. He figured that everyone was so busy with their own jobs that they wouldn't notice him.

Careful to avoid the greenroom and dressing rooms, Angel went to the stage-left wings to look around the less populated part of the theater. According to the signs, the left side of the stage led to the costume shop, paint closet, and electrical room. Most of the doors were tied open to make sure that they did not slam during the performance. Angel could see the costumer in her shop and avoided the room completely.

Once past the costume shop, he entered the paint closet next door. Several cans of paint lined the shelves of one wall while dozens of brushes lined the other. There was a big sink in the middle of the back wall. Nothing could be hiding in that room. Before Angel exited he heard angry voices in the next room straining to remain at a whisper. At first he couldn't make out what they were saying, until they moved out into the hallway.

"I can't believe that you left that mess behind," said a male voice with a familiar tone.

Angel did his best to hide behind the paint room door. Since it was tied open, he couldn't entirely fit, but it did obscure most of his body.

"I couldn't help it," a female voice answered.

"You shouldn't have been striking things until after the show."

"But I needed to, Sam." The female voice gave Angel a name to work with. "Xander's had this whole production so screwed up that I couldn't wait any longer. We missed so much work during the week cleaning up after his mistakes."

"I should have fired him last week, but we'll get rid of him as soon as the show is over," Sam said. "Although, I'm thinking of making Willow a permanent member of the crew."

"She has been doing a great job."

"I've got to get back up to the booth to call the rest of the cues so that Willow can go onstage."

"I should be in the light booth too," the woman said. "See you after the show."

Angel heard one of them quietly pull a door shut and lock it, which he found a little odd.

As they were walking away from the paint room,

Angel stole a glance from behind the door to confirm his suspicions. Although both the man and woman had their backs to him, it was all that Angel needed to see. The badly dyed black hair confirmed that the stage manager was the vampire he had fought in the cemetery.

After they were gone, Angel decided to have a look inside the next room. The old lock on the shop door gave way with only a little push. Once inside, Angel had to wonder what mess Sam was talking about. The room was the electrical closet, where they stored the extra lighting equipment, and it was a shining example of theater efficiency. The extra lamps were hung in rows on the wall and organized piles of the electrical cords were below them, draped over a metal bar. That was when he noticed a bulge in the curtain of cords. When he pulled them aside, the body of a young woman fell into his arms. There were two puncture wounds in her neck.

A distant roar of applause indicated the first act of *Macbeth* had ended.

As soon as the lights came up, Giles and Jenny realized that all doors leading to the backstage area were blocked by the house crew, meaning that they would have to find another route. Having to fight their way through the crowd to get outside, they used up half the intermission on their way to meet Angel. After circling around to the back of the theater, they were happy to find him waiting for them with the door propped open. He ushered them in and closed the door behind them.

"It's the stage crew," Giles said.

"I know," Angel said. "As far as I can tell, there are only the five of them."

"Yes," Jenny said, referring to her program. "A costumer, propmaster, technical director, light designer, and the stage manager."

"He's the one I fought last night," Angel said, taking the program from her and looking down the list of names. "I had a near run-in with him, and I think . . . the light designer, Amy."

"How do we handle five vampires with innocent people around?" Giles asked.

"Divide and conquer," Angel replied.

"Can we wait until after the show?" Jenny asked.

"No time," Angel said. "As soon as the curtain falls, they're going to kill Xander. And, if I'm not mistaken, I think they're going to make Willow one of them."

As if on cue, Willow and Xander appeared beside them.

"Hi, guys!" they said in unison.

"What are you doing here?" Giles asked.

"We're supposed to be here, trespasser," Xander replied easily. "What are *you* doing here?"

"Did you come to wish us luck?" Willow asked. "Because you shouldn't do that. It's bad luck to wish good luck in the theater. I don't subscribe to Elisabeth's positive view on that subject. Not since I had to go onstage tonight."

"Listen to Superstition Girl, please," Xander said, jamming his hands into his pockets. "I'm having enough bad luck as it is. I don't need any more."

"Xander, you're doing fine." Willow reassured him.

"Which is why we came backstage." Giles quickly used her comment for his explanation. "To tell you both how marvelously you're doing."

"Willow, you make a wonderful witch," Jenny said, joining in.

They looked to Angel.

"And . . . Xander . . . the scenes changes are . . . going smoothly," the vampire said.

"Thanks, but you should get back to your seats," Willow said, trying to hike up the costume that was designed for an actress nearly a foot taller. "The second act is about to begin."

"Well, then, by all means," Giles said. "Break a leg, you two."

"Careful, I just might," Xander, prophet of doom, said.

Giles, Angel, and Jenny exited through the stage door, making sure to hold it open a crack so it didn't lock behind them.

"Xander," Giles heard Willow say with gentle exasperation. "Stop being so negative."

"Five seconds into the first act I knocked over the entire props table."

"I'm sure no one noticed," she said unconvincingly.

"Will, I'm lousy at this job," he said. "They've been giving me busywork, and I still blow it. Summer is supposed to be a break from the nightmare of high school. Yet, here I am, the bumbling fool again. I'm tired of being the comic relief. For once, I'd like to be the hero."

Once Giles heard Willow and Xander drift away, he led Jenny and Angel back inside. Still careful not to be seen, Angel took them to an area where they could come up with a plan. Safe in the electrical room, they could barely hear the first lines of the second act.

"On the other side of the stage are the dressing

rooms," Angel explained, unrolling a set of electrical plans that showed a layout of the theater. He pointed out the backstage area. "They should be safe during the performance. I don't think there's anything planned until after the show. There are two curtained sections behind the stage. The larger curtain covers up the set storage, and the smaller one hides the props table. There are also two booths to the left and right side of the stage."

"We saw them from the audience," Giles said.

"The booth stage right is for lighting. I saw the light designer in there earlier. On the left side is the stage manager's booth. Willow's been in and out of there with him all evening."

"What about the others?" Giles asked.

"We passed the costume shop next door," Angel continued. "I think the costumer is in the dressing rooms right now, but she'll probably be back in that room for most of the second act like she was for the first. There are two guys backstage, one doing the scene changes and one working the props. Xander alternates between them."

"We'll start with the costumer and the one in the light booth," Giles said. "They should be easiest to kill without witnesses. Then we'll take on the two backstage, leaving the stage manager for last."

"I'll get the one in the light booth and the one moving sets."

"Which leaves the costumer and propmaster for me and Giles."

"When we're done, we'll meet by the stage door and work out a plan to keep the stage manager away from Willow," Giles said.

With the beginnings of a plan in place, Angel left

the electrical room to go to the light booth. When he reached the costume shop, he motioned back to Giles and Jenny that it was still empty before he continued his mission. Closing the door to the electrical room, they began to hatch their plan.

"I suppose that we should wait a few minutes before leaving," Giles said as he eyed the room for possible weapons. Between the electrical cords, stage lamps, and various tools, there were many to choose from. While looking the room over, he noticed that the body was still peeking out from behind the cords.

"Or we could hide in the costume shop and wait for her to return?" Jenny suggested.

"If we leave the room now, we could accidentally run right into her," Giles said as he strategically draped the cords over the deceased actress. *No need to announce that we were here*, he thought.

"Well, I have my handy-dandy stake in my purse," Jenny said, holding up her purse to accentuate what she was saying. "How do you suggest we take the costumer out?"

"I suppose the simplest plan would be to pretend that we are lost and take her by sur—"

The door burst open, cutting Giles's response short.

"Let me save you some time," the costumer said, standing in the doorway. *"I* am the one whose death you have been plotting. May I suggest that the next time you plan someone's murder, you don't do it in a room that bears the signs of a break-in. You're just asking for someone to come looking into it."

Her face switched from mild-mannered costumer to full-fledged vampire.

* * *

"Xander!" Elisabeth's urgent whisper came from her dressing room door as Xander passed by carrying Macbeth's crown.

As he approached, he quickly realized that the actress was in her underwear.

Don't look. Don't look. Don't look.

"Um . . . can I . . . can I help you?" Xander asked, his eyes looking everywhere but at her.

"What's wrong?"

"Nothing," he said as his face turned a bright shade of red.

"Xander, look at me," she said. "There is no place for embarrassment in the dressing room. I need your help."

He looked up, directly into her eyes. "What can I do?"

"Brenee went to get the nightgown for my final scene, but she hasn't come back yet," she explained. "I need you to go find her. *Quickly.*"

"Got it," he said and was off.

Running through the theater wings, trying not to make a sound, Xander passed the greenroom before slowing down as he started to cross behind the stage. Onstage, he could hear the murder of Lady MacDuff and her son. From backstage, he could hear his name, again being urgently whispered.

"Xander, where's the crown?" The voice came from Mel, the propmaster.

Turning, Xander went behind one of the backstage curtains to the props table. He handed the king's crown to Mel.

"Don't forget to get the daggers from the murderers as soon as they come offstage," the propmaster reminded him.

"I'm on it," Xander said.

Heading to the wings stage left, Xander passed the

murdering extras, grabbed their daggers and continued to the costume shop.

En route, he heard Willow calling the name that he was seriously considering changing.

"What?" he whispered back.

"Sam wants you to help with the next scene change. It's taking Carl too long when he does it himself."

"Got it."

In the costume shop, Brenee was nowhere to be found. After a frantic search of the costume closet, he located the nightgown.

On the way to Elisabeth's dressing room, he stopped by the props table to drop off the daggers.

"What took you?" the propmaster asked.

"Costume emergency," he replied, showing the nightgown.

"Well hurry back," Mel said. "I need your help with the flags for the army scene."

"I have to do the next scene change."

"Then get rid of that costume, because it's coming up."

And off he was again.

"What took you so long?" Elisabeth asked. "Never mind. Where's Brenee?"

"I couldn't find her, but here's the gown."

He started to go.

"Wait. I need help getting into it."

"But I have to be ready for the next scene change—"

"If I'm not in this outfit," she said, "then, scene change or not, the next scene won't be happening."

"Point taken."

She slipped the nightgown on, and Xander began the laborious task of buttoning up the ridiculously numerous buttons in the back.

Perfect, he thought, *here I am finally helping a woman with her clothing, and I'm putting it on, not taking it off.*

While Xander was looking for the costumer, she was keeping Giles and Jenny busy in the electrical room. The attack started with her flinging a metal stage lamp at Giles, knocking him to the ground. While he was out of commission, Brenee went for Jenny's neck.

The move was so fast that Jenny didn't have the chance to grab any kind of weapon, much less reach for the stake that she had in her purse. Pulling at the vampire's hands, she could feel the muscles in her throat constricting as the vampire choked her. Brenee pushed Jenny's head to the side, giving herself access to the flesh.

"I don't know who you are," the costumer said. "And I truly don't care."

As Brenee bore down upon Jenny's neck, Giles managed to extricate himself from the lighting equipment. Reaching for one of the hanging electrical cords, he grabbed it by both ends and looped it around the costumer's neck, using it to pull her away from Jenny.

The costumer struggled to get free, but Giles held tight. Jenny removed her stake from its confines and plunged it into the heart of the vampire.

"That's one," she said.

Conveniently, there was no door to the light booth, so Angel could watch the light designer as she worked the lightboard. Amy's back was to him, which would make a surprise assault much easier. He noticed that she had a headset on, so the attack would have to be fast so that she could not warn the others. Luckily, the mouthpiece was in an up position, indicating that she was not transmitting. A quick stab in the back with his stake, and she would be dust.

"You may not have a reflection in the booth window," the light designer hissed. "But the light you are blocking is casting a shadow on the room."

The headset was off, and she was up and facing Angel in a flash.

"Good eye," Angel said.

"Comes with the job," she replied. "You must be the one that Sam had a run-in with last night."

"Guilty," Angel said. "You shouldn't have taken the headset off without calling for help."

"I think I can handle you alone."

"Shall we take this outside?" Angel asked, since the booth was rather small for fighting.

"I'd rather not. I don't want to miss the next cue. Just one request."

"What?"

"The audience is on the other side of that window. Can we keep this down so we don't interrupt the show?"

"Of cour—"

Angel didn't have time to finish the word before her fist was in his face. The surprise attack caused him to drop his stake.

Weaponless, he returned with a volley of punches to her stomach.

She jumped to the right and hit him with a roundhouse, which he blocked with his arm.

The two broke and circled the booth, facing each other, waiting.

This time Angel started with a kick to her face.

Amy fell back a step, then went at him with her fists in a face-stomach-chest combination.

This was when Angel found his opportunity. Letting loose with his barrage of fists, he backed her closer to the circuit board on the wall. The board had a number of wires attached that fed electricity to the lights above the stage. When Angel had moved her close enough, he took a break from the fists and stepped back, returning with a kick to her chest that knocked her into the board. The electricity coursing through her body knocked her momentarily senseless, giving Angel his opportunity.

Picking up the discarded stake, he plunged it into her heart.

Onstage, the lights flickered, but did not go off. However, the odd lighting effect did not go unnoticed in the stage manager's booth.

"What is going on over there?" Sam asked. "I can't raise Amy on the headset. Willow, go see what's happening."

"I'm on it."

"Take a headset with you in case Amy's is broken."

Willow grabbed one of the cordless headsets on her way out.

When Giles and Jenny peeked around the backstage curtain at the props table, they couldn't help but notice the amount of weapons stored back there. Silently, they moved back to the other side of the curtain.

"I never realized how violent this play was," Jenny whispered.

"A vampire is bad enough," Giles whispered back. "But a fully-armed vampire is even more of a concern. The direct approach will be more dangerous."

"I have an idea," Jenny said. "You take him out once he's distracted."

Without providing a more detailed explanation of the plan, Jenny moved around the curtain and found the propmaster standing over his table of props.

"Excuse me," she said, using her voice to its most seductive potential. "I think I'm a little lost."

"You're not supposed to be back here," he said.

"I know," she replied, moving closer to him, "but I just couldn't help myself. I've never been backstage at a real theater before."

She flashed a smile and let her hair do what it seemed to do naturally.

"Well, Miss, you'll have to go back outside," he said, moving toward her. "We're in the middle of a show."

"Are you in charge of *all* the props?" she asked, idly rubbing a hand down her neck.

"Yes, Miss—"

"Jenny."

Her smile grew.

His eyes focused on her neck, lips parting.

"Jenny," he was starting to warm up to her. "Yes, I do oversee the props."

"And there are so many," she said. "How do you keep track of them all?"

"Well, it can be difficult—"

Got him.

"—but, I manage," he continued. "I do oversee a staff."

While this degrading interaction was taking place, Giles crept up behind the Neanderthal vampire propmaster and, in a moment of irony, picked up one of the daggers.

"And I'm sure that it's a large staff too," she said, knowing that Xander was the only *staff* he oversaw.

The vampire was all but on her neck when Giles brought the dagger down upon his back.

The rubber dagger bent on contact.

With a start, the propmaster turned to find out what had hit him. Jenny pulled her stake out and finished the job.

When Willow got to the light booth, she found it empty.

"No one's here," she said into her headset. "It looks like the circuit board is fried."

"Well, bring up cue seventy-three," Sam said. "The actors won't start the scene until the lights change."

Willow crossed over to the lightboard. She wasn't exactly proficient at working the system, but Amy had shown her the basics earlier that week. Pushing the sliders, she raised the stage lights.

"That's not seventy-three," Sam's tightly controlled voice said over the headset.

"That's all that's coming up," she said back. "I think it's only going to be lights up and down for the rest of the show. Amy must be up in the light grid trying to fix it."

"Well, I wish she would have told someone first," Sam said.

"Do you want me to stay here?" she asked.

"No," he replied. "Get Xander to do it. Then go find Amy and see if she needs any help to salvage the rest of the cues."

"Will do," she said and left the booth.

It only took her a moment to find Xander, who was in a panic at the props table.

"I need your help," they both said.

"You first," Willow said.

"Mel's disappeared and these flags need to be waving from the wings on both stage left and stage right at the start of the next scene. I can't possibly be both places at once."

"He's not the only one missing." She filled him in on the situation.

"Maybe Mel went to help her?" Xander guessed.

"But he wouldn't leave his post without telling you."

"It must have been when I was onstage doing the last scene change," Xander said as he saw Elisabeth exit the stage. "Where I need to be *again*. Here, take these!" He grabbed a pile of flags and handed them to Willow. She ran stage left, trying not to trip on her oversized costume, while he went stage right. Luckily, there was no set change. Instead, there was supposed to be a really cool lighting effect that would signal the new scene. Things being as they were, Xander and Willow just waved the flags frantically and the actors took that as their cue.

Angel found the technical director backstage by the sets, waiting for his next cue. Angel looked over the area behind the back curtain. The only route to the technical director was the direct one. Naturally, Angel took that route without second thought.

The technical director was caught off guard, but was able to defend against the attack he saw coming. Feinting right, he threw his body against Angel, who found himself slamming into one of the sturdier set pieces. When Angel turned, he saw that the technical director had grabbed an unlit torch and was swinging it wildly on the offensive.

Angel managed to block most of the blows until one of them landed square in his chest and sent him back through a fake wall. When Angel extricated himself from the set piece, he found that the technical director had lit his torch. Realizing that it was not safe to be around wooden set pieces with a wild vampire holding a torch, Angel ran from the props storage area with a definite destination in mind.

Making sure that he was still being followed, Angel ducked into the paint closet and waited. As he expected, the attacker assumed that Angel was trapped and recklessly ran into the open doorway.

As soon as the technical director cleared the doorway, Angel threw the contents of a turpentine can at him. As the turpentine met the torch flame, the liquid became fire and engulfed the vampire.

Angel then grabbed a fire extinguisher from the wall and put out the flames that had caught on the doorframe.

Giles and Jenny had seen the flash of light from backstage. They were about to investigate when they saw Angel coming toward them.

"I assume that was you?" Giles asked.

"Two down," Angel replied.

"And we took care of our two," Jenny said. "That leaves the stage manager."

"Duck," Giles said as he saw Willow and Xander about to come their way. Taking the only possible route, they hurried out the stage door. In their haste, they allowed the door to close and lock behind them.

"Do you smell something burning?" Willow asked.

"Now that you mention it."

"Stage left."

The twosome followed the scent and came across the partially charred paint closet. As they surveyed the wreckage, neither of them paid any attention to the extended silence coming from the stage until Willow heard Sam's strained voice over her headset.

"Scene change!"

Without stopping to wonder why no one was at their post, the two novice crew members ran out to complete the last scene change.

Sam watched as Xander and Willow cleared the stage for the final scenes. Throwing his headphones down in anger and disgust, the stage manager went off to find his missing crew. *No reason for me to stay in the booth.* No one was listening for his cues and nothing else was being moved on- or off-stage. The rest of the show was entirely up to the actors.

Knowing his crew well, he was sure that they were off starting the cast party early. He had expected better from them. True, they had killed less than in any of the previous cities, but it was only a short time before they would have free rein over half the audience. In his search, the first person he came across was Willow.

"Where is everybody?" He could barely conceal his anger.

"Xander's on the catwalk," she said. "We can't find Amy, or anyone else, so I gave him my headset and sent him up to work the spotlight for the final scene."

"Willow, that special effect is too important to leave to Xander."

"But I couldn't climb the ladder in this costume."

"Then you should have gotten me." He was trying not to take his anger out on Willow since he knew she was doing her best.

"I know Xander can do it," she said loyally.

"Look, I need you up in the booth watching the show. I'll keep an eye on Xander."

Willow immediately headed for the stage manager's booth, and Sam made his way to the ladder up to the catwalk.

At the same time, Angel was dropping into the theater by way of the window he had used earlier. He quickly opened the stage door to let Giles and Jenny in, hoping that they were not too late.

Thirty feet above their heads, Sam was now on the same catwalk that Angel had been perched on only an hour before. He was nearing Xander, who was fumbling with the spotlight.

The light was intended to represent an otherworldly glow upon the presentation of Macbeth's severed head. Sam heard Willow's cue and watched Xander flip the switch on the spotlight, but nothing happened. From his position behind Xander, Sam could see that the inexperienced crewman had forgotten to plug the cord into the light. While Xander frantically played with the fixture, Sam was moving closer. *That's it,* he thought, *the show's over. Time to get rid of Xander.*

It was then that Xander surprised him by doing something right.

Seeing that the cord was lying beside him, Xander bent to get it and knocked the lamp out of position. When Xander plugged in the cord, the light was no longer focused on the stage but behind him. Quickly he repositioned the light so that it was in the correct spot, but it was too late for Sam. When the white hot spotlight was turned on, it was aimed directly at the stage manger's face. The blinding light had caught Sam so off his guard that he lost his footing and fell from the catwalk. Thankfully, he had fallen to the right and wound up behind the stage curtain rather than on the stage itself.

Sam landed on his back with the wind knocked out of him, but otherwise unscathed. He decided it would be best to rest for a moment while his eyes readjusted to the light, and his body readjusted from the fall.

His eyes cleared up just in time to see the man dressed in tweed bring a stake down upon his heart.

As soon as the curtain fell, Willow was running backstage to congratulate the cast. Xander was the first person she saw as he climbed down from the catwalk.

"You did great, Xander!"

"Thanks, you too."

Elisabeth came running toward them.

"Willow, hurry up. You're going to miss the curtain call!"

"The assistant stage manager doesn't go out for the curtain call," she said.

"No, but the First Witch does. Come on."

"But, Xander . . ."

"Go," Xander said. "You deserve to bask in your applause."

The two actors ran off to the stage.

"I'll just stay here," he said to no one. "Alone."

Turning, he saw Giles, Jenny, and Angel by the stage door. They were applauding.

"You know, you guys have to stop sneaking back here," Xander said as he crossed to them. "You could get us in trouble with the stage manager."

"We promise that we won't do it again," Jenny said with a smile.

"So what did you think of the play?" Xander asked.

"It was, by far, the most exciting night at the theater I've ever had," Giles responded as Jenny and Angel smiled in silent agreement.

"Giles, I did it!" Willow said as she ran up and gave him a big hug.

Giles, unaccustomed to the grand show of emotion, gave a halfhearted hug in return, which Willow immediately noticed as being uncomfortable for him.

"Sorry," she said, letting him go. "Youthful exuberance gone overboard."

"Perfectly understood," Giles said, happy that she was still alive to hug and be hugged.

"Are you all staying for the party?" Willow asked.

The three backstage guests looked at one another waiting for someone to come up with a good reason for them not to attend.

"I have to pack," Jenny said, providing her own out. "I'm going to visit my family for a while . . . among other things."

Willow looked to Giles.

"I should see her home," he explained as he wondered, *What other things?*

Which led her to look toward Angel.

"Parties aren't my thing," he said.

"You don't know what you'll be missing," Xander said, showing them to the door.

"It'll be the highlight of the summer," Willow added.

"Which isn't really hard considering how absolutely boring this summer's been," Xander said, opening the stage door for them.

"Absolutely," Giles said as he walked out the door. "Well, enjoy the party."

"And have a good rest of the summer," Jenny added.

"Bye!" Xander and Willow said in unison.

"Well, let's go find the crew," Giles heard Willow say to Xander as the door began to close. "We should find out what time we have to be here tomorrow to take down the set."

As the door lock clicked, the three fill-in Slayers walked down the alley toward the street.

"Are you sure that you two will be okay with me out of town?" Jenny asked.

"I think we should be fine," Giles said. "Aside from the theater company, things had been relatively quiet for the past few weeks. And Buffy should be back before long."

Angel stopped at the mention of the Slayer's name. "Giles, can I speak with you for a moment?" he asked.

Taking her cue, Jenny said, "You know, in all the commotion, I lost my program. I'm going to see if they have any more up front. I'll meet you there, Giles."

"Have a safe trip," Angel said.

"Thanks," she said as she went to the front of the theater. "I'll see you when I get back."

"Giles," Angel said once Jenny was around the corner. "By now, I guess it's pretty safe to assume that

Buffy won't be getting in touch with me this summer."

"Angel, I—"

"You don't have to come up with an excuse," he continued in his characteristically soft and slightly brooding voice. "Just . . . if you talk to her again . . . Tell her that I hope she's having a good summer vacation."

ABOUT THE AUTHORS

Cameron Dokey is the author of more than twenty novels for young adults. She enjoys her time in the world of the Slayer, and she admits she's not sure what this says about her. When not writing, she's out working in the garden of her Seattle, Washington home. Yes, even when it's raining.

Nancy Holder is the award-winning, bestselling author of many Buffy and Angel titles including *Angel: City of* and *Immortal* (with Christopher Golden). She, Jeff Mariotte and Maryelizabeth Hart recently completed *Buffy the Vampire Slayer: The Watchers Guide 2*. To celebrate, they bought a small villa in Tuscany and fly there on their private jet for the weekends. (That part's not true, but it was fun to write. Just like this short story.)

Yvonne Navarro lives in the Chicago area and has had eleven novels and sixty-plus short stories published since the mid-eighties. She's written about vampires, zombies, plain old people, and the end of the world. She has never been in the military (just as well, since she doesn't think she'd look good in an army uniform), but she has learned to listen and follow orders by studying martial arts. Visit her at www.para-net.com/~ynavarro.

Paul Ruditis was born and raised in Philadelphia and lived there until he moved to California in search of his fortune . . . he's still looking for it. His first book, *The Roswell Pop Quiz,* will be out this fall.

Michelle West discovered Buffy when she caught the last ten minutes of "Angel," in which she got to watch Darla with guns, got to watch Angel save Buffy, and got to watch Buffy and Angel kiss. After that, she made Mike Brooks lend her every single episode from the start of the first season on. Her brother Gary still has to tape them just in case her baby plays with the VCR settings (which has happened twice).

Vital Statistics:

Favorite character: Buffy Summers.

Favorite episode: "Prophecy Girl," although a close second is "Becoming, Part Two."

Favorite couple: Willow and Oz.

Favorite villain: The Mayor.

Favorite character who has the most potential to be something gritty, interesting, and relevant: Faith.

"Wish me monsters."
—Buffy

Vampires, werewolves, witches, demons of nonspecific origin. All of them are drawn to the Hellmouth in Sunnydale, California. And all of them have met their fate at the hands—or stake—of Buffy the Vampire Slayer.

This volume catalogs and explores the mythological, literary, and cultural origins of the endless numbers of ghoulish creatures who have tried to take a piece of the Slayer in the first four years of the hit TV show.

Buffy
the Vampire Slayer ™

THE MONSTER BOOK
by
Christopher Golden
Stephen R. Bissette
Thomas E. Sniegoski

AVAILABLE NOW FROM

POCKET BOOKS

YA FICTION HOW

How I survived My summer
 vacation :
$5.99   09/08/00 ACT-3548

DEC. 26 2000

DEC 20 01

SEP 23 09